THE HUNT

THE HUNT

ANDREW FUKUDA

SIMON AND SCHUSTER

First published in the USA in 2012 by St Martin's Press, 175 Fifth Avenue, New York, NY 10010.

First published in Great Britain in trade paperback in 2012 by
Simon and Schuster UK Ltd,
A CBS COMPANY

This special edition published exclusively for Waterstones, 2013

Simon & Schuster UK Ltd
1st Floor, 222 Gray's Inn Road, London WC1X 8HB

Simon & Schuster Australia, Sydney
Simon & Schuster India, New Delhi

A CIP catalogue record for this book is available from the British Library.

PB ISBN: 978-1-47111-812-8
E-BOOK ISBN: 978-0-85707-543-7

1 3 5 7 9 10 8 6 4 2

Printed and bound by CPI Group (UK) Ltd, Croydon, CR0 4YY.

www.simonandschuster.co.uk
www.simonandschuster.com.au

For Ching-Lee

THERE USED TO be more of us. I'm certain of this. Not enough to fill a sports stadium or even a movie theatre, but certainly more than what's left today. Truth is, I don't think there's any of us left. Except me. It's what happens when you're a delicacy. When you're craved. You go extinct.

Eleven years ago, one was discovered in my school. A kindergarten student, on her first day. She was devoured almost immediately. What was she thinking? Maybe the sudden (and it's always sudden) loneliness at home drove her to school under some misbegotten idea that she'd find companionship. The teacher announced nap time, and the little tyke was left standing alone on the floor clutching her teddy bear as her classmates leaped feet first towards the ceiling. At that point, it was over for her. Over. She might as well have taken out her fake fangs and prostrated herself for the inevitable feasting. Her classmates stared down wide-eyed from above: *Hello, what have we here?* She started to cry, they tell me, bawl her eyes out. The teacher was the first to get to her.

After kindergarten, when you're free and clear of naps, *that's* when you show up at school. Although you can still get caught by surprise. One time, my swimming coach was so enraged by the team's lethargic performance at a school meet, he forced all of us to take a nap in the changing room. He was only making a point, of course, but that point near did me in. By the way, swimming is fine, but don't do any other sport if you can help it. Because sweat is a dead giveaway. Sweat is what happens when we get hot; water droplets leak out like a baby drooling. I know, gross. Everyone else remains cool, clean, dry. Me? I'm a leaky faucet. So forget about cross-country, forget about tennis, forget about even competitive chess. But swimming is fine, because it hides the sweat.

That's just one of the rules. There're many others, all of them indoctrinated into me by my father from the time I was born. Never smile or laugh or giggle, never cry or get teary-eyed. At all times, carry a bland, stoic expression; the only emotions that ever crack the surface of people's faces are heper-cravings and romantic-lust, and I am obviously to have nothing to do with either. Never forget to apply butter liberally all over your body when venturing out in the daytime. Because in a world like this, it's a tough task explaining a sunburn, or even a suntan. So many other rules, enough to fill a notebook, not that I ever felt inclined to write them down. Being caught with a "rulebook" would be just as damning as a sunburn.

Besides, my father reminded me of the rules every day. As the sun was going down, over breakfast, he'd go over a few of the many rules. Like: don't make friends; don't inadvertently fall asleep in class (boring classes and long bus rides were especially dangerous); don't clear your throat; don't ace your exams, even though they insult your intelligence; don't let your good looks get the better of you; no matter how the girls might throw their hearts and bodies at you, never give in to that temptation. Because you must always remember that your looks are a curse, not a blessing. Never forget that. He'd say all this while giving my nails a quick once-over, making sure that they weren't chipped or scratched. The rules are now so ingrained in me, they're as unbendable as the rules of nature. I've never been tempted to break any of them.

Except one. When I first started taking the horse-drawn school bus, my father forbade me from looking back at him to wave goodbye. Because people never do that. That was a hard rule for me, initially. For the first few nights of school, as I stepped onto the bus, it took everything in me to freeze myself, to not look back and wave goodbye. It was like a reflex, an insuppressible cough. I was just a kid back then, too, which made it doubly hard.

I broke that rule only one time, seven years ago. It was the night after my father staggered into the house, his clothes dishevelled as if he'd been in a tussle, his neck punctured. He'd been careless, just a momentary lapse, and now he had two clear incisions in his neck. Sweat poured down his face, staining his shirt. You could see he already knew. A frenzied look in his eyes, panic running up his arms as he gripped me tight. "You're alone now, my son," he said through clenched teeth, spasms starting to ripple across his chest. Minutes later, when he started to shiver, his face shockingly cold to the touch, he stood up. He rushed out of the door into the dawn light. I locked the door as he'd instructed me to do and ran to my room. I stuffed my face into the pillow and screamed and screamed. I knew what he was doing at that very moment: running, as far away from the house before he transformed and the rays of sunlight became like waterfalls of acid burning through his hair, his muscles, his bones, his kidney, lungs, heart.

The next night, as the school bus pulled up in front of my house, steam gushing from the horses' wide and wet nostrils, I broke the rule. I couldn't help myself: I turned around as I stepped onto the bus. But by then, it didn't matter. The driveway was empty in the dark birth of night. My father was not there. Not then or ever again.

My father was right. I became alone that day. We were once a family of four, but that was a long time ago. Then it was just my father and me, and it was enough. I missed my mother and sister, but I was too young to form any real attachments with them. They are vague shapes in my memory. Sometimes, though, even now, I hear the voice of a woman singing and it always catches me off guard. I hear it and I think: *Mother had a really pretty voice*. My father, though. He missed them terribly. I never saw him cry, not even after we had to burn all the photos and notebooks. But I'd wake up in the middle of the day and find him staring out the unshuttered window, a beam of sunshine plunging down on his heavy face, his broad shoulders shaking.

My father had prepared me to be alone. He knew that day would eventually come, although I think deep down he believed it was he who would be the last one left, not me. He spent years drilling the rules into me so I knew them better than my own self. Even now, as I get ready for school at dusk, that laborious process of washing, filing my nails, shaving my arms and legs (and recently, even a few chest hairs), rubbing ointment (to mask the odour), polishing my fake fangs, I hear his voice in my head, going over the rules.

Like today. Just as I'm slipping on my socks, I hear his voice. The usual warnings: *Don't go to sleepovers; don't hum or whistle*. But then I hear this rule he'd say maybe just once or twice a year. He said it so infrequently, maybe it wasn't a rule but something else, like a life motto. *Never forget who you are*. I never knew why my father would say that. Because it's like saying don't forget water is wet, the sun is bright, snow is cold. It's redundant. There's no way I could ever forget who I am. I'm reminded every moment of every day. Every time I shave my legs or hold in a sneeze or stifle a laugh or pretend to flinch at a slip of stray light, I am reminded of who I am.

A fake person.

The Heper Lottery

BECAUSE I TURNED seventeen this year, I'm no longer mandated to ride the school bus. I walk now, gladly. The horses – dark, gargantuan brutes that came into favour long ago for their game-finding ability but are now consigned to pulling carriages and buses – can detect my unique odour. More than once they've swung their noses in my direction, singling me out, their nostrils gaping wide, like a wet, silent scream. I much prefer the solitude of walking under the darkening dusk sky.

I leave home early, as I do every night. By the time I walk through the front gates, students and teachers are already streaming in on horseback and carriages, grey shapes in a murky blackness.

It is cloudy tonight and especially dark. "Dark" is this term my father used to describe the night-time, when things get covered over in blackness. Darkness makes me squint, which is one reason it's so dangerous. Everyone else squints only when eating something sour or smelling something putrid. Nobody ever squints just because it's dark; it's a dead giveaway, so I never let so much as a crease cross my brow. In every class, I sit near the mercurial lamps that emit the barest suggestion of light (most people prefer grey-dark over pitch-black). That cuts down on the risk of an inadvertent squint. People hate those seats near the lamps – too much glare – so I can always find a seat by one.

I also hate getting called on in class. I've survived by blending in, deflecting attention. Getting called on in class puts the spotlight solely on me. Like this morning, when I get called on by the teacher in trig class. He calls on students more than anyone else, which is why I detest the man. He also has the puniest handwriting ever, and his faint scribbles on the board are near impossible to see in the grey-dark.

"Well, H6? What do you think?"

H6 is my designation. I'm in row H, seat 6: thus my designation. My designation changes depending on where I am. In my social studies class, for example, I'm known as D4. "Mind if I pass on this one?" I say.

He stares blankly at me. "Actually, I do. This is the second time in a week you've done this."

I look at the blackboard. "It's got me stumped." I resist trying to make out the numbers on the blackboard, afraid I might accidentally squint.

He closes his eyelids lightly. "No, no, I won't accept that. I know you can do it. You always ace the exams. You can do this equation in your sleep."

Students are now turning to look at me. Only a few, but enough to make me nervous. Including the person in front of me, Ashley June. Her designation in this class is actually G6, but in my mind I've always called her *Ashley June*. From the first time I saw her years ago, that designation has stuck.

She turns around, looks at me with her opulent green eyes. They seem comprehending, as if she's at last caught on: that I've often gazed longingly from behind at her lush auburn hair (the magnificent, dazzling colour!), wistfully recalling their silky feel in my hands so many moons ago. She holds my gaze, surprise lighting in them when I don't flick my eyes away the way I've been doing for years now. Ever since I sensed her interest in me, ever since I felt a pull in my own heart tugging towards her.

"H6?" The teacher starts tapping the chalk on the board. "Give it a shot, come on now."

"I really don't know."

"What's got into you? This is basic stuff for you." He peers at me. I'm one of the smarter students in school, and he knows that. Truth is, I could easily be the top student if I wanted to – grades come that easily to me, I don't even have to study – but I deliberately dumb down. There'd be too much attention at the top. "Look here. Let's work together on this. Just read the question first."

Suddenly the situation has intensified. But nothing to panic over. Yet.

"Guess my brain's not quite awake yet."

"But just read the question. That's all." His voice now holds an edge of sternness.

Suddenly I don't like this at all. He's beginning to take it personally.

More eyes start to peer back at me.

Out of nervousness, I begin to clear my throat. Then catch myself. Just in time. People never clear their throats. I breathe in, forcing myself to slow down time. I resist the urge to wipe my upper lip where I suspect small beads of sweat are starting to form.

"Do I need to ask you again?"

In front of me, Ashley June is staring more intently at me. For a moment, I wonder if she's staring at my upper lip. Does she see a slight glisten of sweat there? Did I miss shaving a hair? Then she puts up an arm, a long slender pale arm like a swan's neck arising out of the water.

"I think I know," she says, and gets up from her seat. She takes the chalk from the teacher, who is taken aback by her forthrightness. Students don't usually approach the board uninvited. But then again, this is Ashley June, who pretty much gets away with whatever she wants. She gazes up at the equation, then writes with a quick flourish in large letters and numbers. Moments later, she's done and adds her own check mark and an "A+" at the end. Dusting off her hands, she sits back down. Some of the students start scratching their wrists, as does the teacher. "That was pretty funny," he says. "I like that." He scratches his wrist faster, demonstrably, and more students join him. I hear the *rasp rasp rasp* of nails scratching against wrists.

I join them, scratching my wrists with my long nails, hating it. Because my wrists are defective. They don't itch when I find something humorous. My natural instinct is to smile – smiling is this thing I do by widening my mouth and exposing my teeth – and not to scratch my wrist. I have sensitive nerve endings there, not a funny bone.

A message on the PA system suddenly sounds over the loudspeakers. Instantly, everyone stops scratching and sits up. The voice is robotic, man-female, authoritative.

"An important announcement," it blares. "Tonight, in just three hours at two a.m., there will be a nationwide Declaration made by the Ruler. All citizens are required to participate. Accordingly, all classes held at that time will be cancelled. Teachers, students, and all administrative staff will gather in the assembly hall to watch the live broadcast from our beloved Ruler."

And that's it. After the sign-off chimes, nobody speaks. We're stunned by this news. The Ruler – who hasn't been seen in public in decades – almost never makes a TV appearance. He usually leaves Palatial and other administrative announcements to the four Ministers under him (Science, Education, Food, Law) or the fifteen Directors (Horse Engineering, City Infrastructure, Heper Studies, and so on) under them.

And the fact that he is making a Declaration is missed by no one. Everyone starts speculating about the Declaration. A nation-wide Declaration is reserved for only the rarest of occasions. Over the past fifteen years, it's happened only twice. Once to announce the Ruler's marriage. And second, most famously, to announce the Heper Hunt.

Although the last Heper Hunt occurred ten years ago, people still talk about it. The Palace surprised the public when it announced it had been secretly harbouring eight hepers. Eight living, blood-filled hepers. To lift morale during a time of economic depression, the Ruler decided to release the hepers into the wild. These hepers, kept under confinement for years, were fattened and slow, bewildered and frightened. Cast out into the wild like lambs to the slaughter, they never had a chance. They were given a twelve-hour head start. Then, a lucky group chosen by lottery were permitted to give chase after them. The Hunt was over in two hours. The event generated a surge in popularity for the Ruler.

As I walk to the cafeteria for lunch, I hear the buzz of excitement. Many are hoping for an announcement of another Heper Hunt. There is talk of a lottery for citizens again. Others are sceptical – *haven't hepers become extinct?* But even the doubters are drooling at the possibility, lines of saliva dripping down their chins and under their shirts. Nobody has tasted a heper, drunk its blood, feasted on its flesh, for years now. To think that the government might be harbouring some hepers, to think that every citizen might have a shot at winning the lottery for the Hunt . . . it sends the school into a tizzy.

I remember the Hunt from ten years ago. How for months afterwards I didn't dare fall asleep because of the nightmares that would invade my mind: hideous images of an imagined Hunt, wet and violent and full of blood. Horrific cries of fear and panic, the sound of flesh ripped and bones crushed puncturing the night stillness. I'd wake up screaming, inconsolable even as my father wrapped his arms protectively around me in a strong hug. He'd tell me everything was all right, that it was just a dream, that it wasn't real; but what he didn't know was that even as he spoke, I'd hear the lingering sounds of my sister's and mother's wretched screams echoing in my ears, spilling out of my nightmares and into the darkness of my all-too-real world.

The cafeteria is packed and boisterous. Even the kitchen staff are discussing the Declaration as they scoop food – synthetic meats – onto plates. Lunchtime has always been a challenge for me because I don't have any friends. I'm a loner, partly because it's safer—less interaction, less chance of being found out. Mostly, though, it's the prospect of being eaten alive by your so-called friend that kills any possibility of shared intimacy. Call me picky, but imminent death at the hands (or teeth) of a friend who would suckle blood out of you at the drop of a hat . . . that throws a monkey wrench into friendship building.

So I eat lunch alone most of the time. But today, by the time I pay for my food at the cash register, there's barely a seat left. Then I spot F5 and F19 from maths class sitting together, and I join them. They're both idiots, F19 slightly more so. In my mind, I call them *Idiot* and *Doofus*.

"Guys," I say.

"Hey," Idiot replies, barely looking up.

"Everyone's talking about the Declaration," I say.

"Yes," Doofus says, stuffing his mouth. We eat silently for a while. That's the way it is with Idiot and Doofus. They are computer geeks, staying up into the wee hours of the day. When I eat with them – maybe once a week – sometimes we don't say anything at all. That's when I feel closest to them.

"I've been noticing something," Doofus says after a while.

I glance up at him. "What's that?"

"Somebody's been paying quite a bit of attention to you." He takes another bite into the meat, raw and bloody. It dribbles down his chin, plopping into his bowl.

"You mean the maths teacher? I know what you mean, the guy won't leave me alone in trig—"

"No, I meant somebody else. A girl."

This time, both Idiot and I look up.

"For real?" Idiot asks.

Doofus nods. "She's been looking at you for the past few minutes."

"Not me." I take another sip. "She's probably staring at one of you."

Idiot and Doofus look at each other. Idiot scratches his wrist a few times.

"Funny, that," Doofus says. "I swear she's been eyeing you for a while now. Not just today. But every lunchtime for the past few weeks, I see her watching you."

"Whatever," I say, feigning disinterest.

"No, look, she's staring at you right now. Behind you at the table by the window."

Idiot spins around to look. When he turns back around, he's scratching his wrist hard and fast.

"What's so funny?" I ask, taking another sip, resisting the urge to turn around.

Idiot only scratches his wrist harder and faster. "You should take a look. He's not kidding."

Slowly, I turn around and steal a quick glance. There's only one table by the window. A circle of girls eating there. The Desirables. That's what they are known as. And that round table is theirs, and everyone knows by some unwritten rule that you leave that table alone. It is the domain of the Desirables, the popular girls, the ones with the cute boyfriends and designer clothes. You approach that table only if they let you. I've seen even their boyfriends waiting dutifully off to the side until granted permission to approach.

Not one of them is looking at me. They are chit-chatting, comparing jewellery, oblivious to the world outside the sphere of their table. But then one of them gives me a lingering look, her eyes meeting, then holding, mine. It is Ashley June. She looks at me with the same kind of wistful, longing glance she's shot at me dozens of times over the past few years.

I flick my eyes away, spin back around. Idiot and Doofus are scratching their wrists maniacally now. I feel the heat of a dangerous blush begin to hit my face, but they are thankfully too busy scratching to notice. I quell my face, taking deep, slow breaths until the heat dissipates.

"Actually," Idiot says, "didn't that girl have a thing for you before? Yeah, yeah, I think that's right. A couple of years back."

"She's still pining after you, she's got the hots for you after all this time," Doofus wisecracks, and this time the two of them start scratching each other's wrists uncontrollably.

Swimming practice after lunch – yes, my coach is a maniac – is almost called off. None of the squad members can concentrate. The locker room is abuzz with the latest rumours about the Declaration. I wait for the room to clear before getting changed. I'm just slipping out of my clothes when someone walks in. "Yo," Poser, the team captain, says, ripping off his clothes and slipping into his extra-tight Speedos. He drops down for push-ups, inflating his triceps and chest muscles. A dumbbell sits in his locker awaiting his biceps curls. His Buffness the Poser does this before every practice, jacking up to the max. He has a fan club out there, mostly freshmen and sophomores on the girls' squad. I've seen him let them touch his pecs. The girls used to gawk at me, the braver ones sidling up and trying to talk to me during practice until they realized I preferred to be alone. Poser has thankfully drawn away most of that attention.

He does ten more push-ups in quick succession. "It's got to be about a Heper Hunt," he says, pausing halfway down. "And they should forget about doing it by lottery this time. They should just pick the strongest among us. That would," he says, finishing his push-up, "be me."

"No doubt about," I say. "It's always been brawn over brains in the Hunt. Survival of the fittest—"

"And winner takes all," he finishes as he pushes out ten more push-ups, the last three on one hand. "Life distilled down to its rawest essence. Gotta love it. Because brute strength always wins. Always has, always will." He runs his hand over his bicep, looking approvingly, and heads out of the door. Only then do I fully remove my clothes and put on my trunks.

Coach is already barking at us as we jump in and continues to berate us for our lack of focus as we swim our laps. The water, always too cold for me even on a normal day, is freezing today. Even a few of my classmates complain about it, and they almost never complain about the water temperature. Water at cold temperatures affects me in a way it doesn't anyone else. I shiver, get something my father called "goose bumps". It's one of the many ways I'm different from everyone else. Because despite my near identical physiological similarity with them, there are seismic fundamental differences that lie beneath the frail and deceptive surface of similarity.

Everyone is slower today. Distracted, no doubt. I need more speed, more effort. It takes everything in me to stop shivering. Even when the water is at its usual temperature, with everyone splashing away, it usually takes a full twenty minutes before I'm warm enough. Today, instead of getting warmer, I feel my body getting colder. I need to swim faster.

After a warm-up lap, as we are resting up in the shallow end, I am almost overcome by a sudden urge to kick off and swim the forbidden stroke.

Only my father has seen me use it. Years ago. During one of our daytime excursions to a local pool. For whatever reason, I dipped my head underwater. It is the first sign of drowning, whenever even the nose and ears dip below the surface. Lifeguards are trained to watch for this: see half a head submerge underwater, and they're instantly reaching for their whistles and life preservers. That's why the water level, even at the deep end, goes up only to our waists. It's the depth that gets to people, renders them incapacitated. If their feet can't touch the bottom without their jaw line sinking below water, a panic attack seizes them like a reflex. They freeze up, sink, drown. So even though swimming is considered the domain of adrenaline junkies, those willing to flirt with death, really, it's not. Here in the pool, you can simply stand up at the first sign of trouble. The water is so shallow, even your belly button won't drown.

But me that day, dipping my head underwater. I don't know what possessed me. I ducked my head below and did this thing with my breath. I don't know how to describe it except to say I gripped it. Held it in place in my lungs behind a closed mouth. And for a few seconds, I was fine. More than a few seconds. More like ten. Ten seconds, my head underwater, and I didn't drown.

It wasn't even scary. I opened my eyes, my arms pale blurs before me. I heard my father yelling, the sound of water splashing towards me. I told him I was fine. I showed him what to do. He didn't believe at first, kept asking if I was OK. But eventually, he came around to doing it himself. He didn't like it, not one bit.

The next time we went swimming, I did the same thing. And then some. This time, with my head underwater, I stretched out my arms, stroked them over my head, one after the other. I pulled on the water, kicked my legs. It was awesome. Then I stood up, choking on water. Coughed it out. My father, worried, waded towards me. But I took off again, arms reaching up and over, pulling the water under me, legs and feet kicking the water, my father left in my wake. I was flying.

But when I swam back, my father was shaking his head, with anger, with fear. He didn't need to say anything (even though he did, endlessly); I already knew. He called it "the forbidden stroke". He didn't want me to swim that way anymore. And so I never did.

But today I'm freezing in the water. Everyone is just going through the motions, even chatting to one another, heads smiling above water as hands and feet paddle underneath like pond ducks. I want to stroke hard, kick out, warm up.

And then I feel it. A shudder rippling through my body.

I lift up my right arm. It's dotted with goose bumps, grotesque little bumps like cold chicken skin. I paddle harder, propelling my body forward. Too fast. My head knocks up against the feet of the person in front. When it happens again, he shoots a glare back at me.

I slow down.

Cold seeps into my bones. I know what I have to do. Get out of the water before the shivering gets out of control, escape into the locker room. But when I lift my arms, goose bumps – disgustingly like bubble wrap – prickle out, obvious to all. Then something weird happens to my jaw. It starts to chatter, vibrate, knock my teeth together. I clench my mouth shut.

When the team completes the lap, we rest up before heading out for the next lap. We've all paced ourselves too fast and have twelve seconds before the next lap. It's going to be the longest twelve seconds of my life.

"They forgot to turn on the heat," somebody complains. "Water's too cold."

"The maintenance crew. Probably too busy talking about the Declaration."

The water levels off at our waists. But I stay crouched, keeping my body underwater. I trail my fingers over my skin. Little bumps all over. I glance up at the clock. Ten more seconds. Ten more seconds to just fly under the radar and hope—

"What's the matter with you?" Poser says, gazing at me. "You look sick." The rest of the team turns around.

"N-no-nothing," I say, my voice chattering. I grip my voice and bark it out again. "Nothing."

"Sure?" he asks again.

I nod my head, not trusting my voice. My eyes flick at the clock. Nine seconds to go. It's as if the clock is stuck in Super Glue.

"Coach!" Poser yells, his right arm motioning. "Something's wrong with him."

Coach's head snaps around, his body half a beat behind. The assistant coach is already moving towards us.

I raise my hands, up to the wrists. "I'm OK," I assure them, but my voice trembles. "Just fine, let's swim."

A girl in front of me studies me closely. "Why is his voice doing that? Shaking like that?"

Fear ices my spine. A soupy sensation steals into my stomach, churning it upside down. *Do whatever it takes to survive,* my father would tell me, his hand smoothing down my hair. *Whatever it takes.*

And in that moment with the coaches coming towards me and everyone staring at me, I find a way to survive. I vomit into the pool, a heaving green-yellow mess filled with sticky spittle and gooey saliva. It's not a lot, and most of it just floats on the surface like an oil spill. A few colourless chunks drift downward.

"That's so *disgusting*!" the girl shrills, splashing vomit away as she jumps backward. The other swimmers also move away, arms and hands slapping at the water. The green slick of vomit floats haphazardly back towards me.

"You get out of the water now!" Coach yells at me.

I do. Most people are too distracted by the vomit in the pool to notice my body. It's ridden with goose bumps. And shaking. Coach and his assistant are making their way to me. I hold up my arm, pretend I'm about to upchuck again. They stop in their tracks.

I run into the locker room, bent over. Inside, I make retching sounds as I towel off and throw my clothes on. I don't have much time before they come in. Even with the clothes on, I'm still shivering. I hear them getting closer now. I jump down onto the floor and start doing push-ups. Anything to get my body warmer.

But it's useless. I can't stop shivering. And when I hear the first voices cautiously enter the locker room, I grab my bag and head out. "I don't feel well," I say as I walk past them. Disgust pulls their faces down as they step aside, but that's OK. I'm used to it, that look.

It's the way I look at myself in the mirror when I'm alone at home.

You live too long trying not to be something, eventually you wind up hating that thing.

In English literature class right before the Declaration, no one can concentrate. All we want to do – including the teacher, who jettisons any pretence of teaching – is talk about the Declaration. I'm quiet, trying to thaw out, coldness still dug in deep in my bones. The teacher insists the Declaration is about another Hunt. "It's not like the Ruler is going to marry again," she says, her eyes stealing up to the clock, counting down the minutes to two a.m.

Finally, at one forty-five a.m., we're led to the auditorium. It's bubbling over with excitement. Teachers line the sides, shifting on their feet. Even janitors loiter at the back, restless. Then two a.m. arrives and the screen above the stage is filled with our nation's symbol: two white fangs, standing for Truth and Justice. For a frightful moment, the projector sputters and blanks out. A groan ripples across the rows of seats; technicians fly to the projector that sits, heavy and unwieldy, like all audiovisual equipment, in the centre of the auditorium. Within a minute, they have it up and running again.

Just in time. The Ruler, sitting at his desk in the Circular Office, is beginning his speech. His hands are clasped, his long fingers interlaced, the nails gleaming under the spotlights.

"My dear citizens," he begins. "When it was announced earlier this evening that I would be speaking, many of you" – he pauses dramatically – "if not all of you, were intrigued, to say the least. My advisers have informed me that concern spread across this great land, and that many of you were overwrought with speculation and even undue worry. I apologise if that happened; it was not my intent. For I come to you with news not of war or distress, but of great tidings."

Everyone in the auditorium leans forward at this. All across the land, over five million citizens huddle around TVs and large screens with bated breath.

"My announcement to you, gentle people, is that this year we will once again hold that most esteemed of events." His tongue slips out, wets his lips. "For the first time in a decade, we will once again have a Heper Hunt!"

At that, everyone's heads snap back and forth, side to side, loud snorts issuing out of their noses. The auditorium, filled with the staccato movement of snapping heads and the sound of suctioned air, reverberates with excitement.

"Now, before I sign off and the Director of the Heper Institute furnishes you with the details, let me say that such an event is emblematic of who we are. It encapsulates all that makes this nation transcendent: character, integrity, perseverance. May the best succeed!"

A raucous stomping of feet fills the auditorium. As one, we stand with him, placing our hands over our throats as his image on the screen fades out. Then the Director of the Heper Institute speaks. He is a wiry, sharp man, officious in demeanour, dressed to the nines.

There will be a hunting party of between five and ten this year, he tells us. "This is a democracy we live in, where every person counts, where every person matters. Thus, *every* citizen over the age of fifteen and under the age of sixty-five will receive a randomly assigned sequence of four numbers. In exactly twenty-four hours, the numbers of the sequence will be randomly picked and publicly announced live on TV. Anywhere between five to ten of you will have this winning sequence."

Heads snap back, spines crack. *Five to ten citizens!*

"The lottery winners will be immediately taken to the Heper Institute of Refined Research and Discovery for a four-night training period. Then the Hunt will begin." The auditorium breaks out in hisses and snarls. The Director continues. "The rules of the Hunt are simple: the hepers will be given a twelve-hour head start into the desert plains. Then the hunters will be released. The goal? Chase the hepers down, eat more of them than any other hunter." He stares into the camera lens. "But we're getting ahead of ourselves, aren't we? First, you have to be one of the few lucky lottery winners. Good luck to you all."

Then more foot stomping, silenced with an uplifted hand. "One more thing," he says. "Did I mention anything about the hepers?" He pauses; everyone leans forward. "Most of the hepers were too young for the previous Hunt. They were mere babies back then, really. It would have been cruel, barbaric, and, well, simply unfair to have babies as prey." A cruel glint perches in his eyes. "But since that time, we have raised them in the most controlled of environments. To ensure not only that they will provide us with succulent flesh and rich blood, but that they will also be more . . . dexterous than last time. Finally, as we speak tonight, they are ripe and ready for sport and consumption."

More wrist scratching and drooling.

"Good citizens," the Director continues, "there is no time like the present. Most of you will receive your lottery numbers at your workstation within a minute. Mothers at home, your numbers will be sent via e-mail to your official account. And for those in high school and college, your numbers are awaiting you back at your desk. Good luck to you all." His image fades out.

Usually we are led out in orderly fashion, row by row. But today there is pandemonium as the student body – a slippery, sloppy soup – gushes out. The teachers, usually lined up along the side directing traffic, are the first ones out, hurrying to the staff room.

Back in my homeroom, everyone is maniacally logging in, long nails tapping against the glass deskscreen. I am all fakery as I put on my act of shaking my head and drooling. At the top of my inbox, in large caps and in crimson red, is the lottery e-mail:

Re: YOUR HEPER HUNT LOTTERY NUMBERS

And these are my numbers: 3 16 72 87.

I couldn't care less.

Everyone shoots off their numbers to one another. Within a minute, we realize that the first number in the sequence ranges from only 1 to 9; the remaining three numbers in the sequence range from 0 to 99. A meaningless tally over the first number is drawn up on the blackboard:

First sequence number	# of students with that number
1	3
2	4
3	1
4	5
5	3
6	2
7	4
8	3
9	2

Irrational theories are quickly developed. For whatever reason, 4 – being the most common number in our classroom – is surmised as having the best chance of being the first number selected. And 3, with only one hit – me – is quickly dismissed as having no chance.

All fine with me.

It's dark when I arrive home, a hint of grey smearing the sky. In another hour, the morning sun will peek over the distant mountains to the east. A siren will sound; anyone outside will have only five minutes to find shelter before the sun's rays turn lethal. But it's rare for anyone to be outside by that point. Fear of the sun ensures that by the time the sirens sound, the streets are empty and windows shuttered.

As I slip my key into the keyhole, I suddenly sense something is off. A fragrance? I can't put my finger on it. I scan the driveway and streets. Other than a few horse-drawn carriages hurrying home, no one's around. I sniff the air, wondering if I imagined it.

Somebody was just here. A few moments before I arrived.

I live alone. I have never invited anyone here. Other than me, nobody has even stood at the front door before. Until today.

Cautiously, I make my way around the perimeter of the house, looking for signs of disturbance. Everything looks fine. The stockpile of cash left by my father and secreted in the floor boards, though slowly diminishing, is untouched.

Closing the front door, I stand listening in the darkness of my home. No one else in here. Whoever was standing outside never came in. Only then do I light the candles. Colours break out.

This is my favourite time of day. When I feel like a prisoner taking his first steps of freedom or a diver rising from the depths of the mythical sea, drawing in his first gasps of air. This is the moment, after the endless grey-black hours of night, I see colour again. Under the flickering light of the candle, colours burst into being, flooding the room with pools of melted rainbows.

I put dinner in the microwave. I have to cook it twenty times, because the timer only goes up to fifteen seconds. Hot, slightly charred, is my preference, not the tepid, soppy mess I'm forced to eat outside. I remove my fangs, place them in my pocket. Then I bite into the burger, relishing the heat as it attacks my teeth, savouring the solid feel of charred crispiness. I close my eyes in enjoyment.

And feel dirty, ashamed.

After my shower – showering is this thing you do where you rub gobs of hand sanitiser and pour water over your body to get rid of odour – I lie on the sofa, my head propped up on folded sweatshirts. Only one candle is alight; it casts flickering shadows on the ceiling. Sleep-holds dangle above me, placed there years ago merely for show on the off chance a visitor might drop by. The radio is on, the volume set low. "Many experts are speculating that the number of hepers will be in the range of three to five," the radio analyst says. "But because the Director was silent on this issue, there really is no way of knowing."

The radio programme continues, with a few callers chiming in, including a crotchety woman who speculates that the whole thing is rigged: the "winner" will end up being someone with deep pockets and close friends in high places. Her call is suddenly cut off. Other callers weigh in about the number of hepers in the Hunt this time. Only one thing is for certain: it has to be at least two, because the Director – in a voice loop that has been played over and over – used the plural tense: heper*s*.

I listen to a few more callers, then get up and switch off the radio. In the quiet that follows, I hear the gentle *pit-pat* of rain on the shutters.

My father sometimes took me out in the daytime. Except for the times he took me swimming, I hated going outside. Even with sunglasses, the brightness was overwhelming. The burning sun was like an unblinking eye, spilling light like acid out of a beaker, turning the city into an endless flash. Nothing moved out there.

He would take me to empty sports stadiums and vacant shopping malls. Nothing was locked, because sunlight provided the best security. We'd have the whole Core Park to fly kites or the empty public pool to swim in. He told me this ability to withstand sun rays was a strength, made us superpowerful. *We can withstand what kills them*. But to me, it was only something that made us different, not stronger. I wanted to be like everyone else, cocooned in the dome of darkness that was home. Blackness comforted me. It hurt my father to hear that, but he didn't say anything. Gradually, we stopped going out.

Except when a certain awful need hit us.

Like right now. I open the door. The rain has stopped.

I venture out.

The city is fast asleep behind shuttered husks of darkness. I "borrow" a horse from a neighbouring yard and ride down empty streets under an overcast sky.

I head out today because every few weeks I get the urge. When my father was alive, we'd venture out together. The shame was mutual because we'd never speak, wouldn't even look each other in the eye. We went far, past the city borders, to the Vast Lands of Uncertain End. That's a mouthful, and most people simply call it the Vast.

It's an endless stretch of desert plains. Nobody knows how far it goes or what lies beyond it.

Because I live in the outer suburbs, far from the tall office buildings of the Financial District and farther yet from the centre of the metropolis where towering governmental skyscrapers clutter the landscape, it doesn't take long before the city is well behind me. The city boundary is vague: there's no wall to demarcate the beginning of the Vast. It arrives indiscernibly. Scattered homes give way to dilapidated poultry farms, which in turn cede to crumbling shacks long ago abandoned. Eventually, it's just the spread of empty land. The Vast. There's nothing out there. No place to flee. Only the cruellest of elements, the three Ds: desert, desolation, and death. *There's no escape for us out here,* my father would say, *no sanctuary, no hope, no life for us at all. Don't ever come out here thinking there's escape to be had.*

I don't dilly-dally out here but head north. About an hour out, an isolated mound of soft green fuzz sits there in the middle of the Vast, an aberrational oddity discovered years ago by my parents. And what I need is in the green fuzz. By the time my feet hit the soft grass, I'm sprinting towards a glade of trees. I reach for a red fruit hanging off a branch. I tear it off, shut my eyes, and sink my teeth through the skin. The fruit crunches in my mouth, watery and sweet, my jaws working up and down, up and down. When my father and I ate the fruit, we'd eat with our backs to each other. We were ashamed, even as we chewed, bite after bite, juice running down our chins, unable to stop.

After my fourth fruit, I force myself to slow down. I pluck away at the different offerings of fruit, tossing them into a bag. I pause for a minute, gazing up at the sky. High above me, a large bird glides across the sky, its wings oddly rectangular. It circles around me, its form strangely unchanging, then heads east, disappearing into the distance. I pick a few more fruit, then head over to our favourite spot, a large tree whose leaves spread lush and high. My father and I always sat under this tree, munching fruit, back against the trunk, the city in the far distance, darkened and flat. Like a dirty puddle.

Years ago, we would explore the green fuzz for signs of others like us. Signs like rutted cores of discarded fruit, trampled grass, snapped branches. But we almost never found anything. Our kind was careful not to leave any giveaway signs. Even so, I'd occasionally find that unavoidable and clearest of signs: less fruit on trees. That meant others had been there as well, plucking and eating. But I never saw any of them.

Once, between bites, I asked my father, "Why don't we ever see other hepers here?"

He stopped chewing, half turned his head towards me. "Don't use that word."

"What word? Heper? What's wrong with—"

"Don't use that word," he said sternly. "I don't want to hear that word coming out of you ever again."

I was young; tears rushed to my eyes. He turned fully towards me, his large eyes swallowing me whole. I tilted my head back to keep the tears from rimming out. Only after my tears dried did he turn his eyes away. He gazed afar at the horizon until the rocks stopped churning inside him.

"*Human*," he finally said, his voice softer. "When we're alone, use that word, OK?"

"OK," I said. And after a moment, I asked him, "Why don't we see other humans?"

He didn't answer. But I can still remember the sound as he bit off large chunks of apple, loud crunches exploding in his mouth as we sat under a tree drooping with ripe fruit.

And now, years later, there's even more fruit hanging off the trees, an overabundance of colour in the verdant green fuzz. So sad, to have colours signify death and extinction. And that's how I eat now, alone in the green fuzz, a solitary grey dot among splashes of red and orange and yellow and purple.

Dusk arrives, the night of the lottery. Inside every home, young and old are awake, jittery with excitement. When the night horn sounds, shutters and grates rise, doors and windows fling open. Everyone is early to work and school tonight, to chit-chat and tap impatiently on computer screens before them.

At school, there's not even an attempt at normality. In second period, the teacher doesn't call the class to order but simply disregards us as she taps away on her deskscreen. Halfway through class, a citywide announcement on the intercom is made: because work productivity in the city has fallen so drastically, the announcement of the lottery numbers has been moved up a few hours. In fact, it will now be broadcast live in a few minutes. "Have your numbers in front of you," the announcer ends cheerily, as if everyone hasn't already memorised them.

Instantly, delirium breaks out in the classroom. Students rush back to their seats, eyes fastened on deskscreens.

"Are you ready for the lottery yet?" the news anchor says a few minutes later, all aplomb abandoned in his excitement. "I have mine right here," he says, holding up a sheet of paper with his numbers. "Tonight might just be my night, I woke up with a feeling in me."

"As did every citizen of this great city, no doubt," chimes in his co-host, a slim woman with jet black hair. "We're all so excited. Let's go now to the Heper Institute, where the numbers are about to be picked." She pauses, her finger reaching up to her earpiece. A feral glint invades her eyes. "We're getting word now of a surprise. This is a whopper, folks, so sit down."

In the classroom, heads snap back and then lurch forward. No one says a word.

"Instead of having the Director pick the numbers, the Palace has decided a captive heper will pick the numbers."

Somebody snorts loudly; several students suddenly leap onto their desks.

"You heard that right, folks," she continues, and her voice is wetter now, with a slight lisp. "We're getting a live feed . . ." She pauses again. "I'm hearing that it's coming from a secret location from within the Heper Institute. Take us there now."

Instantly, the view of the newsroom switches to that of a bare, cavernous indoor arena. No windows or doors. Placed in the centre of the arena is an empty chair. Next to it, a large hemp sack and a glass bowl. But nobody is looking at the sack or the chair or the glass bowl. All our eyes are fastened on the blurry image of a male heper crouched in the corner.

It is elderly and wiry, but its stomach is fat-marbled and protrudes disproportionately to its thin frame. Hair plasters its arms and legs, and the sight of the hair sends a river of lip smacking through the classroom.

The videocamera zooms in and then out on the heper. But clearly the camera must be running unmanned, on autopilot. If anyone were in the arena with the heper, the heper would have been devoured within seconds. The newest wave of videocameras – weighing a relatively spry two tons – is capable of autozooming, a technological advancement unimaginable just a decade ago.

The camera zooms in now, capturing the heper's uncertainty as it gazes upward at something offscreen. Then, as if instructed, it gets up and walks to the chair. There is indecision in its every step, caution. Emotions pour nakedly off its face.

A student shakes his head violently, drool trapezing outward, some of it landing on me. Saliva pours out of our mouths, collecting in small pools on desks and the floor. Heads are half cocked sideways and back, bodies tensed. Everyone in a trance *and* a heightened sense of alertness.

The news anchors have been silent.

The heper reaches the chair, sits down. Again, eyes bulging wide, it looks offscreen for direction. Then it reaches into the hemp sack and takes out a ball. A number is printed on it: 3. It holds the ball up to the camera for a second, then puts it in the glass bowl.

It takes a moment before we realize what's just happened. The news anchors break their silence, their voices wet and blubbery with saliva. "We have the first number, folks, we have the first number. It's three!" Loud groans all around, fists crumpling sheets of paper. The teacher in the back of the classroom whispers a cuss.

I stare down at my own paper: 3, 16, 72, 87. Coolly, I cross out the number 3. Only a few classmates are still in the running. It's easy to spot them. Their eyes are sparkling with anticipation, drool running down their exposed fangs. Everyone else is unclenching now, muscles relaxing, mouths and chins being wiped. They slump in their chairs.

The heper nervously reaches for another number.

16.

More groans. I take my pen and cross out 16, a slight tremor in my fingers. Must hold the pen tighter, get my fingers under control.

As far as I can tell, that last number took out the remaining contenders in the class. Except me. Nobody has noticed yet that I'm still in the running. I kick out more saliva, let it run down my chin. I hiss a little, cock my head back. Heads flick towards me. Before long, a crowd has gathered around my desk.

The heper pulls out the next number.

72.

There is a momentary, stunned silence. Then heads start bopping, knuckles cracking. My next number – 87 – is chanted like a mantra. Somebody runs out, tells the adjacent classroom. I hear chairs scraping against the floor; moments later, they come flying in, crowding around me. Drool splatters on me from above; a few are hanging upside down from the ceiling, staring down at my screen. News flies up and down the hallways.

My heart, like a claustrophobic rat in a cage, is out of control. Fear grips me. But for the moment, no one is looking at me; everyone is fixated on the screen. Something is wrong with the heper. It's shaking its head from side to side now, almost violently, eyes wide with fear. A naked, overwhelming display of emotion. A fruit suddenly falls from a small opening in the ceiling. A red fruit, and the heper leaps for it, devouring it within seconds.

"So disgusting," somebody says.

"I know, I can barely watch."

The heper takes a few steps towards the sack, is about to pull out the last number, when it pauses. It drops the sack and retreats to the far corner, where it crouches, hands over ears, eyes snapped shut. For a second, it lifts its head and stares offscreen. Then its eyes widen with fear, and its head shakes violently. It pins its head between its knees.

"It doesn't want to pick the last number," a student whispers.

"I told you," my teacher says, "these hepers are smarter than they look. It somehow knows these numbers are for the Hunt."

The screen blacks out. The next shot is of the newsroom. The anchors are caught off guard. "Looks like we're having technical difficulties," the male anchor says, quickly wiping his chin. "We should be back on air shortly."

But it takes more than a few moments. Video of the heper picking the first three numbers is looped over and over. Word spreads around school about me; more students crowd the classroom. Then more news: another student in the school is still in the running. As I pump out more saliva down my chin and jerk my head in staccato fashion, I make some rough maths calculations in my head. The odds that I have the last winning number are 1 in 97. That's just a little over 1 per cent. *A comfortingly low chance,* I tell myself.

"Look!" someone says, pointing at the deskscreen.

The TV channel has shifted away from the newsroom to an outdoor location. The male heper is gone. In its stead is a female heper, young. This heper is sitting outdoors in a chair, a hemp sack and glass bowl on the ground next to it. The image is glassy and shiny, as if a glass wall stands between the heper and camera. Behind the heper, distant mountains sit under the few stars that dot the night sky. Unlike the other heper, this female heper is looking not nervously offscreen, but directly at the camera. With a collectedness in its gaze, a self-possession that seems odd in a captive heper.

Some of the boys lurch up on desks. A female heper is known to be the choicer morsel of the two genders. The flesh meatier, fattier in parts. And a teenage one – as this one appears to be – is the most succulent of all, its taste beyond compare.

Before the hissing and drooling kicks up again, the heper is already reaching into the sack. It calmly removes a ball, holds it with outstretched arm towards the camera. But it's the eyes I'm looking at: how focused they seem to be on mine, as if they see me in the camera lens.

I don't need to see the ball to know the heper has picked number 87. An explosive *hiss* curdles out from classmates, followed by a *phat-phat-phat* of smacking lips. The congratulations begin: ears brought down to mine, rubbing up and down, side to side. A minute later, between ear hugs, I glance down at the deskscreen. Amazingly, the heper is still holding the numbered ball up to the camera, a look of quiet defiance imprinted on its face. The picture starts to fade out. But in the moment before it does, I see the heper's eyes moistening, its head slanting forward ever so, hair bangs falling over its eyes. Its defiance seems to melt into a sudden, overcoming sadness.

Before too long, they come. Even as my classmates are still congratulating me, I hear their officious boots thumping along the hallway. By the time they open the door to my classroom, every student has taken his or her seat, standing up at attention as the team of four walks in. They are all immaculately dressed, silk suits with tight, clean lines.

"F3?" the squad leader asks from behind the teacher's desk. Like his suit, his voice is silky, pretentious, but with undeniable authority.

I put my hand up.

All four pairs of eyes swivel and fasten on me. They are not hostile eyes, just efficient.

"Congratulations, you have the winning lottery combination," the leader murmurs. "Come with us now, F3. You will be taken directly to the Heper Institute. Your ride is awaiting you in front of the school. Come now."

"Thank you," I say. "I feel like the luckiest guy in the world. But I need to pick up a few items from home, clothes." And my shaver and scrubber and nail clipper and fang cleaner—

"No. Clothing will be supplied at the Institute. Come now."

I've never been in a stretch carriage, much less one drawn by a team of stallions. The stallions are sleek black, merging seamlessly with the night. They turn towards me as I approach the carriage, their noses sniffing me out. I climb inside quickly. Students and teachers spill out of the school from the east and west wings, rushing over to gawk. But they all stand a respectful distance away, silent and still.

Because of the darkly tinted windows, it's unnerving how pitch-black it is inside. I restrain the urge to stretch out my arms or to widen my eyes. Head bent down, I slide my body forward slowly until my knees hit the soft front of the leather seat. I hear more bodies following me in, feel the seat sag under the weight of their bodies.

"Is this your first time inside a stretch?" a voice next to me asks.

"Yes."

Nobody says anything.

Then another voice: "We will wait for the other winner to get here."

"Another student?" I ask.

A pause. "Yes. Shouldn't be long now."

I stare out of the tinted window, trying not to give away the fact that I can't see a thing in here.

"Some papers to sign," says yet another voice. A faint rustle of papers, the unmistakable snap of a clipboard. "Here you go."

My eyes still trained outside, I swing my right arm in a wide arc until I hit the board. "Ooops, I'm such a klutz sometimes."

"Please sign here and here and here. Where the Xs are."

I stare down. I can't see a thing.

"Right where the Xs are," yet another voice chimes in.

"Can we just wait a bit? I'm kind of caught up in the moment—"

"Now, please." There is a firmness in that voice. I sense eyes turning to look at me.

But just then, the limo door opens. "The other lottery winner," someone whispers. A faint grey light from the outside spills inside. Not a moment to lose. I whip my eyes down, barely catch sight of the Xs, scribble my name down. The carriage tilts with the added weight. Then, before I can see who entered, the door swings shut and the interior is plunged into blackness again.

An ankle jams into my shin.

"Would you watch where you put your legs!" a voice snaps at me. It's a girl's voice, somewhat familiar.

I stare out of the window, not even trying to meet her eyes.

"Do you two know each other?" a voice asks.

I decide the safest action is to shrug and scratch my wrist. Something ambiguous that could be interpreted a number of ways.

The sound of wrists scratching in response. I'm safe for now.

"Please sign these papers. Here, here, and here."

There is a momentary pause. Then she speaks with command. "My friends are outside. The whole school is outside. This is the best moment of my life. Can you please roll down these windows so they can see me? It'd be good for the school, for the community, to join us in this wonderful time."

For a long time, there is no response. Then the window rolls down and the grey outside light ambles in.

Sitting across from me is Ashley June.

We ride in silence and darkness, the officials dispensing with small talk. The stallions stop at a stoplight; the *clip-clop* of their hooves comes to a momentary cease. The muffled, rumbling sounds of the crowd outside filters through: bone snaps, teeth grinding, the crackle of joints and ankles. Hundreds, if not thousands, of people line the streets, watching our passage.

Ashley June is silent but excited. I can tell. Snaps of her neck crack out in the darkness in front of me. I throw in a few snaps of my own, cracking my knuckles once or twice.

This is not the first time Ashley June and I have been in the dark in close quarters. It was a year or two ago, before I became the recluse I am today and just as Ashley June was beginning her meteoric rise in the ranks to the Desirable club. It was raining that night and the class was cloistered inside the school gym. Our gym teacher never showed, and nobody bothered to let the office know. Somehow – these things just have a way of happening – everyone started playing spin the bottle. The *whole* class, all twenty or so of us. The class divided into two circles by gender. The words – *This is so lame, I'm outta here* – were on my lips when the guys suddenly spun the bottle and got things going.

It whirled around in a blur, then slowed, coming to a stop at the boy sitting across from me.

Then it continued to inch forward slowly, as if through glue, until the bottle mouth, like the gaping mouth of a dying goldfish, came to a stop. Pointing right at me, dead centre, no question about it.

"Suck fest," the boy next to me said bitterly. "So close to me."

And it was as though an electric jolt shot through the girls' circle. They started whispering, heads huddling together, casting me luring, excited looks. In a flash, a girl reached forward and spun the bottle. The bottle twirled fast, then broke into a slower blur. When it was crawling through its final rotation, girls leaning back in disappointment as the bottle passed them, and just as it was slowly passing by Ashley June, she reached forward and stopped it with her foot, the mouth of the bottle pointing at her.

"Wow," she said, "figure that." And because it was Ashley June, they let her get away with it.

A minute later, Ashley June and I were inside the closet. We stood mere inches apart, the walls enclosing us tightly. The smell of pine was thick inside, the darkness complete.

Neither of us moved. I heard the others talking outside the door, their voices miles away. I stared down at my feet, breathing through my nose in long, controlled breaths.

I thought to speak to her, this being the perfect – the *only* – opportunity to express what had been bottled up in me for years. *Ashley June, I've had feelings for you for a long time. Since the first time I ever saw you. You're the only one I've ever been drawn to, the only one I think of every day.*

"Should we get a move on?" she asked in the darkness, her voice whispery and surprisingly low. My opportunity, so fleeting, gone.

We bumbled awkwardly in the confined space as we took off our arm sleeves. I grabbed the zipper, pulled at it, felt it give.

With our sleeves off, we paused. Now was the moment. Was she waiting for me to move first? Then the sound of her neck cracking, a loud bony snap. A low rumbling in her throat, then a snarl, so close, the hiss wetting the walls and ceiling and floor of the blackened closet enclosing me.

I let my mind go blank, an erasure, then a replacement with a primal urge manufactured in the imaginings of my mind. I opened my mouth and a snarl hurled out, its raw savagery and urgency catching me by surprise. My arms flew forward towards her and our forearms collided, nails gashing against skin. For a second, alarm shot through my mind: if blood was spilt, her ardour would quickly – in a microsecond – shift, and she would be at my neck, her fangs sinking razor quick through my skin, and the others outside would pour in just seconds later, diving inside in an orgy of blood. But caught up in the moment, I did not stop, we did not stop, but brusquely brushed aside arms, so many impeding us, shoved elbows and shoulders away, jostled for position. We knocked up against the walls confining us on every side, hollow thumps thudding as our elbows and knees hit against the invisible walls.

I got there first. Before she could regain her footing, I shoved my elbow into the socket of her armpit. The way I had read about in books, seen in movies. I had her. Her body tensed in anticipation as my elbow locked into her armpit. And just like that, her body lost all tension and softened. I swivelled my elbow in long, luxurious circles, and her body moved in rhythm. Salivary wetness slivered between and around her snarling teeth. I concentrated hard after that, keeping up with appearances, making sure that the snarls came out in the right fevered pitch, that my body oscillated with enough passion and frenzy.

Afterwards, Ashley June and I bent down to find our arm sleeves. In the dark, our arms bumped into each other; and in one unforgettable second, our hands briefly touched. The skin of her fingers brushed against the open palm of my hand. We both flinched back – I in surprise, Ashley in revulsion. She was quiet, perhaps collecting herself. I was about to push the closet door open when she spoke.

"Wait?"

I paused. "What is it?"

"Can we just . . . stand here for a bit?"

"OK."

A minute passed. I could not see her in the dark, what she was doing.

"Are you . . ." she began.

I waited for her to continue. But for a long time she did not say anything.

"Do you think it's still raining hard?" she said finally.

"I don't know. Maybe."

"It's supposed to rain all night, the forecast said."

"Did it?"

And again, she was quiet before speaking again. "You always walk to school, don't you?"

I paused. "Yes."

"You brought your umbrella tonight?"

"I did."

"I walked to school tonight," she said, and we both knew she was lying. "But I left my umbrella at home."

I did not say anything.

"Do you mind walking me home?" she whispered. "I hate getting wet."

I told her I did not mind.

"Meet me by the front gates after school, OK?" she said.

"OK."

She then pushed open the closet door. We did not look at each other as we joined the group. The guys kept looking at me expectantly, and I gave them what they wanted: I mouthed, "Wow!" and bared my fangs. They scratched their wrists.

Later that night, after the last bell rang and the students poured out of school, I sat at my desk. I stayed there even as the din of the hallways subsided, even as the last students and teachers vacated the school, the *clip-clop* of horse hooves fading into the distance. Rain gushed down in thick columns outside, splattering against the window. Only after the dawn siren rang hours later did I get up and leave. The front gates were empty of people as I walked past, as I knew they would be. It was frigid by then, the rain still pouring down heavily, as if trying to fill the void of the emptied streets. I did not use my umbrella. I let the rain soak my clothes, seep all the way through to my body, the wet cold licking my chest, stinging my skin, freezing my heart.

The Heper Institute

THE RIDE IS long. Even the stretch carriage becomes uncomfortable and jarring after the first couple of hours – it's not built for long-distance travel. Long travel is very rare: the appearance of the deadly sun every twelve hours restricts travel. But for the sun, travel distances would be much longer, and locomotive technology would probably have supplanted horses long ago. In a world where, as the saying goes, "death casts its eye on us daily", horses more than sufficiently meet the short-distance travel needs.

Nobody speaks as we travel through the outskirts, along roads that get bumpier by the minute until they yield to the give of desert sand. Finally, some five hours out, we pull up in front of a drab government building. I step out, legs stiff and unsteady. A desert wind blows across the darkened plains, hot but somehow refreshing, sifting through the bangs of my hair.

"Time to go." We are escorted towards the grey building, the officials' boots kicking up slight puffs of dust. Several other carriages are parked off to the side, the horses tied but still jaunty from their journey, their noses wet and wide with exertion, heat steaming off their bodies. I quickly count the carriages: including the one I shared with Ashley June, there are five others. That makes seven lottery winners.

Nothing about the spare grey of the building's exterior prepares me for the opulence of the interior. Marble floors glow with the ebony hue of old world craquelatto. Interior Ionic columns, scrolls curling off top and bottom, stretch high to impossibly tall ceilings that are outlined by a plaster cornice etched with curled fronds. A labyrinth of hallways and staircases criss-crosses in a dizzying disorientation. We walk single file, a few officials in front, a string of them tailing behind us, our boots *click-clock*ing on the marbled floor, flanked by lines of mercurial lamps. Ashley June walks directly in front of me, an arm's length away. Her hair is like a torched fire, leading the way.

The hallway leads to a large set of silver-crested double doors set between two Corinthian columns. But before we reach them, the lead official suddenly turns to a door on the left. The procession comes to an awkward halt as he knocks on the door. A moment later, the door swings open.

The cavernous hall is dark. In the middle is a circle of curved-back velvet chairs dotted about like the numerical digits of a clock; all but two of the chairs are occupied. Ashley June, in front of me, is escorted to an empty chair. I'm taken to the chair next to hers and sat down. The officials take their place a few yards behind us, standing at attention.

Seven of us sit in the murky greyness, hands laid on kneecaps, staring directly ahead, the tips of our fangs jutting out slightly. The hunters. We are perfectly still, as if the molecules in the air have been glued together, fastening everything in place.

The official, when she appears, catches us all by surprise. Instead of being dressed in military garb, she wears a flowery dress, the long sleeves adorned with pictures of dandelions and roses. She floats gracefully from the dark periphery to the centre of the circle, where a high-backed chair slowly ascends from the floor. Her bearing is one of homespun goodness, more matronly than military. She seats herself gracefully on the chair that continues to revolve slowly upward. As it makes a full circle, she makes eye contact with each person in turn, taking us in, studious yet affable. When her eyes meet mine, friendliness spills out towards me like the rays of a summertime dusk.

She speaks, and her voice is soft yet clear. "Congratulations to you all. Each of you gets to partake in a rare and splendid experience that the rest of the world only dreams of." She pauses, her ears perching up. "Everyone will be dying to hear about the Hunt afterwards; you'll all be plenty busy afterwards dealing with the media, especially the one of you who hunts down the most hepers." She spins slightly on her feet; her dress sashays around her legs.

"To that end, we've prepared a potpourri of activity for you all. You'll have *so* much to share with the media afterwards. Over the next few nights, your schedule will be jam-packed with events, from dusk to dawn. You might get restless, your mind on the Hunt in five nights. I understand." A few heads flick back, almost indiscernibly. She pauses, and when she recommences, there is a seriousness lining her words. "But between now and then, I need to stress the importance of maintaining your focus over the next few nights. With the training. Learn your necessary skills, absorb the tidbits of advice we give you. These are not ordinary hepers, the classic hepers you've read about or been told about. These hepers are different, special: they've been trained in the art of evasion, they know how to be on the run and, when necessary, to strike back. Over the past few months, we've supplied them with weapons – primitive fare like spears and daggers – but you'd be surprised by how adept they've become at using them.

"So keep your focus. If you start daydreaming too much about their blood, about the taste of their warm flesh under you, the feel of their hearts beating swiftly under your nails, the skin of their necks just about to break under the sharp pricks of your fangs" – a glazed look enters her eyes – "the taste of that first squirt of blood in your mouth, gushing into a stream . . ." She shakes her head, clearing her eyes. "That is what you need to avoid. Focus on your training so that you can help yourself be the victor. Because remember: you're training not only to hunt down the hepers, but also to beat out the other hunters. We've found from past Hunts that usually only one hunter comes to dominate the Hunt, who devours most, if not all, of the hepers. Out there in the desert, there's no community spirit, no spreading the wealth. You get to the hepers first, last thing you'll want to do is share the riches. No, inevitably, you'll find yourself gorging on the embarrassment of riches set before you. You want to be that hunter, you want to be the winner. So train hard. Focus. To the swift go the spoils."

Her face then breaks into rainbows. "You'll be taken to your rooms momentarily. Rest well, because tomorrow will be a real treat. A sumptuous breakfast, then a tour of this facility. You'll see the training grounds, the artillery room, the Control Centre, the meditation lounge, the dining area. And finally, at the end of the night, we'll take you to . . . the heper village."

Officials step forward from outside the circle and stand next to each hunter. The official on my right is a sullen grey statue. In his hand is a package.

"That's right," she says, still seated in the centre slowly revolving, "take the package. Read it when you get to your room. It has some invaluable information. Your escort will take you to your rooms now. You've all had an exciting and long night. Try to get some rest today. Turn in early."

She gets up and disappears into the dark. At that, we stand and follow our beckoning escorts. Our circle disintegrates as we disperse, quietly, swiftly. We are taken down different hallways, through different doors, until all that remains are the emptied chairs still positioned like the numbers of a handless, dysfunctional clock.

My escort leads me brusquely down a hallway, up a flight of stairs, along another hallway, and then down another flight of stairs without speaking. We walk the length of yet another hallway, dimly illuminated by candle, until we stand directly outside a large door. The escort pauses, turns to me. "I've been told to extend to you apologies. On behalf of the Heper Institute. Due to the number of lottery winners and the lack of rooms here, one of you has to be housed in . . . unique accommodations. It came down to the two youngest – you and your fellow schoolmate – and chivalry demands the girl be given the last guest room in the main building. Your room is actually in a small building a short distance removed. Unfortunately, the only way to get to it is by walking outside. Under the open sky."

Then, before I can respond, he pushes open the door and steps out. The expanse of the night sky – the desert plains spread underneath – catches me a little. Stars, pinpricks of silver, are scattered about like spilt salt. My escort mutters a curse and slips on a pair of shades. The moon hangs just above the mountains to the east; it is crescented, its lopsided smile reflective of my own pleasure at being outside. Truth is, I'm glad to be separated from the main building, from everyone else.

We're on a brick path that leads to a distant small slab building, single storey. "What did you say this place is?"

"It's a conversion," he answers without looking at me. "Used to be a small library. But we've spruced it up into a comfortable living quarter for you. It's up to snuff with everyone else's."

I take a quick glance back at the main building. Isolated patches of mercurial light are dotted about its face. Otherwise, the building is completely dark. "Look," my escort says, observing me, "I know you're wondering why we couldn't put you in the main building. It's got more unused rooms than hairs on a heper. I wondered the same thing myself. But I just do what I'm told. And so should you. Besides, there's a perk that comes with being housed here."

I wait for him to continue. But he shakes his head. "When we get there. Not right now. You'll like it, I promise. And you will want me to demonstrate how to use it, of course, won't you?"

Each brick of the path thrums with a vibrant red, like translucent containers of fresh blood. "This path was put down two days ago," he says, "to make this walk a little more pleasant for you." He pauses for effect and then says, "You'll never guess who did the job."

"I have no idea."

He turns to look at me for the first time. "Hepers."

I resist the impulse to widen my eyes. "No way," I say, snapping my head to the side a little. *Click*.

"Absolutely," he says. "We set them to work. In the daytime, of course. Our guys worked the night shift; but once it became clear we couldn't get it ready in time, we got the hepers to help out. They worked in the daytime for two days straight. We rewarded them with some extra food. Those things will do anything for food."

"Who supervised them? Who could have . . . you let them just roam freely?"

My escort just shakes his head with a "you've got a lot to learn, kid" look.

He pushes open the front doors and walks in. The interior is surprisingly spacious and airy. But the conversion from library to guest room is incomplete. It's really still a library, the only modification being a set of sleep-holds newly attached to the ceiling. Otherwise, the whole library looks virtually untouched: shelves still full of books, old, yellowed newspapers hung in cherrywood holders, and reading desks positioned evenly about the floor. A musty smell hangs over everything.

"The sleep-holds," he says, gazing upward. "Just installed yesterday."

"Hepers?"

He shakes his head. "That one we did. Hepers would never come inside. Too afraid of a trap. They're dumb, but not stupid, know what I mean?"

He shows me around at breakneck speed, pointing out the reference section, the mercuric light switches, and the closet filled with clothes for me and explaining how the shutters work automatically by light sensors. "They're super quiet, the shutters," he tells me. "They won't wake you." He speaks hurriedly. It's obvious he has something else on his mind. "You want to try out the sleep-holds? We should try them, make sure they fit."

"I'm sure they're fine, I'm not fussy that way."

"Good," he says. "Now, follow me, you're going to like this."

He leads me down a narrow aisle, his footsteps quick and eager, then turns sharply to the back of the library. Lying on a bureau next to a small, square window is a pair of binoculars. He picks it up and peers out of the window, his mouth open, drool sloshing audibly in his mouth. "I'm demonstrating how to use these binoculars because you asked me to. I'm only responding to your request," he says robotically, his index finger turning the zoom dial. "It's only because you asked me to."

"Hey," I say, "give me a look."

He doesn't respond, only continues to peer intently through the binoculars. His eyebrows are arched like the wings of an eagle.

"You can adjust the zoom by turning this dial," he mumbles. "Up and down, up and down, up and . . ." His voice drifts.

"Hey!" I say, louder.

"And on this side is the focus dial," he mumbles, his slim fingers sliding over the control. "Let me explain to you how this works. Since you asked. It's complicated, let me explain carefully. This might take a while."

Finally, I snatch the binoculars out of his hands.

His hand snaps around my forearm. I don't see it happen, he moved too fast. His nails pierce my skin, and for one horrible, sickening moment, I think those nails are about to slice through and draw blood. He lets go immediately, of course, even takes a step or two back. A glazed, distant look is still clouding his eyes, but it is dissipating fast.

Three nail indentations are planted in my wrist, dangerously deep. But no blood.

"Apologies," he says.

"Don't worry about it." I hold my arm behind my back, feeling the indentation with the fingers of my other hand. Still no moisture: still no blood. If a drop of a drop of blood had seeped through, he'd already be at me.

"Did I demonstrate it well enough for you?" His voice is pleading. "Do you understand how to use the binoculars now?"

"I think I can give it a try."

"Perhaps one more demonstration will—"

"No. I can handle it." Keeping the binoculars behind my back, I turn to look outside. A crescent moon shines behind a scrim of clouds, its thin, sickly light falling down. "What am I supposed to be looking at?"

He doesn't say anything, so I turn to look at him. For a moment, the clarity in his eyes turns slightly opaque again. A line of drool that hasn't yet been wiped away thickens down his chin. "Hepers," he whispers.

I don't want him hovering behind me, pestering me for another "demonstration", so I wait until he leaves. I'm filled with a strange dread but also an excitement as I pick up the binoculars. Other than my family, I've never laid eyes on a heper.

At first, I'm not sure what I should be looking for. Then moonlight spills through a break in the clouds, illuminating the swathe of land. I swivel the binoculars slowly, searching: a brief burst of cactus, a boulder, nothing—

A small collection of mud huts sitting inconspicuously off in the distance. The heper village. My guess is it's about a mile away. A pond of some sort – no doubt man-made; no body of water could possibly survive in this terrain – lies in the centre. Nothing moves. The mud huts are as nondescript as the desert.

Then I see something.

Moonlight glimmers above the mud huts in a concave shimmer. Then I realise: there's a transparent dome covering it. It rises high, about fifty yards at its highest point above the mud huts. Its circumference encapsulates the entirety of the village.

Of course; it all makes sense now.

Without the dome, the hepers would be a free-for-all. What would prevent the people from marauding the mud huts at night when the hepers lay asleep and unprotected? Who could stop themselves from feasting on them unless they were sealed in completely? They'd never have survived a single night hour without that dome of protection.

I zoom in on the mud huts, searching for some sign of life. But nothing moves. The hepers are asleep. Not a chance of seeing them tonight.

A heper steps out of one of the huts.

Even with binoculars, I make out very little. A thin figure, walking towards the pond, female. It appears to be holding a bucket of some kind. When it reaches the edge of the pond, it bends over, fills the bucket. I play with the dial until it comes sharper into focus. Then I recognise it: the female heper on TV, the one that picked out the last lottery number.

I watch as it stands up, takes a sip of water from cupped hands. Its back is to me, its head staring east at the mountains. For a long time, it does not move. Then it bends down, cups its hands, takes another sip. Its movement, even for so simple an act, is graceful and sure. Its head suddenly swings in my direction; I flinch back. Perhaps it has caught a reflection off the binoculars' lens. But it is looking past me, at the Institute. I zoom in on the face. Those eyes: I remember them from earlier this evening, on my deskscreen, their brown tone like the trunk of a wrongly felled tree.

After a few moments, it turns around and disappears into a mud hut.

Hunt Minus Four Nights

I AM CURIOUS about the library they've lodged me in and intend to stay up through the day hours to explore. But the night's activities have worn me out; no sooner have I sat down to read the welcome package than I find myself waking up, hours later.

Somebody is pounding at the door. Startled, I jump up, my heart hammering. "Give me a minute!" I shout. I hear a mumbled response.

Fear douses me awake. I'm realising now. My face. I'm not ready. My fingers reach for my chin: a faint stubble just breaking the skin. Enough to be noticed. And what of my eyes? Are they bloodshot with fatigue? And do my fake teeth need to be whitened, my body washed?

Never forget to shave. Get enough sleep to avoid bloodshot eyes. Never forget to whiten your teeth every morning before you leave. And wash every day; body odour is the most dangerous—

My father's instructions. I've abided by them every single day of my life. But my razor blades and eye drops and fang whiteners and underarm ointments are stashed miles away at home. Given the right mix of other products, I could cobble together what I need. For example, three sheets of aluminium foil dissolved in horse shampoo with a liberal application of baking soda will, after a fortnight, congeal into a serviceable bar of underarm deodorant. Trouble is, I don't have these ingredients at hand. Nor do I have a fortnight to spare.

The door pounding gets louder, more insistent. I do the only thing I can. Grab my penknife and quickly raze my chin, making sure not to chafe my skin. That would be a fatal mistake. Then I grab my shades and head to the front door. Just in time, I catch myself. My clothes. They're creased from being slept in, a telltale sign that I didn't sleep in the sleep-holds. I run to the closet, throw on a new outfit.

The escort is not happy. "I've been knocking for five minutes. What's the matter with you?"

"Sorry, overslept. Sleep-holds were comfy."

He turns, starts walking. "Come now. The first lecture is about to begin. We have to hurry." He takes another glance back at me. "And lose the shades. It's cloudy tonight."

I ignore him.

The Director of the Heper Institute is as sterile and dry as his surroundings, which is saying a lot. His face has a plastic sheen, and he likes to stand wherever it is dark. He exudes an austere authority that is both quiet and deadly. He can whisper a rat to death with the razor-sharp incisions of his carefully nuanced words.

"Hepers are slow, hepers like to hold hands, hepers like to warble their voices, hepers need to drink copious amounts of water. They have an expansive range of facial tics, they sleep at night, they are preternaturally resistant to sunlight. These are the rudimentary facts about hepers." The Director speaks with a practised élan. He pauses dramatically in the dark corner, the white glow of his eyes disappearing, then reappearing, as he opens his eyes. "After decades of intense study, we now know significantly more about them. Much of this information is known to only a few of us here at the Heper Institute of Refined Research and Discovery. Because you will be hunting hepers in four nights, it has been determined that you, too, will become privy to the latest research. Everything we know about hepers, you will know. But first, the waivers."

We all sign them, of course. The papers are handed out by officials in grey suits who emerge from the darkness behind us. *All information learned over the next few weeks will not be disclosed or disseminated to any person after the Hunt is completed unless the Heper Institute expressly grants permission.* I initial next to it. *You may not sell your story for publication or option said story for a theatrical production unless the Heper Institute expressly grants permission.* I initial next to it. *Compliance is total and irrevocable.* I initial next to it. *Upon punishment of death.* I sign and date it.

The Director has been watching us carefully as we sign, each hunter in turn. His eyes are black holes, sucking in observations with a slippery, keen acuity. He never misses a thing, never guesses wrong. As I hand over my waiver papers, I feel his eyes clamp down on me like a suddenly jammed stapler. Just before the papers are taken from me, they dangle off my hand, shaking ever so slightly. His eyes flip to the papers, to the way they are quivering. I know this without looking, from the piercing cold burn on my wrist where his eyes settle. I grip the papers tighter to still them.

Then I feel his stare shift away, the cold burn on my wrist evaporating. He has moved on to the next hunter.

After all the papers have been collected, he continues without missing a beat. "Much of what is known about hepers is more fictional than factual. It's time to debunk these myths.

"Myth one: they are wild beasts at heart and will be continual flight risks. Fact: they are easily domesticated and are actually quite afraid of the unknown. Truth is, during the day while we sleep and the Dome is retracted, they are unsupervised and free to roam. The whole stretch of the plains, as far as you can see, free for them to escape, far and away. If they choose. But they never have. Of course, it's easy to understand why. Any heper who leaves the safety of the Dome is – come night-time – free game. Within two hours, it would have been sniffed out, chased down, and devoured. In fact, this has happened. Once or twice." He does not elaborate.

"Myth two: they are passive and submissive, ready to lie down rather than fight back. Ironically, this myth has been perpetuated by previous Hunts when the hepers showed anything but resistance. Historical accounts of that Hunt reflect how useless they were: first, the initial flight, where they proved to be slow and disorganised; and second, their submissive surrender when surrounded by us. Even when we were two miles away, they just gave up. Stopped running. And when we came on them, not a single one fought back, not so much as even a single raised arm. Practically lay down and let us have at them.

"What our research has demonstrated, however, is that hepers can be trained to be aggressive. They've demonstrated surprising acumen with the weapons provided. Primitive weapons, mind you, mere spears, knives, daggers, axes. And, quite endearingly, they've even fashioned leather guards that they place around their necks for protection. Those naive darlings." He starts scratching his wrist, then stops. He jots something down in his notebook. "Not sure how they got the leather. Surprisingly resourceful, they can be."

We sit still as he finishes writing. He snaps the notebook shut, starts speaking again.

"Myth three: they are a male-dominated society. This is another myth perpetuated by previous Heper Hunts. You've all heard about it, how it's always the men who take charge – futilely; the men who make all the decisions – the wrong ones, as we also know. The women typically do nothing but follow. Followers. Submissive. We thought this was simply how they were genetically wired: men dominate, women submit. But our research has produced some startling results. Currently, we have five hepers in captivity, all but one of which is male. Four males, only one female. Want to wager a guess who's the leader?" His eyes sparkle with excitement.

"This is one of the more surprising discoveries. In fact, it was I who was the first to spot the trend. Even early on, when the hepers were mere toddlers, it was I who noted that the sole female heper seemed to be in the forefront of everything. A natural-born leader. Today, she is without question the leader of the pack. They look to her for . . . well, everything. Where she goes, they follow. What she commands, they obey. During the Hunt, if you want to cut off the head from the body, you take her out first. With her out of the picture, the group will quickly disintegrate. Easy pickings, thereafter."

He licks his lips.

"This girl. All of you have seen her, in fact. On TV – she was the one who picked the last number. That wasn't supposed to happen, of course. We would never have put a female on the airwaves, especially one so young. We know the effect a young female heper has on people. It was supposed to be a little boy heper. But she . . . well, before we knew it, she took control of the situation and put herself in front of the camera. That girl . . ." His words grow slithery with saliva. Spittle collects at the corners of his mouth. His eyes grow distant; he is lost in some dreamland. When he speaks, his voice is soft with desire. "She would be delicious, so . . ."

He snaps out of it with a quick flick of his head. "I digress. My apologies. The official who let that happen is no longer with us." He scratches his wrist, once, twice.

"There are other myths," he continues, "and other discoveries we will disclose to you over the next few days. But for now, absorb what we've just told you. Use this new knowledge to aid you in the Hunt: first, hepers are afraid to flee into the unknown; and second, they can be trained to be aggressive. And they do not mind having a woman lead them. Not this one, anyway."

He slips away deeper into his dark corner; blackness swallows him. Nothing happens for the next few minutes. Nobody moves, nobody speaks. We sit, blasé faces and glazed stares. Waiting for someone, something, to break the silence.

Then I sense it. A prick at the back of my neck: someone from behind is staring intently at me. The last thing to do – I hear my father's voice instructing me – is turn around. Moving so drastically while everyone else is stationary will only draw attention. *Unwanted* attention, as if there were any other kind.

But the prick sharpens until I can take it no longer. I let a pen in my hand fall to the ground; as I slowly swivel around to pick it up, I shoot a quick glance back.

It's Ashley June, her eyes death green in the mercurial light. She's sitting *right* behind me. I almost startle in my seat – "startle" is this reflex where we jump a little in fright – but tamp it down just in time. I close my eyelids halfway – a trick my father taught me to make sure my eyes don't widen too much – and turn around.

Did she see me startle? *Did she see me startle?*

Somebody is at the lectern. Frilly Dress from yesterday. "How are we all tonight? Having fun?" She takes out a notepad, scans it, then looks up, smiling. "We have a busy schedule tonight. First, we'll tour the facilities – should take most of the night. Then, time and darkness permitting, we'll cap it off with a visit to the heper village just shy of two miles from the main building. If we're running late and it gets too close to sunrise, then we'll have to push it off till tomorrow." She looks at each of us, reading our expressions. "Somehow I don't think you're going to allow that to happen. Shall we move on, then?"

What follows for the next few hours is a mind-numbingly tedious tour of the facilities. It's nothing more than an amble along dark, endless hallways. And emptiness. That's what strikes me the most: how still and empty everything is – the rooms, the hallways, the very dank air we inhale, mere remnants and echoes of a busier, fuller, livelier era. Our escorts follow us, silently. The second floor is where the staff and hunters are housed, and we bypass it. The third floor is the science floor, for obvious reasons: from one end to the other, it's lined with laboratories. A smell of musky formaldehyde permeates the whole floor. Although the guide speaks glowingly about each laboratory – this one used to study heper hair, this one to study heper laughter, this one heper singing – it is obvious the laboratories have fallen into disuse.

"This whole thing's a crock, you know that, right?"

"Excuse me?" I turn to the elderly man next to me. One of the hunters. We are in a lab previously used to study heper hair and fingernails. The man is leaning towards me, his gaunt frame tilting like a snapped pencil, his head slanted close to a sample of heper fingernails encased in a glass plate. His bald head is as shiny and hairless as the plate, but mottled over with age marks near his forehead. A few wisps of hair are combed across his gleaming head, like thin strands of night clouds across the moon. We are alone at the back of a laboratory; everyone else is clustered near the front of the lab, where the (apparently) more exciting samples of heper hair are on display.

"A crock," he whispers.

"These fingernails?"

He shakes his head. "This whole tour. This whole training period."

I take a sideways glance at him. This is the first time I'm seeing him up close, and he is older than I thought. Hair wispier, wrinkles deeper, the curve of his back more pronounced.

"Why do we need training?" His voice is gravelly. "Just let us have at the hepers, already. We'll devour them in a minute. We don't need training. We have our instinct, we have our hunger. What else do we need?"

"We need to draw this out. Savour the moment. Anticipation is half the enjoyment."

It's his turn to look at me. A brief look, but one that absorbs. I feel the suction of his brain taking me in. And then his approval.

I've been watching him a bit since yesternight. He stuck out, and I now know why. He doesn't want to be here. Every other hunter (except me, of course) is ecstatic, has just literally won the lottery of a lifetime. But his feet drag just so, his eyes fail to shine with the glee the others have, and everything about him seems to spell r-e-l-u-c-t-a-n-c-e. In short, he's everything I'm feeling inside. A thought comes to my mind, but I dismiss it outright: *There's no chance he's a heper.* A real heper (like me) would be covering up those feelings (as I'm doing), not letting them hang out like dirty underwear for all to observe.

As I study him – his stiff, arthritic gait whittled down by age – it hits me why he's so sullen. He knows he doesn't stand a chance.

Not against the younger hunters, who'll outrun and outgun him. By the time he gets to the hepers, there won't even be bones left to gnaw on. This Heper Hunt is torture for him, to be so close yet so far. No wonder he's bitter. He's a starving man at a banquet who knows there won't even be crumbs left on the floor for him.

"There's more going on here than meets the eye," he says, still bent over the glass plate.

I'm not sure what to say, so I wait for him to continue. But he doesn't; he shuffles to the front of the lab and joins the others, leaving me standing all alone.

After touring the laboratories on the third floor, we are taken to the fourth floor. We go through it quickly; it's really nothing more than a series of unused classrooms, the chairs inside propped upside down on desktops. At the far end is the auditorium. We stick our heads through the door to take a look. I smell a dusty dankness. Nobody wants to venture in, and we move on.

Eventually we wind up on the top floor, the fifth. The Control Centre spans the full length and width of this floor. The hubbub here is markedly different from the deadness of the lower floors. Clearly, this is the nerve centre to the whole operation. Numerous computers and TV monitors glow from one end to the other. Staffers are up and about, clipboards in hand, walking briskly between desks and cubicles and computer terminals. They're all men, dressed in navy blue single-breasted jackets with peaked lapels and double vents, but slim to the fit and streamlined. Three buttons run down the front of their jackets, emitting a dim mercurial light. They're curious about us, and I catch them stealing furtive glances. We're the heper hunters, after all. We're the ones who get to eat and drink heper flesh and blood.

Instead of concrete walls, large panel windows stretch from ceiling to floor, giving us an almost uninterrupted 360-degree view of the outside. From up here, it feels as if we're hovering above the moonlit plains spread below us.

The group moves over to the windows facing east. The Dome. They all want to see the Dome.

It sits small in the distance, a marble sliced in half, glimmering slightly under the stars.

"There's nothing to see," an escort says. "All they do is sleep at night."

"They never come out?"

"Hardly ever at night."

"They don't like the stars?"

"People. They don't like people watching them."

We stare in silence.

"It's almost like they know we're watching," one of the hunters whispers.

"Bet there's a bunch of them staring back at us. From inside one of those huts. Right now, as we speak."

"They're just sleeping now," says an escort.

We're all straining forward, hoping to catch some movement. But all is still.

"I heard the Dome opens at sunrise."

The escorts glance at one another, not sure if they're allowed to respond.

"Yes," says an escort. "There are sunlight sensors that trigger the Dome. The Dome rises out of the ground two hours before dusk and retracts into the ground one hour after dawn."

"So there's no way to manually open the Dome?" asks Ashley June. "From in here? A button to press or lever to pull that would open it?" There's a protracted, intense silence.

"No. Everything is automated," says an escort. "It's all been taken out of our hands." He has more to say, but he's biting his tongue.

"Do you have any binoculars?"

"Yes. But there's nothing to see. The hepers are all asleep."

Everyone is so caught up with the Dome, nobody observes Ashley June slide away.

Except me.

I follow her from the corners of my eyes, turning my head when she slips altogether from my vision.

She drifts towards the back of the room where three rows of security monitors line the wall. Under the monitors sits a staffer, his head swivelling slowly from side to side and up and down as he scans the monitors above him. She stands very close behind him, edging closer, slowly, until a few strands of hair graze the side of his forehead.

He moves quickly, a slide to his right. She scratches her wrist, apologising, scratching harder, making sure the moment becomes light and accidental. On his chair, he swivels around to face her, then stands. He's baby-faced and inexperienced, and his bleary eyes take a while to take in what's before him. A young lady, and a beautiful one at that. This man, his world filled with an endless onslaught of digital screens, is taken aback by this sudden intrusion of flesh. Ashley June scratches her wrist more, trying to set him at ease. A moment passes, and he begins to scratch his wrist in return, cautiously at first, then faster and surer. His eyes begin to gain focus and brighten.

She says something, but I'm too far away to hear. He answers, energy now beginning to course through his body, and points at a number of different monitors. She asks another question, her body turning slightly towards the monitors, inching closer to the man.

He notices. And when he answers, his head bobs enthusiastically on his narrow shoulders.

No doubt about it, she's good at this flirtation game. And she's up to something.

She raises her long arm, pointing at one of the monitors. Her arm stretches out effortlessly upward like the exclamation point at the end of a sentence that reads: *I'm gorgeous!* That arm has always done a number on me, all those years sitting behind her, especially in the summer months when she wore sleeveless shirts and I could view the whole length of her wonderful, perfectly sculptured arms. They were neither too thin nor too thick, just the perfect dimensions with perfect ridges that exuded both assurance and grace. Even the light freckles that sprinkle her arm, exploding in a splattering of dots as they disappear into her shirt, are more seductive than imperfect.

Slowly, I edge closer to Ashley June, positioning myself behind a small pillar. I peer around the pillar; she's moved even closer to him. Above them, images from security cameras shine with a dull blur. At least a good half of them centre on the Dome.

"Can't believe they're running all the time."

"Twenty-four/seven," he answers proudly.

"And is there always someone watching these monitors?"

"Well, we used to station a staffer here. But, well, it became . . . there was a policy change."

"A policy change?"

There is a long pause.

"Oh, c'mon, you can tell me," Ashley June says.

"Don't tell anyone," the staffer warns, his voice hushed.

"OK. Our secret."

"Some staffers became so lost in these images of the hepers that they'd . . ."

"Yes?"

"They lost their senses, they were driven mad with desire. They'd rush out at the heper village."

"But it's enclosed by the Dome."

"No, you don't understand. They'd rush out in the daytime."

"What?"

"Right from this very seat. One moment they're staring at the monitors, and the next they're rushing down the stairs and out of the exit doors."

"Even with the sun burning?"

"It's like they forgot. Or it just didn't matter to them anymore." Another pause. "So that's why there was a policy change. First, no more recordings—illegal bootleg copies were somehow winding up on the streets. And second, now everyone leaves this floor before dawn."

"It's completely unstationed during the day?"

"Not only is it unstationed, but look, the windows have no shutters. They were taken down. So now, the sun pours in during the daytime. The best security system. Nobody's coming in here after dawn. Nobody."

There is a pause, and I think that's the end of the conversation when Ashley June speaks again. "And what's that big blue oval button over there?"

"I'm not really supposed to say."

"Oh, c'mon, it's safe with me."

Another pause.

"Like everything else you've told me, all the stuff you could get fired for disclosing, it's all safe with me," says Ashley June, this time with a hint of a threat in her voice.

"It's the lockdown control," he says tersely after a moment.

"What's that?"

"It shuts the building down, locks all entrances, shutters all windows. There's no leaving the building once lockdown has been deployed. Push it to set the system, push again to cancel—"

His voice gets drowned out by the approaching tour group, which has moved away from the windows and is now mumbling its way towards the back of the floor, towards the monitors. I slink back into the mix. Nobody's noticed my absence. I don't think.

By the time the group reaches the monitors, the staffer is back in his seat, his head swivelling back and forth, up and down. One of the escorts is speaking in a monotone voice, talking about the function of the monitors, how every square inch of the Institute is covered by a camera. But nobody is listening, they're all staring at images of the Dome in the monitors. They're still looking for hepers.

Except me. I'm watching Ashley June.

She's slinked away again and is wandering around. Or at least pretending to. Something about her bearing – maybe the way she turns her head just so to read documents on desks or bends over as she passes by a control panel filled with switches and buttons – seems purposeful and deliberate. And she's trying to go about unnoticed, but it's near impossible. She's a heper hunter, she's female, she's beautiful. She's sizzling hot oil on your brains. Before long every male staffer around her has taken notice. She realises this, too, and before long, gives up. She rejoins us at the monitors, tilting her head up. She stands very still, immovable, unreadable.

I stare from behind, the line of hair streaming down over the nape of her neck, dark with a dull gleam. She's up to something here in the Control Centre; I can't shake that feeling. Digging for information. Looking for something. Seeking confirmation. I'm not sure. But what I am sure of: she's playing a game the rest of us don't even realise has begun.

Lunch is late that night; it's well past midnight before we are taken down to a large hall on the ground floor and seated at a circular table. None of the escorts sit with us; instead, they retreat to their own table in the peripheral darkness. Without their hovering presence, the hunters are set at ease: our backs relax, we become more talkative. Lunch offers the first time I'm really able to meet the other hunters.

It's the food we talk about initially. These are meats we've never tasted before, only read about. Jackrabbit, hyena, meerkat, kangaroo rat. Fresh kills from the Vast. Or so they say. The flagship dish is a special treat: cheetah, typically eaten only by high-ranking officials at weddings. Cheetahs are difficult to catch, not because of their speed – even the slowest person can outsprint a fleeing cheetah – but because of their rarity.

Each dish, of course, comes wet and bloody. We comment on the texture of the different meats on our tongue, the superior taste to the synthetic meats we usually eat. Blood oozes down our chins, collecting in the drip cups placed below. We will drink it all up at the end of the meal, a soupy collection of cold animal blood.

What I most need is absent from the dinner table: water. It's been over a night since my last drink at home, and I can feel my body desiccating. My tongue, dry and thick, feels like a wad of cotton wool stuffed in my mouth. The past hour or so, spells of dizziness have whirled in my mind. My drip cup gradually fills with mixed blood. I will drink it because it is liquidy and watery enough. Kind of.

"I heard they stuck you in the library." It's a man in his forties, sitting next to me, beefy with broad shoulders; he's the president of SPHTH (Society for the Protection and Humane Treatment of

Horses). His generous potbelly protrudes just above table level. My designation for him: *Beefy*.

"Yup," I say. "Sucks the big one, having to walk outside. You guys are probably partying up in here all day while I'm cooped up all by my lonesome, bored as anything."

"It's the sunrise curfew that would get me," Beefy says, his mouth full of flesh. "Having to leave everyone and everything, drop of the hat, forced to leave. And all alone out there, surrounded by desert and sunlight in the day hours."

"You got all those books," Ashley June says next to me. "What's there to complain about? You can study up on hunting techniques, get a leg up on us."

I see the elderly, gaunt man I'd met in the lab earlier scratch his wrist ever so slightly. He jams a piece of hyena liver into his mouth. His designation: *Gaunt Man*.

"I heard," says another hunter, "that the library belonged to a fringe scientist with some pretty loony theories on hepers." The woman, who looks fit for her age – I place her in her mid-thirties, a dangerous age, equal parts fit and savvy – sits across from me; she barely looks up from her plate as she speaks. Jet black hair, greased up, accentuating her angular pale chin. Her lips are luscious and full, crimson with the dripping of flesh blood, as if her own lips were bleeding profusely down her chin. When she speaks, her lips part across her teeth at an angle, as if only one side of her lips can be bothered to move. Like a lazy snarl. I think: *Crimson Lips*.

"Where did you hear that?" I ask.

Crimson Lips looks up from her bloody plate and holds my gaze, measuring me. "What, the library? Because I've been asking about you," she says, her voice cool and difficult to read, "and why you were put there. My escort knows everything. Quite chatty, once you get him started, actually. Told me, too, lest we start feeling too sorry for you, of the great view you have."

"Same view you guys get. Except I'm out in the middle of nowhere."

"But you're closer, though!" Beefy says, blood spraying out of his mouth and speckling down his chin. A wad of half-chewed rabbit liver flies out, landing near Crimson Lips' plate. Before Beefy can move, she snaps up the chunk and puts it into her mouth. He glares at her briefly before turning his attention back to us. "You're closer to the Dome. To the hepers."

At that, it's as if every head turns to look at me.

I quickly bite off a large chunk of meat; I chew it slowly, deliberately, buying time. I scratch my wrist rapidly. "With about a mile of daylight between me and them. And at night, an impenetrable glass dome insulating them from me. They might as well be on a different planet."

"It's cursed, that place," says Crimson Lips. "The library, I mean. Eventually, it gets to you, drives you batty. It's the proximity. Being so tantalisingly close, being able to smell them but not get to them. Every person who's stayed there has lost it, sooner or later. Usually sooner."

"I heard that's what happened to the Scientist," says Beefy. "He got the itch one night. A few months ago. At dusk, he ventured out, went right up to the Dome. Was pressing his face against the glass like a kid outside a candy store. He simply forgot the time and then . . . *well, hello, sunrise!*" He shrugs. "At least that's the theory. Nobody saw it happen. They found a pile of his clothes halfway between the library and the Dome."

"Good riddance, is what I hear," Crimson Lips says. "He was absolutely useless. They looked at his research after he disappeared. Notebooks and journals filled with absolute dreck."

Dessert arrives, ice cream. This is one of the few foods for which I don't have to fake an appetite. I scarf it down, slowing down only when a sharp pain pinches my forehead. The other hunters continue to stuff their faces, especially the two sitting on my left.

They're in their twenties, both students at the College. He's a phys ed major, she's undeclared. Physical specimens, both of them, to say the least. He's rippling in muscles, although he doesn't flaunt it. She's more of an exhibitionist, wearing daring cut-offs that show off her abdominal muscles. Lookers, too, with crystalline skin, high-bridged noses, and doorknobs for cheekbones. Both Phys Ed and Abs have a natural bounce to their step that speaks of effortless strength and agility. But dumb as doorknobs. One thing's instantly clear: they're the top contenders. One of them is going to win the Hunt. The other is going to finish whatever hepers are left over. No wonder Gaunt Man is unhappy.

Frilly Dress springs in from nowhere, her shrill voice ringing across the hall like a shattered plate. "And did we all have a stupendous lunch?" she asks. It's apparent she has: her chin is still dripping with fresh blood. "Time to move on to the next part of the tour. In fact, we've been moving so fast, we have almost nothing left on today's agenda. My, my, my, you all really should pace yourselves slower. You won't learn anything at this breakneck speed!"

I catch Gaunt Man shoot me a knowing look, as if to say: *Didn't I tell you? This whole thing is a meaningless exercise in redundancy.*

"So," continues Frilly Dress, "the only thing left remaining on tonight's itinerary is the visit to the Dome. This is going to be a real treat. Mind you, we'll likely not see any hepers since they sleep at night, but their odours are really pungent there. To die for, really."

A few necks twitch around the table.

"So, shall we? Make our way now?"

And like that, we're all standing, waiting for our escorts. And then, away we go.

By the quick pace of our feet rushing down the stairs; by the force with which the exit doors are flung open; by the look of excitement on even Gaunt Man's face; by the spasmodic and minuscule vibrations of our heads – I know we are excited. I know we are desirous.

As if by tacit agreement, no one speaks. We are silent, our shoes first padding the hard marble floors and then, once outside, lilting on the softer give of the brick path. Even as we walk past the library, nobody says anything. Only Gaunt Man peers inside, curiously, then at me, perhaps wondering why I, of all of them, have been housed in there. When the brick path comes to an end and our shoes hit the hard, dusty gravel of the Vast, it is as if nobody dares even breathe, we are so wordless.

"It never gets old," an escort finally says. And at that, the pace quickens even more.

I worry that the collective excitement will spring everyone into running. It wouldn't take much to set them off. If that happens, I'll be exposed. Because I can't run, at least not as fast as everyone else. Not by half, in speed or stamina. I still remember in first grade how all my classmates used to zoom past me, and all I could do was plod along as if I were in a vat of mercury. *Always fall,* my father would say, *always pretend to trip and sprain your ankle. Then you can sit out*.

"Hey," I say to no one in particular, to everyone in particular, "there's no way we can get inside the Dome, right?"

"Nope," answers my escort.

"Probably won't even see any hepers, right?"

"Nope. They're all sleeping this time of night."

"So we'll see exactly what we're seeing now, but closer up?"

"What?"

"Well, just mud huts, a pond, laundry lines. That's all, right?"

"Yup."

"Boring," I say daringly.

But the group buys it, at least enough to dampen their excitement. The pace slows.

Fifteen minutes later, we're nearing the Dome. Its scale as we approach takes me by surprise: it towers above us and cups over much more acreage than I previously thought. Crimson Lips starts twitching as she walks in front of me. Abs' shoulders hike up, stiffening with excitement. Phys Ed, walking next to her, is elevating his nose into the air, sniffing.

"I smell them. I smell heper," Gaunt Man shouts, his gnarled voice exploding into the night's quiet. Other heads snap up with a *crack,* noses pointed upward and around, sniffing.

About fifty yards out, they crash through the tipping point and break into a stampede. I plod behind them, running as fast as I can. They are blurs, a haphazard menagerie of black oscillations and grey smudges, legs springing and pumping, arms swinging upward and out. There is no grace or order about their movements, just a random assortment of cuts, springs, leaps.

By the time I catch up with them, they're pressed up against the glass, too fixated by the Dome to notice my late arrival. Inside the Dome are about ten mud huts. They're dotted evenly around the compound, about half of them clustered near a pond. And the pond is remarkable: first, for its very existence smack bang in the middle of the desert; but also for the perfectly symmetrical circle it makes. Man-made, without a doubt.

Next to the technological wizardry of the pond and Dome, the mud huts look like prehistoric relics. The walls are cratered and rough, punctured by small, unframed windows. Each hut sits on two encircling rows of rectangular stones, coarsely fitted together.

"Can't see a thing inside," Beefy says.

"Probably all just sleeping, anyway," an escort says.

"But take a whiff, I can smell them. Stronger than usual," says my escort, standing next to me.

"Just a bit," another escort says, at the other end of the group.

"More than just a bit," my escort says. "It's pretty strong tonight. They must have been running around a lot, sweating earlier." But a frown crosses his face. He turns in my direction, takes another sniff. "Very strong tonight. Odd, that."

I force myself to remain calm. It's me who's giving off the smell, I know that, but I can't move or do anything too drastic. So I try to distract. With a question: "How deep is that pond?"

"Not sure," he says. "Deep enough to drown in, I suppose. But no heper has ever drowned. They're like fish, those things."

"No way that pond's natural," I say.

"Genius in the midst of us," Gaunt Man says, then spits in the dusty, hard ground.

"Is this glass Dome porous?" Abs suddenly asks. She's been so quiet, it takes me a second to realise the pretty voice belongs to her. "Because I can smell heper. So much better than the artificial smells they sell."

"It does seem to have got stronger over the past few minutes," Phys Ed says.

"Must be porous. I can really smell them!" Abs says excitedly.

"Didn't think so, but the air really is thick with their odour . . ." my escort says distractedly. "Daylight was hours ago. Almost eight hours ago. Shouldn't be this much odour lingering." His nostrils are working faster now, flaring with alarming wetness. Those nostrils start turning towards me, like eyes widening with realisation.

I shift away from the group. "I'm going to walk around the Dome, see if I can see anything on the other side." Thankfully, no one follows me. On the other side, hidden by the mud huts, I spit into my hands, then vigorously rub my armpits. Pretty disgusting, but so is the alternative, which is being ripped apart into a hundred pieces.

When I return to the group, they're ready to head back. "Smell's gone," Gaunt Man says with a hangdog expression, "and nothing to see. Hepers are all asleep."

We start to head back, despondency dragging our feet. No one says a word. I take the back of the line, downwind.

"Starry night," someone says to me.

It's Ashley June, peering back at me.

"A bit too bright for my liking," I say.

She scratches her wrist ambiguously with a glance upward. "Those hepers are just like zoo animals," she says, "sleeping all the time."

"The escorts say they're naturally shy."

"Stupid animals," she spits. "It's their loss."

"How so?"

She surprises me by slowing down until we're side by side. "Think about it," she says, her voice congenial. "The more the prey knows about the hunter, the more of a strategic advantage it gains. If those things were awake, they'd know how many of us there are, how many men, how many women, our ages—"

"You're assuming they know about the Hunt."

"They must. They've been given weapons."

"Doesn't mean anything. Besides, a 'strategic advantage' isn't going to help them one bit. No matter what, this Hunt's over in two hours tops."

"One hour, if I have anything to do with it," she whispers. It's clearly meant for only me to hear. I steal a sideways glance at her. Since we've arrived at the Heper Institute, she's been less brash, less front and centre, than the starlet I know at school, hardly a blip on the radar, in fact. She still commands attention, of course, on account of her attractiveness, but she hasn't flaunted it the way she does at school.

A breeze sifts across the Vast, blowing strands of hair across her pale cheekbones. Her eyes, hardened under the stony night light, seem restless. She suddenly bends down to tie her laces. I stop with her. She takes her time, untying and then retying the laces on her other shoe as well.

By the time she stands up, the group has moved on ahead. "You know, I'm so glad you're here," she says softly. "It's just so good to have a . . . friend."

The sound of the desert wind fills the silence between us.

"I think we should team up," she says. "I think we can really help each other."

"I work best alone."

She pauses. "Did you read a lot about the Hunt ten years ago?"

"Yeah, just like everyone else," I lie. I avoided every book, every article, every sentence, every word.

"Well, I've been studying this Hunt thing. A lot more than anyone else. Like, religiously. It's been an obsession of mine for years. I've read books, subscribed to journals, scoured the library for tidbits of information on the topic. Even listened to radio interviews with former winners, though they tended to be plenty brawny but pretty dumb. Anyway, just to say, whatever you might learn over the next five days, I already know. Knew it years ago."

"That's nice to know," I say, not sure where this is going. But she's not lying. She a member of all kinds of heper societies and clubs at school.

"Listen. This is the open secret. Most people here already know it, but you seem clueless, so let me fill you in. It's all about alliances. The winner always comes out of the strongest alliance. Always. It's true for the last Hunt, and it's true for every Hunt before that. If you team up well, you'll do well. Simple as that."

"Why don't you partner up with one of the other hunters? Everyone knows that raw strength and physical prowess always wins the Hunt. And the other hunters are better contenders than me in that department. Take the two college students, for example: they're athletically and physically imposing. Even the cagey old guy is a stronger hunter than me; where he might be lacking in the strength department, he more than makes up for it with his guile and street smarts. And what about the woman – she looks like she knows how to handle herself. She's got it both: she's mentally wily *and* physically dexterous. You'd do well with her."

"It's a trust issue. You're the only one here I can trust."

"Well, trust me on this one. With me, you'll lose."

"Why, you're not going to even try?"

"Of course I am! I want those hepers just as much as anyone else. But I'm a realist."

"Look," she says, putting a hand on my chest and stopping me. "You can go at it alone and have no chance, or you can team up with me, and together we might have a chance. But you go into this without any kind of plan, and you're going to end up empty-handed."

She's right, but not in the way she thinks. Because I, more than anyone else, know that if I go into this without a plan, I lose. And not just the Hunt. But my life. Without a strategy, the Hunt will expose me for what I am.

I do have a plan, and it's quite simple: survive. That's it. Over the next few nights, lie low, don't attract attention. Then, the night before the Hunt, feign an injury. A broken leg. Actually, I'll have to do more than feign – I'll have to *actually* break my leg. I'll make a big fuss about the bad luck of getting taken out of the Hunt. Punch and kick and claw at the administration as the hunters head off into the distance while I lie in bed, cast wrapped around my leg. And then go on with life. So yes, she's right: I do need a plan. And I already have one. But it doesn't involve teaming up with her.

"Look, I understand. But I . . . work better alone."

I think I see something flash in her eyes, some kind of breakage. "Why do you keep doing this to me?"

"What?"

"Pushing me away. All these years."

"What are you talking about? We don't even really know each other."

"And why is that?" she says, and paces forward to catch up with the group, her hair billowing behind her in the breeze.

Against my better judgment, I quicken my steps until I catch up with her. "Wait, listen."

She turns to look at me but keeps walking.

"We *should* talk. You're right."

"OK," she replies after a moment. "But not here. Too many prying eyes, curious ears. Let's stop by the library."

Our escorts are none too happy with this. "Any deviance from protocol is not permitted," they recite, almost in unison. We ignore them; as the group passes the library, we break from it, walking through the front doors. Our escorts, miffed, follow us in. They know there is little they can do to stop us.

We walk through the foyer, stopping in front of the circulation desk. The escorts stand with us. We stare at one another.

"Well," I say to Ashley June after a prolonged period, "this is a little awkward."

She tilts her head towards me with eyes that seem to sparkle a little more. "Give me a tour," she says, then glares back at the escorts. "Alone." She walks away, past the tables and chairs, farther into the main section, observing the décor and furniture. "So this is the Shangri-la resort we've all been hearing about," she says, standing on a worn-down floral rug in the centre of the large room.

"How did *that* happen?" I ask. "A few hours ago, everyone was calling this place a hellish solitary confinement, and now it's a resort? No, really, I'd so much rather be in the main building," I lie, walking over to her. The escorts, thankfully, don't follow.

"Trust me, you'd rather not. The constant bickering, the complaining, the pettiness, the watchfulness, the stalking – and that's only among the staffers. It's pretty oppressive. Wouldn't mind it myself, getting away from it all. And from all the questions."

"Questions?"

"About you. People are wondering why you've been set apart here, why you're getting the special A-list treatment. And since they know we go to the same school, they assume I know you well; they've all been peppering – more like bombarding – me with questions about you. What you're like, your past, whether you're smart, ad nauseam."

"What do you tell them?"

Her eyes meet mine, at first seriously, then with a softness that surprises. She walks to the floor-to-ceiling windows, the point farthest from the escorts, and gives me a beckoning look. I follow, coming to stand with her at the windows. And now, far removed from the escorts, it's just the two of us, bathed in the silver glaze of moonlight pouring in. Our chests less constricted, the air lighter.

"I tell them what I know," she says, looking out of the window and then back at me. Her eyes, awash in the moonlight, radiate out, her irises delineated and clear. "Which isn't a lot. I tell them that you're a bit of an enigma, a loner, that you keep to yourself. That you're crazy smart even though you try to hide it. That even though all the girls whisper about you, you've never so much as dated a single one. They ask if we've ever been together, and I tell them no."

My eyes flick to hers. She holds my stare with a kind of quiet desperation, as if afraid I might break away too quickly. The air between us changes drastically. I can't explain it, other than it feels like both a hot quickening *and* a calming softness.

"I wish I had more to tell them," she whispers. "I wish I knew you better." She sags her body against the window as if suddenly fatigued by an invisible weight.

It is this leaning – it looks like a surrender – that cracks something in me, like ice splintering on the first day of spring. Pale in the moonlight, her skin is a glowing alabaster; I have a sudden strong urge to run my hands down her arms, to feel its cool clay smoothness.

For a few minutes, we gaze outside. Nothing moves. A rind of moonlight falls on the distant Dome, bejewelling it in a glint of sparkles.

"Why is it that this is the first time we've really talked?" She reaches up, tucks some loose hair strands behind her ear. "I've always wanted something like this with you, you must have known that. I think a hundred of these moments have passed us by."

I stare outside, unable to meet her eyes. But my heart is beating faster and hotter than it has in a long time.

"I waited for you that rainy night," she says, her voice barely audible. "For almost an hour at the front gate. I got completely drenched. What, did you sneak out of the back entrance after school? It was a few years ago, I know, but . . . have you forgotten?"

I fix my eyes on the eastern mountains, not daring to meet her eyes. What I want to tell her is that I have never forgotten; that not a week goes by that I don't imagine I made a different decision.

That I'd walked out of the classroom as the bell rang and met her at the front gates and walked her home, rain slicking down the sides of my trousers, our shoes sloshing through puddles, hands together holding the umbrella above our heads, useless against the downpour, but the wetness not minded in the least.

But instead of speaking to her, I hear my father's voice. *Never forget who you are*. And for the first time, I realise what he meant by that. It was just another way of saying, *Never forget who* they *are*.

I don't say anything, only stare out at the night stars, their lights blinking down with abject loneliness. So close together, these clustered stars, their lights brushing, overlapping; but their proximity is only illusory, because in reality they are impassably far apart, separated by a thousand million light-years of emptiness between them.

"I don't think I . . . know what you're talking about. Sorry."

She doesn't respond at first. Then she suddenly jerks her head to the side, her auburn hair veiling her face. "Light's too bright tonight," she says, her voice brittle as she slides on a pair of large oval moonglasses. "Hate it when there's a full moon."

"Let's step away from the windows," I say, and we move back to the rug, back within earshot of the watching escorts.

We stand awkwardly in front of each other. My escort steps forward.

"We need to get back to the group. It's dinnertime."

At dinner, most of us are pretty spent. We're too tired to engage in anything more than middling conversation, a far cry from the gabfest we had at lunch. I worry about my body odour and discreetly sniff my underarms from time to time. I eat quickly, mindful of my proximity to others. Gaunt Man seated next to me is given to occasional twitches. He doesn't say anything, but a couple of times, his nostrils enlarge in my direction.

Ashley June sits on my other side. I am conscious of her every move: the closeness of her elbow to mine, every time she picks up and puts down her utensils, the sway of her hair as she ties it into a ponytail to keep it from falling into the drip cups. Mostly, I notice her silence. A strong urge pulls in me to look at her. And to move away from her, keeping my odour from her.

By midmeal, I'm more than worried about my body odour. And the more nervous I get, the more odour I emit. A quick and quiet exit is what's needed. I stand up; all eyes at the table immediately turn to me. Stepping away from the table, I look for my escort sitting at his own table somewhere in the surrounding darkness. He emerges from behind me a few moments later.

"Everything OK?"

"Yes, fine. I should be heading back to my lodging. I'm worried about the sunrise."

He looks at his watch. "It's not due for another hour."

"Even so, I'm a worrier. I don't want to chance getting caught outside by a premature sunrise." Everyone at the table is staring at us now.

"I assure you, our dawn–dusk calculations are never wrong," he says.

I cast my eyes downward, realising I actually don't have to feign tiredness. I'm truly worn to the bone. "If there's nothing else for tonight, I think I'm going to retire early. Pretty pooped."

I sense him staring at me, trying to understand. "But the food – there're so many more succulent dishes to come."

I realise what's going on. "You know you don't have to escort me back. Stay and eat. To your fill. Really. I know my way back from here. Two flights down, left down the hallway, right, another left, then out of the double doors with the Institute emblem."

"You don't want to stay for dessert?"

"No, I'm fine, really."

"But the choicest, bloodiest meats are yet to come!"

"Just knackered, is all. Really, don't you worry about me."

"You sure you're fine getting back without assistance?"

"I got this." And before he can object, I leave. And as I walk away, I shoot a quick look at the table.

They're all supposed to be eating, ignoring my conversation with the escort, stuffing their faces. But instead they're looking at me with befuddlement. No; more than befuddlement. This is *bewilderment*, the kind that nests in people's minds, keeps them wondering.

"Stupid, stupid, stupid," I mutter to myself as I walk down two flights. *Idiot, idiot, idiot*, I inwardly reprove myself as I head down the hallways. "Moron, moron, moron," I say out loud as I push open the double doors to the outside. And then it is my father's voice in my head: *Don't do anything out of the ordinary, don't do anything that sticks you out from the crowd. Avoid anything that'll draw attention.*

Even when I reach the doors to the library a few minutes later, I am still chastising myself. *Imbecile, stupid, moron, doofus.*

Back in the library, I roam the aisles, the back rooms, hidden corners, scour every inch. But it's useless. There's no drinkable liquid of any kind in the library, not so much as a drop. And in the restroom, like in all bathrooms, there's nothing but hard sanitising dispensers. Knowing better, I dab a few drops of the sanitiser on my tongue. The sanitiser drops scour my tongue with an acidic burn that leaves a foul aftertaste. I'm really worried now. Away from my supplies stashed at home, from all my instruments of subterfuge – my shavers, bottles of water, odour suppressors, teeth whiteners, nail filers – things are deteriorating quickly. The lack of water is causing my head to spin. I can't concentrate. On things. All my thoughts are jagged. Short thrusts. A pounding headache.

I lift up my arm, take a sniff of my armpit. There. Even *I* can smell it now. And if I can smell it, they can. No wonder Gaunt Man and Beefy were so distracted at dinner.

I don't know if anyone suspects me yet. Gaunt Man and Beefy might have smelled something at dinner, but I don't think they've connected the dots to me yet. But by tomorrow, I'll be reeking.

I head over to the leather couch and plop down. My head: still pounding, spinning. Outside, a hint of dawn presses against the windows. The shutters will close soon.

I throw my elbow over my eyes, not wanting to think but knowing I need to face reality. Plan A seemed perfect not so long ago: fly under the radar during training period, break a leg right before the Hunt. But now, things have changed. With my body sending out eat-me smells and my tongue as dry and coarse as sandpaper, I won't make it to the Hunt four nights away. I'll either die of thirst or be savagely devoured. Probably the latter.

Lying on the couch, a numbed alarm pressing down on me, I begin to drift. Actually, it's more like a plummet into a deep canyon of sleep.

Thirst awakens me. I cough: a thousand splinters pierce my parched throat.

Slowly, I peel my draped arm away from my face. The library is dark: the shutters have closed. But something is odd. I can still see, with a dim clarity, the interior of the library. As if a candle is burning.

Impossible. I spin around, drowsiness quickly shaken off. I see the light source.

It's right there. A single, thin beam of sunlight shooting from a hole in the shutter behind me. The beam shoots past my ear, reaching to the far wall of the library. It is a piercing line of light, laser-like, seeming to carry a physical heft. I hadn't noticed it yesterday. But then again, I was on the other side of the library, fast asleep during the day hours.

I walk over to the shutter. Tentatively, I reach towards the hole. I half expect the light to sear my skin. But there's just a pinprick of warmth where the beam hits my skin. The hole in the shutter is a perfect circle, smooth along the edges. Very strange. This is no accident, no result of the building's aging process. This hole was intentionally made – *drilled* – through a two-inch steel-reinforced shutter. But for what purpose? And by whom?

The kooky Scientist. That part is not difficult to figure out; no one else has ever lived here. But why would he do it? A beam of sunlight like this would not only keep a person from sleeping, but cause permanent retinal and intestinal damage. None of this makes sense.

Or perhaps the Scientist had nothing to do with this. Perhaps the hole was drilled by the staffers later, after he'd disappeared. But why? And if they knew they were going to house me in the library, surely they would have patched it up before I moved in. Again, none of this makes any sense.

And then a thought blizzards into my mind, chilling me.

I shake my head, as if to banish the thought. But it's latched on to my brain, irrevocably now. And the more I think about it, the more likely it seems.

Somebody drilled this hole. Tonight.

To test me. To flush me out.

To find out if I'm a heper.

It makes sense. Tonight, with my unwashed body giving off an odour, suspicion is aroused. But more proof is needed before I can be accused. Sending a surreptitious sunbeam into the library during the day is perfect. Subtle yet dispositive. A sunbeam so small that it wouldn't awaken a heper, but enough to jolt any normal person awake, making him flee to the far side of the library and demand a new room at first dark. The perfect litmus test.

I pace down the aisles, trying to keep fear at bay. My fingertips brush against the dusty spines of leather covers. There's a flaw in my thinking, I realise. The only people who could possibly be on to me are those who've been in proximity. That would be the hunters and the escorts. But they've been with me all night long; we've never left one another's sight. Nobody has had the opportunity to slip away and drill a hole through two inches of reinforced steel.

I head back to the hole and study it even closer. The edges are weathered and dulled, not shiny or sharp as they would be after a fresh cut. I bend down to the floor, looking for any fresh shavings. Nothing. This hole has been here a while.

That leaves me in a bit of a pickle. If I feign anger tomorrow and complain about the hole, staffers will come over to take a look before sealing it up. But that hole will invite questions about my first day of sleep – why hadn't I complained after that first day? On the other hand, if I say nothing and this is indeed a ploy to trap me, then I'd be flushed out.

Then something clicks inside my head. Perhaps the beam is just a side effect of something more important. Maybe it's the hole – and not the beam – that is really the key to this whole mystery.

I peer intently at the hole now, taking in every tiny scratch near it, its height from the floor, its small diameter.

But of course. It's the perfect size.

To peer through.

But when I look through the hole – the light outside blinding – it's a nothing. Just the bland, monotonous Vast, stretching endlessly in front of me, the hot sun bleaching whiteness into it. Not even the Dome is in sight. Dust and dirt and sand and light. That's it. There's nothing to see.

For the next hour, I pace the floor, study the sunbeam, peer through the hole; but it's useless. I can't figure it out. What kills me is the feeling that I'm so close, that I'm actually staring at the answer. Eventually I sit down, my aching feet worn to the nub. I close my eyes to focus; and when I pry them open some hours later, the sunbeam is gone, the shutters have opened, and somebody is pounding at the door. Dusk has arrived.

Hunt Minus Three Nights

HEPERS ARE BELIEVED to be anywhere between five and ten millennia behind us on the evolutionary ladder." The Director's voice drifts from the lectern with antiseptic detachment. "Certainly, hepers display the more primitive behavioral traits that our ancestors discarded many centuries ago. Think, for example, of their exceptional swimming ability. That trait harkens back to their relatively recent amphibian origins, when they dwelled in the sea from which all life derives. Their fishlike ability to manoeuvre in water testifies to the relative lack of evolutionary progress from that elementary stage. Think, too, of their beastlike ability to endure the sun's rays. This ability to withstand sunlight is a genetic relic from the pre-cave era, when land-roaming animals lacked the intelligence to seek shelter in caves. They built up a resistance to the sun, although said resistance inhibited the evolutionary development of the brain. A shame, that."

His words float to me like seaweed in murky water. I am sitting near the back of the lecture hall, as distanced from people as possible. I had a quick change of clothes (while my escort banged away at my door), but I'm worried about my odour. Nobody seems to have smelled anything – everyone is stationary, no one twitching. I got through breakfast, early evening lectures, and a tour of the grounds, lunch, without anyone noticing. A large window to the left of the podium is thankfully open, a breeze blowing steadily in, dissipating any odour inside. So I hope.

"Their facial expressions – so slippery with unrestrained and unfettered emotions – harken back to the pre-linguist, pre-language era, when expressions served as a kind of sign language. Next slide."

A photo of the legs of a male heper, covered in hair. Everyone leans forward. Drool starts to line slowly downward from their fangs, like spiders descending to desktops.

"A vestigial genetic artifact from an era predating the discovery of fire. Without the capability to build fire, hair was their only mechanism to ward off the winter cold. Elite scholars have postulated that this evidence of body hair predates even the stone era, when primitives would have been able to fashion rudimentary weapons to hunt and then use fur for clothes. I have written a book on this topic, the first in my field to postulate this now well-supported theory. Next slide."

A photo of a heper eating a fruit, red skinned with yellow substance inside. I see heads flinch back in revulsion.

"Ah, yes. Quite inexplicable, this trait, to say nothing of its ghastliness. It bespeaks their lack of predatory skills, their inability to really kill anything larger than vermin. So they must hunt those things that do not flee: the things of the earth, vegetables and fruits. This trait in time became *in extremis* to the extent that their bodies eventually required fruit and vegetables. Deprive them of vegetables and fruit, and their bodies begin to break down. Reddish spots appear on their bodies, sores attack their lips, then gums, leading eventually to the loss of teeth. They become immobilised, fall into a depressed, vegetative state. Next slide."

A photo of the group of hepers under the Dome. They are sitting around a campfire, their mouths open, heads cocked to the side, eyes closed.

"Nothing has mystified and beguiled scholars as much as the hepers' ability to warble their voices with words, and with such remarkable consistency. Studies undertaken at the Institute have found that hepers are able to duplicate these ululations – what they call 'singing' – with astonishing accuracy. In fact, a song can be replicated minutes, days, months, even years after it is first sung with near identical sonic frequencies. There are a plethora of theories out there; none are satisfactory save one, which I presented at the Annual Conference on Heper Studies last year. In short, hepers developed this 'singing' ability under the mistaken belief that it helped the growth of vegetables and fruits. That is why we see them 'sing' most commonly when tending to the farmland or plucking fruit off trees. Some scholars posit that hepers may also believe 'singing' helps to sustain the burning of a fire and to cleanse the body better. This is evinced in their tendency to warble their voices when assembled around a fire or when bathing at the pond."

I sit in my seat, hiding my inner amusement. Everything the Director says about hepers has the ring of truth and a learned authority about it, but I suspect it's nothing more than speculative nonsense. I suppose it's easy to so widely miss the mark when it comes to hepers, to quickly slide from honest scientific inquiry to unsubstantiated theories. After all, if the roles were reversed and it was people who became extinct, people theories would likely be rife with exaggerations and distortions: instead of sleeping in sleepholds, they'd sleep in coffins; creatures of the night, they'd be so invisible to the eye that even in front of mirrors, they'd lack a reflection; pale and emaciated, they were weak and benign beings who could coexist peacefully alongside hepers, somehow restraining themselves from ripping hepers to ribbons and sucking down their blood; they'd all invariably be incredibly good-looking with perfect hair. There'd probably be some outright confabulations as well: their ability to swim with dizzying speed *under* water; and ludicrous and laughable notions about people-heper romances.

Two rows in front of me, Phys Ed's head suddenly twitches violently backward. A short line of saliva flies off his fangs and swings upward, splatting across his face diagonally. He shakes his head.

"Pardon me," he murmurs.

The Director stares at him, then proceeds. "Another aberration is their rather grotesque tendency to leak minuscule beads of salty water when they get hot or are under stress. Under these extreme conditions, they also emit large amounts of odour, especially from the underarm region, which itself, especially in male adults, contains a nest of body hair. It is common for them—"

Phys Ed's head snaps back again. "Sorry, sorry," he says, "didn't mean to interrupt. But can no one else smell it? Heper odour?" He turns around, and for one awful moment, his eyes settle on mine. "Don't you?"

"A little. Just a little," I offer.

The Director's eyes turn to me. A chill spreads down my body.

Controlled breathing; keep eyelids halfway down; don't dart my eyes back and forth.

"It's really thick, it's getting into my nose, into my head, it's hard to concentrate." Phys Ed points to an open window. "Mind if we close the window? I can barely concentrate—"

Abs, sitting two seats away from him, suddenly jerks her head back, snaps it forward again. "Just now. I smelled it, too. Heper.

Pretty strong odour. It must be wafting in from outside through the open windows. What is it, heper mating season?"

The Director heads over to the open window. His face is placid, unreadable, but he's clearly thinking deeply. "I smell something as well. The breeze is bringing it in?" His voice rises indecisively at the end. "Here, let me close the window, see if that helps. The hepers must be really sweating it during the day. Wonder what they're up to."

The lecture continues, but barely anyone is listening anymore. Everyone is curious, sniffing the air. Far from cutting off the heper odour, closing the window has only intensified the odour. It's me; the smell is emanating from me. How long before the others realise this? Their fidgeting and agitated head shakes grow more frequent and violent by the minute. I'm not helping matters – or myself – much: I've got to keep up the act, and my own head shakes and neck snaps are an exertion that in turn releases more odour.

Ashley June suddenly speaks up. "Maybe they've been sneaking in here during the day. Into this building. That's why their odour is everywhere."

We look to the podium to see what the Director will say. He's gone. Uncannily. And in his place is Frilly Dress, who, as usual, has materialised out of nowhere. "Impossible," she says, her voice shriller than usual. "There's no way a heper would come in here, into the hornets' nest. It's certain death."

"But the odour," Ashley June says, her mouth watering. "It's so strong."

Suddenly her head snaps back, viciously. Slowly she turns around, her head lowering. She gazes at all of us, at me. "What if one of the hepers snuck in here last night? What if one of the hepers is still hiding in this building?"

And just like that, we are flying out of the doors, the escorts right next to us, at first trying to coax us back into the lecture hall, but then, as we spin around corners and leap down floors ("The odour's getting stronger!" shouts Crimson Lips next to me), the escorts join in the frenzy, feed into it. Gnashing teeth, saliva trailing us, hands shaking in the air, nails grating against the walls.

It's hard to separate myself from the group. That's my plan: to peel away, steal back to the library, and hope no one thinks much of my absence. But every time I turn a corner to get away, they're right there with me. It's my odour. And with all this running around, it's only getting worse. I was hoping they'd all sprint past me, giving me the opportunity to fly down the stairs and out of the door before they can double back. But they stay right with me. It's terrifying, to be so close to their teeth and claws. They will not be unaware for much longer.

What causes the group to leave me is more by accident than design. I black out – probably for no more than a second or two. One moment I'm running, the next I'm flat on the ground, the group sweeping past me and disappearing around a corner. The lack of water. It's parched my throat, dried my muscles, ossified my brain now. I'm past my breaking point.

When I come to – it's really more a greyout than a blackout – I know I have to move. The group will double back when they lose the scent; they'll follow the trail right back to me, lying weakened and prone on the floor, sweat on my forehead, the odour running off me in rivers. *Move,* I tell myself, *move*. But it's tough even to prop myself up. I feel as dry as attic dust, yet as heavy as a waterlogged sack of flour.

There is silence in the hallways, then the sound of footsteps growing louder. They're realising. They're coming back now.

Fear jump-starts my body. I roll over, leap to my feet. Doors. I need to put as many doors between me and them. It'll slow them down, cut off my scent even a bit. Every little bit counts.

I push doors out of my way; seconds later, I hear those same double doors slammed open, like shotguns popping. I'm not even racing down flights of stairs anymore; I'm leaping down them, one flight at a time. The pain ricochets up my legs, shoots up my back.

They're catching up. No matter how fast I try to push myself, no matter how treacherously I bound down the stairs, the sound of the group behind me looms ever closer. Hard, scrabbling sounds, quick whispers of clothes being whisked this way and that. Only a matter of time now.

Unless . . .

"It's this way!" I shout. "The scent is this way, it's really strong now, I think I'm on to it!"

"How did he get so far ahead of us?" someone shouts, a floor above.

I slam through a set of doors, run halfway across the hallway, then plunge through another set of doors and start leaping up stairs, three at a time.

"Wait for us!" someone shouts right below me.

"No way! I'm virtually on top of it now."

"How's the slow kid beating us?" Gaining so fast, just a matter of seconds.

Through another set of doors, a mad sprint down the long hallway. I take a quick look backward: the horde is coming on me like a rabid wave, Gaunt Man leaping from floor to wall to ceiling, Phys Ed darting along the crease where wall meets ceiling, the others all apace, their faces stoic, their fangs bared. Three seconds.

I throw myself through the set of doors in front of me. They swing open with a weird touch of familiarity. I see why: I'm back in the lecture hall. I've made full circle. The hall is completely empty. Everyone has joined the chase.

Where do I want to die? I wonder. *At the back? Standing dramatically on a desk? Near the lectern?*

And that's when I see the window.

Jump up, heave it open.

Not a millisecond later, the group flows in like a black wave. They're so synchronised: on the walls, the floor, the ceiling, there's no jostling for position, no elbowing. Just a coordinated rapid sweep into the lecture hall, eyes spinning, nostrils flaring.

"It jumped! It jumped outside!" I yell, perched in front of the open window, pointing out. Even before I finish yelling, four of them are up there on the perch, jostling for position, peering through the window with me, their heads disconcertingly close to mine. A strong breeze thankfully picks up, gusts through the window.

"I can smell it everywhere! It's like it's right here, hiding, where?"

"It's gone—"

"We can chase it down, can't have got far—"

"Maybe," I say. "If we go quick, we should be able to get to it."

They are bunching their legs, readying to leap out of the window, when a whisper freezes them in place.

"You've been had." A wet, quiet, sinister whisper, seething with threat.

It is the Director.

He's not looking at us, merely glancing at his nails, marvelling at their pastel gleam in the moonlight. His voice is quiet, seemingly indifferent to whether anyone is listening.

"Some of you here think you're so smart," he purrs. "You think you're such a quick study, that you know better than the experts here. A couple of days at *my* establishment and suddenly you think you're smarter than the specialists who've devoted their lives to this fine Institute. Did you really think that the Institute *I* run would be so careless as to allow a heper to be on the loose, to roam unchecked through the grounds?" He studies his nails.

A pause, then he continues, his voice even softer now. "And did you really think a heper would be so stupid as to be caught outside the protection of the Dome after dusk?" He puts his right hand down. "They might be animals, but they're not stupid. Like some of you here."

It is deathly quiet. "There is arrogance and ignorance in spades here. Funny how often they go hand in hand. You need to remember who you are. You were selected by luck – not by merit, not by demonstrated ability, not by anything earned. *Dumb* luck. And now you saunter into *my* Institute and think you run the whole damn place.

"There is no heper. Yes, there is a discernible smell of heper that has blown in from the outside. It is more pungent than usual, yes. But there is no heper, not inside, not the way you think. You've all been victims of mass hysteria."

Beefy, despite the Director's words, suddenly shivers. With desire. He can't hold back, he can't deny the heper smell in his nose. Saliva from Phys Ed, hanging from the ceiling, drips down onto a chair. They can still smell me. They can't help themselves.

"Ah," continues the Director, observing these reactions, "the power of mass hysteria. Once you've been told there's a face of a heper imprinted on a tree bark, you can't unsee that image so easily, can you? No matter what we say, you'll still see a heper. The conviction proves to be . . . sticky. Not so easy to unring a bell once it's been rung. Look at you all. You've almost got me convinced."

Something lands on my hair, sticky and slightly acidic. I glance up; Abs is up there, hanging upside down. She's gazing at the Director, trying to control herself. More saliva drifts down, silvery and shiny like a spider's thread.

"It's understandable, your susceptibility to mass hysteria. You're all heper virgins: you've never seen, smelled, or even heard a heper before, not a live one, anyway. So at the first hint of suggestion, you're all gone, lemmings charging off a cliff. And there's no breaking out of it now. We've seen this happen time and again here at the Institute, with the new hires. They come here, wet behind the ears. Some come to see a heper behind every shadow and lose their ability to function. Eventually, they lose the ability to perform even the simplest of tasks."

His head revolves, looking at each of us in turn. "We are not without our options, however." At this, he glides away into the peripheral darkness. Frilly Dress emerges moments later, her face beaming.

"It's a programme I came up with. The new hires were getting too distracted, so we had to come up with a way to, well, desensitise them. The option of sniffing acidic powder to numb the smell nerves in the nostrils was considered, but not seriously. My plan was more humane." She nods towards the back of the lecture hall.

A beam of mercuric light cuts through the lecture hall. An image lights up on a screen above her. We see a large room, like an indoor arena of sorts. Dotted around the perimeter are wooden posts sticking out of the ground like tree stumps. Thick, hardy leather straps are tethered to each post. Even on video, a palpably ominous air hangs over everything. A sense of sour dread seeps off the projected image. *Nothing good happens in there,* I think. My insides contract and chill, become lined with a film of frost.

The place looks strangely familiar. I search my memory banks, trying to—

And then I recall. The lottery pick. The old, emaciated heper picking out the numbers. It was filmed right from this arena.

Frilly Dress, sensing the rapt attention, pauses dramatically. She tugs on her earlobe. "This converted work space is now affectionately called the Introduction. The name says it all. It is where you will be introduced to your first live heper. In the flesh, in the blood, right before you."

Crimson Lips lets rip a huge snarl. Beefy starts grunting. Drool streams down now from the ceiling in rivulets.

"Calm down. Nobody is going to be eating a heper. Not today, anyway. Not one fang, not one finger, will so much as touch heper flesh. The leather straps that bind you to the posts will ensure that." She picks up a long ruler and uses it to indicate a circular trapdoor on the ground that looks very much like a manhole. "The heper will emerge from this door on the ground. It will come out, after you've all been secured to your posts, and for about five minutes, you will get to see and hear and smell the heper. The only senses you will not be using – for now – are touch and taste, obviously. But that heper will be sufficiently up close and personal. And you will be able to smell it – real heper, rather than your hysterical imaginings. It will set you straight. The Introduction has been incredibly successful with our new hires. After this exposure, they're no longer heper virgins. Their ability to focus and not be distracted by faint heper odours is much improved. We think the programme will be just the ticket for you all."

"So there is heper in this building!" Gaunt Man says, his voice loud and gruff. "That's why heper smell is so strong!"

"There's one heper. And you haven't been smelling it. It stays in its quarters. And that door you see in the photo is steel-reinforced and locks from the inside. It is completely safe in there. Has been for the past three years. And the silly thing has enough food stored up in there to last a month."

"But how do you get it to come out at the Introduction? How do we know it's going to come out when we're there?"

She scratches her wrist. "Let's just say that we offer choice morsels it can't refuse. Fruits, vegetables, sweet chocolate. Besides, it knows it's in no danger. It's done this a dozen times, knows that everyone is securely tethered to their posts. As long as it stays in the safe zone and doesn't stray too close to a post, it's fine. Nobody can touch it. It's free to gather up the food to its heart's content."

"Is it the one who—"

"Now, really," Frilly Dress interjects. "Do you really want to keep asking me questions, or would you rather move on down to the Introduction?"

Judging by the speed with which we zoom out, turns out it's a rhetorical question.

We are as giddy as schoolchildren on a field trip to the amusement park. It takes us five minutes to get to the arena, or rather, to descend there. Turns out, the four floors above ground are just the tip of a very cold, black iceberg. Whole flotillas of floors exist beneath the ground. The farther we descend, the colder and darker it becomes. There is no sign that anyone lives or works or uses or visits these ghost floors anymore. We descend into the depths of the earth, the pull of claustrophobia closing in on me.

By the time we arrive at the bottom floor, I'm spent. My knees feel as if a jackhammer has done a number on them, and my head spins crazily from the spiralled descent. No one else is fatigued; if anything, the energy level has risen as anticipation draws to a climax. There's a lot of chatter, a lot of teeth grinding.

"Are there enough posts for all of us?" Ashley June asks. Everyone is jostling for position in front of the closed double doors.

"Don't you worry, any of you," Frilly Dress answers. "There are ten posts inside. Only seven of you. The posts are equidistant from the centre, none has an advantage over another. A food item is placed near each post so all of you will get a chance to see the heper up close and personal."

Despite her words, they're still pushing. I separate myself inconspicuously to the side.

"What are we waiting for?"

"Just a bit longer. Paperwork needs to be processed upstairs. They'll let us know when we're good to go."

"How?"

Frilly Dress shakes her head. "You'll see."

"Is it really as great as she put it?" Phys Ed asks his escort.

"Better than advertised. *So* much better."

"I can smell it!" Beefy says. "Stronger than ever!"

"Nonsense," chides Frilly Dress. "The heper's still in its chambers." But she seems uncertain, her nostrils moistening and flaring.

"It's the same smell! We've been smelling *this* heper all this time."

I take two steps back, slowly moving away from them.

"Getting stronger by the second." More drool and shivers.

I play along. But those doors had better open soon, because this is a small enclave we wait in, and in such tight, unventilated quarters, my odour is amplified.

Gaunt Man's head flicks violently towards me. He's not just hissing; he's slobbering in his saliva. Foolishly, I meet his eyes. He is staring at me with a dawning realisation, his eyes blinking, blinking, blinking with a new—

At that very moment, the double doors swing open, an expulsion of steam and smoke enveloping us.

Shouts of excitement as we sweep into the room. The expanse, with its high arching ceiling (rounded and ballooned like an indoor sports stadium) and wide spread of the dusty ground beneath, catches me by surprise. The heper's door is on the ground, in the very centre of the arena, shaped and sized like a manhole. Ten wooden posts are spaced evenly around it. We disperse quickly, each of us running like kids choosing horses on a carousel. As Frilly Dress said, there's more than enough for all of us, but that doesn't stop general bedlam from ensuing. It's the morsels. Hunters are fighting over posts positioned before morsels deemed most attractive to the heper. Abs and Ashley June are having a feline fight over a post in front of a bunch of bananas.

"I was here first," snarls Ashley June.

"Well, I'm already strapped in," Abs hisses back. She snaps shut a latch in the strap around her ankles. "There. Locked in. Can't get out now even if I wanted to. And I don't."

Across from me, Crimson Lips and Phys Ed are bickering over a post in front of some ears of corn. My attention shifts over to Gaunt Man, whose eyes are glowing at me like a bat's. I can't read his expression, but I sense confusion. He's still trying to figure me out, questioning if he really did smell heper odour coming off me.

I ignore him, busy myself with the straps. There are four metallic cuffs that lock around our wrists and ankles. Each cuff is tethered to the post by thick leather straps. Even strapped in, we have quite a lot of room to range: about a body length from the post. As long as the heper doesn't stray past the perimeter delineated by the morsels, it'll be safely out of our reach.

An escort walks in, stoic faced, and hands each of us a pair of shades. "Lights will be turned up in a moment," he murmurs, "so the heper can see." He checks each of our straps, spending the most time on Gaunt Man, whose straps are way too loose. Gaunt Man objects, raising his arm; as he does so, his shirt becomes untucked and he quickly reaches down to tuck it back in.

But not before I see it. A dull glint coming from his belt, curved and long like a dagger's blade.

An uneasy feeling touches the back of my neck. When the escort checks on my straps, it's on the tip of my tongue to say something. But the escort walks off before I can speak. He stops at the very centre of the arena and says, "Welcome to the Introduction, ladies and gentlemen." Before walking out, he stamps his boot heavily on the circular door three times, a deep boom sounding. The lights inside the arena turn brighter. We throw on our shades.

And wait.

A mechanical whirring sounds from the circular door in the ground, followed by a series of robotic beeps. The door opens, just a crack. And then, just as swiftly, it drops shut, coughing up a puff of dust. Heads cock to the side. Then the door opens not a second later, a little wider this time. Enough to see the outline of a head. The twin dots of eyes peering out.

All the hunters explode towards the heper. Almost in unison, bodies snap against the restraints, flip in the air, and fall to the ground.

The door, again, falls shut.

In a blink, everyone is upright and lurching against the restraints. I pull against my mine, frothing at the mouth as I swing my head wildly to and fro. My shades fly off.

I blink at the sudden brightness of the arena, now awash in vivid, keen colours. I see the hunters with a clarity that seems to enliven them. They are animals, bestial and overtaken with heper lust. Phys Ed and Crimson Lips have given to scratching their necks, leaving long white etches where their nails rake into skin. Their mouths gape wide, then snap shut like a steel trap, the harsh, rocky sound of teeth gnashing against teeth filling the fetid air.

The trapdoor opens again; a fully extended arm holds up the

door. A head emerges from underneath, peering around like a periscope. Apparently assured, it steps out, leaving the door opened, all the better for a quick escape.

For a moment, all is quiet. The sloshing of saliva ceases; the crack of necks and knuckles and spines stop. We study the heper with an almost innocent curiosity, as if we don't mean to pillage its intestines and suck its blood and gorge on it at the drop of a hat. It is the same heper as the one on TV, frail and wispy. It blinks, surveys the piles of morsels distributed around it.

Then Ashley June lets loose a horrific scream of desire into the air. Within seconds, we're all yowling and mewling.

The heper is unmoved by the cacophony as it walks to the first pile of food. Two loaves of bread, placed in front of Crimson Lips' post. The heper picks up a loaf, rams it into its mouth, and tears off a mouthful. It moves efficiently, businesslike, as it grabs the other loaf and tosses it into the open door without so much as a glance at the hissing Crimson Lips. It's done this before. It shuffles over to the next pile, bottles of water. It twists open a cap, hoists the bottle upside down, and guzzles down water. Doesn't linger. Cradling the remaining bottles in the crook of its arm, it carries them over to the open door and drops them in. Then it is up and moving to another pile, the candy. All the while, even with snarls and screams about it, the heper never looks up. It is coolly minding its own business.

The heper moves past a stack of notebooks in front of Gaunt Man and towards the candy. My eyes catch a glimmer of stale light from Gaunt Man's waist. The dagger; Gaunt Man is taking it out now. White veins in his bony hand bulge out like sickly squirming worms as he grips the dagger and starts filing away at the leather strap. He knows he has to move fast: the heper isn't exactly laying out a picnic mat to dine in our midst. It's simply going to throw all the food and drinks and notebooks into its chamber and then disappear. It'll be gone in less than a minute. A rage fills the arena, an explosion of frustration at the feeling of being cheated. Ashley June gives another bloodcurdling scream. She strains against the straps, a desperation attending her desire.

Gaunt Man attacks the straps with extra fervour. He pulls taut the strap tethered to his left wrist while his right arm pistons back and forth, sawing away.

And just like that, the strap falls in two. He stares stupidly at it dangling in half. Then it hits him; I see his body go erect. Fantasy is now a dusking reality. And he's hunched over again, filing away at the straps tied to his legs, his right arm a blizzard of speed.

The heper has no idea. It is standing over the pile of candy. It's unwrapping a candy, sucking on it, oblivious to what's going on behind it.

Gaunt Man has sliced through the two leg straps. He switches hands, starts sawing away at the final strap on his right wrist.

The heper pauses, lifting its head into the air like a dog catching a scent.

Then it bends down and picks up another piece of candy.

The last strap is giving Gaunt Man some trouble. Perhaps in his excitement he's not focusing, or perhaps it's on account of having to use his left arm. But he's slower, and it's frustrating him. He lets out a scream of frustration that knifes into my eardrums.

The heper winces, then spins around. It sees Gaunt Man, the sliced straps dangling from his left arm and ankles, and it understands the situation immediately. In a blink, it spins, dropping the candy, its legs already pumping to the door in the ground. Just five paces to get there.

At that very moment, Gaunt Man slices through the final strap. He spins around. He is twenty paces from the trapdoor. The heper is flying towards it, now only three paces away.

Before the heper takes another step, it is tackled by Gaunt Man.

They roll in the dirt, Gaunt Man's tackle carrying them ten yards. They separate briefly: the heper leaps to its feet, lunges for the trapdoor.

Gaunt Man sideswipes it, sends it back down to the dirt. The heper scrabbles against the ground like a rabid crab; Gaunt Man leaps atop it. They're about the same size, but it's no match. Not even close. Gaunt Man's fingers sink sickeningly into the heper's back; blood quickly spreads on its shirt.

The sight of heper blood so close, the smell of it rushing into the air, sends the other hunters into hyperdelirium. The screams rip into my eardrums, threatening to shatter them. *Don't cover your ears! Don't cover your ears!* I do the only thing I can: I raise my head, look to the rafters, and scream. At the pain, at the horror I know is taking place. My scream joins the others around me. For a few moments, it is my scream that fills my ears, covers over all the jackal- and hyena-like howls around me. That is all I want. For just a few moments to be free of their screams.

Then, for the first time, the heper makes a sound. A scream, so different from the screams of desire and hunger around it. This is a cry of horror and a burrowed resignation. It haunts me. It is the amplification of what has lived in my own bones for years.

I hear the sound of bone crunched and then snapped. Gaunt Man has broken one of the heper's legs. He's toying with it, like a cat with an injured mouse, biding his time. And he's doing it to nettle the other hunters as well, teasing us with the prize that is so out of reach for us but so inevitable for him. The heper crawls now on its two arms and one leg, its left leg dragging in the dirt, its eyes delirious with unimaginable pain.

"Throw me the knife!" Abs shouts. She is looking at Crimson

Lips, who has recovered the knife that Gaunt Man tossed away. Crimson Lips is a blur; nobody's noticed until now that she's been sawing away at the straps.

"Throw me the knife!"

"The knife – listen to me, throw me the knife!" someone else yells.

Gaunt Man's head snaps up, takes in what is happening. He can't take his time anymore. Within seconds, Crimson Lips is going to cut through her restraints, will be charging toward the heper. With a cry of anger, he leaps on the heper and sinks his fangs into the back of its neck.

Abs cuts through her fourth strap; even as it is falling away, she is already spinning around, leaping in one cheetah-like pounce to the heper. Her aim is off; she ends up upending Gaunt Man, and the two of them bounce away from the suddenly freed heper.

The heper scuttles on hands and foot, blood trailing behind it, frantically trying to find the door opening. Its eyes are pools of fevered dread and pain. It is disoriented, blinded by the blood pouring into its eyes. In its confusion, it is coming right at me.

Abs and Gaunt Man are on their feet, pouncing towards the heper. They land on it at exactly the same time, knocking it off its feet. Right into me.

Its head knocks into my shoulder a split second before its body slams into mine. Weirdly, it embraces me, its arms encircling my waist. Instinctually, my arms swing around its body. I am holding it up, Abs and Gaunt Man right behind it, their nails sinking into its skin, their fangs bared and a second away from slashing downward and into it.

It looks up, and for one dreadful moment, our eyes meet. I will never know if its eyes suddenly widened because of the flood of pain surging through its body or because of recognition. Of another heper.

Eventually, when it is all over, the hunters are released. A staffer, speaking gravely, instructs us to return to our rooms for the remainder of the night. By then, there is hardly anything left of the heper, just its shredded clothes. Its blood has been licked off where it splattered; even the dirt, coagulated with the heper's spilled blood, has been dug up, stuffed into mouths, chewed, and sucked on.

My escort is waiting outside the Introduction. "Go put on a change of clothes," he tells me, his nostrils twitching. "I smell heper all over you."

The openness of the Vast is what I relish. After I climb the endless flight of stairs, lagging far behind everyone else, I finally reach the ground floor. The others move on up to their quarters. I walk out into the open, the night sky filled with stars. An easterly breeze blows, billowing my clothes, wafting through my hair. I stagger towards the library, grateful to be able to get away, to be alone. Grains of sand blow against my face, but I barely notice.

Halfway back, I collapse to the ground.

I am so sapped of strength, I can't get up. I lay my head back down on the bricked walkway. It's the lack of water. My desiccated brain lies shrivelled in my skull, a sour plum. Greyness takes over.

Minutes later—or is it hours?—I come to. I feel better, strength returned to my limbs. The sky is less dark, the stars fewer in number and dimmer. I glance back at the Institute. Nobody has noticed me.

Even though I know it's futile, I do another walk-through the library, hoping to find something to drink. A half hour later, I collapse on the lounge chair, body feeling like a crisp autumn twig, not a molecule of moisture within. My heart hammers away in alarm as if it knows what I'm trying to deny. That my situation is desperate. I won't last another night. They'll come for me after dusk when I don't show up and find me flopped on the floor. It'll be over moments later.

A metallic click rings through the library, then a soft churning sound. The shutters. Pulling down darkness, like my eyelids slowly closing. In the blackness, the air grows chilly. My body odour rises to my nose, a sickening stench of heper. I lift my arms, smell my pits. Ripe. Tomorrow, after the sun sets and the moon rises, I'm a dead man.

A dead heper.

Images of the heper's death fill my sleep: feverish reinterpretations, the screams louder, the colours sharper. In my nightmare, the heper leaps into my arms, its blood running over my cheekbones, down my cheeks. In my thirst, my pasty-dried tongue reaches out reflexively, dabbing at the blood. I suck on the blood, letting it soak into my tongue like mountain spring water into a dry sponge, then draw it down my parched throat, feeling its energy ripple through my sapped body. As my body begins to tingle warmer, the heper screams louder – until I realise the scream is coming not from the heper, but from the other hunters, all of them still tied to their posts, pointing at me, screaming, as I kneel bent over the dead heper in my arms, its skin pasty and blotchy blue.

I shudder awake, the backs of my dry eyelids scraping against my eyeballs.

It is still the middle of the day. The beam of sunlight has returned, streaming across the library again, an illuminated tightrope from one end to the other. It is even brighter and thicker than I remember it.

I'm too tired to do anything but watch it. My thoughts scatter in haphazard, incoherent penumbras. It's all I can do, just mindlessly watch the beam of light. So I do that, for minutes (hours?). The beam shifts ever so with the passing time, travelling in a diagonal fashion along the far wall of the library.

Then something interesting happens. As the beam moves along the wall, it suddenly hits something that causes it to bounce off at an angle; the beam is reflected diagonally to the adjacent wall. At first, I think it's just my mind playing tricks on me. I blink. It's still there, only more obvious now. The original beam shooting across to the far wall and now the shorter, reflected beam, bounced to the right wall.

It's enough to rouse me out of the lounge chair. I make my way to the far wall, my painful knees churning in sockets like cactus scraping on concrete. Where the beam hits the far wall is a small circular mirror, no bigger than the palm of my hand, nailed to the wall. It is angled slightly, reflecting the beam off to the side wall.

As I make my way to that side wall, it happens again. That second reflected beam is in turn reflected: now there are three sunbeams bouncing around the room. The third beam is weak and momentary. It grows brighter for about ten seconds, then fades. As it does, I hurry to the spot it is shining at, a faint dot of illumination on the spine of a book. I walk over and hook out the book. Feel its leathery feel in my hand, smooth and worn. I carry it to the first beam of sunlight, the second beam itself now fading away. I hold the book to the light, flip it around to the front cover.

The Heper Hunt, it reads.

Many moons ago, the heper population – which in eras past, according to unsubstantiated theories, once, unfathomably, dominated the land – fell to dangerously low numbers. By Palatial Order 56, hepers were rounded up and farmed on the newly built Heper Institute of Refined Research and Discovery. To appease a disgruntled populace, citizens in good standing were randomly chosen to participate in the annual Heper Hunt. It was a resounding success.

The first sign of corruption was seen in the decreasing number of hepers at the annual Hunt. Typically ranging between twenty and twenty-five hepers, that number soon dwindled down to about fifteen. Eventually, only ten hepers were released, then only seven; finally, on a night few have forgotten, the Palace released a statement: there were no more hepers in captivity at the Heper Institute.

And yet. Hushed rumours of secret hunting expeditions persisted: clandestine meetings at the Heper Institute for high-ranking Palace officials; convoys of carriages arriving there in the last hours of dusk; odd wails heard coming from across the Vast. Rumours circulated and grew that corruption reached "all the way to the top".

But then, after a few years, even those rumours ceased.

On the eleventh day of the sixth month of the fourth year of the 18th Ruler, it was announced that hepers had become extinct.

The journal cover is made of charcoal lambskin mottled with minuscule grooves. It is smooth and broken in, looped by twin twines. The pages inside, with mercury-gilt edges, crinkle and differentiate easily when I turn them. Thousands of pages of handwritten notes, the penmanship clean and assured. But there's nothing original in these pages. And, notwithstanding the title on the cover, hardly any material about the Heper Hunt. Only a brief history of the Hunt scrawled on the first couple of pages, then the matter is dropped, like an impulsive manuscript quickly jettisoned. The remainder of the journal is hand-copied and regurgitated material copied from the thousands of textbooks in the library. Long lists of genealogies; ancient poems; well-known fables. Even detailed diagrams that must have taken days to copy, meticulously duplicated.

The Scientist. Clearly, he's the author of this journal. But why he spent thousands of hours needlessly filling its pages is a mystery. I remember what others said about him: his mental instability, his mysterious disappearance.

And then there's the beam of light, dimmer now with the approaching dusk. Why had he gone to such lengths to create that beam – and the two others – to point to the journal? The journal was meant to be found, that's obvious, but by whom and why are not so obvious.

I'm shutting the journal closed when I notice a blank white page smack bang in the middle of the journal. What an odd omission. The hundreds of pages before and after this page are filled from top to bottom; yet this page, back and front, has been left blank. Not a dot of ink. Its whiteness is almost a shout. The last sentence on the preceding page isn't even complete – it's cut off midway and then continues on the page after this blank sheet, picking up exactly where it left off. I tap the spine of the book, pondering, confused. Like the reflected beams of light that pointed me to this book, the very blankness of this page seems to be purposefully directing my attention here. But as much as I examine it, I can't make heads or tails of it.

I flop down, tired. The room is suffocating; I grasp around my neck, feel the scrim of sweat and dirt under my jawline. I don't even need to lift my arm to smell the odour exuding off me like a dog in heat.

It will be my escort who'll make the discovery. When he comes to summon me after dusk, he'll smell my odour flowing out through the cracks along the door frame. He'll sprint around, look inside through the windows, the shutters having already been retracted. He'll see me still sitting in this chair, sullen and tired, my chest rising and falling, breathing hard, eyes wide because I will, though resigned, still be very afraid. He will see the emotion pouring off me in waves. And then he'll understand. He will not call for the others. He will want me for himself. He will leap through the glass windows – so frail in the face of his desire, like thin ice before a blowtorch – and even before the shattered shards have reached the ground, he will be upon me. And then he will have me, devouring me with fangs and nails in just a few—

And then, just like that, I realise something.

The blinding whiteness of the outside feels like acid dropped on my eyeballs. I let the light leak in a little at a time, until I can see without blinking, then without squinting.

It is hours before dusk, when the sun has just begun its descent. The sun isn't going quietly: bleeding red into the sky, it infuses the plains with an orange-and-purple hue. Without the Dome to cover the heper village, the mud huts look exposed and inconsequential in the plains, like rat droppings. Soon the light sensors will detect the arrival of night and the glass walls will arc out of the ground, form a perfect dome, and protect the hepers from the world outside. I must hurry.

There's a glimmer in front of the mud huts, like a hundred diamonds twinkling in the twilight. The pond. It's been staring me right in the face the whole time, while thirst ravaged and odour oozed off my body. How could I have been so blind? All the water I could possibly want, for drinking and washing, within easy access. The only danger would be the hepers, of course, who might not take kindly to my intrusion. They'll be confused, of course, on the arrival of a stranger somehow able to withstand sun rays. But I know how to handle them. Bare my fangs, snap my neck side to side, click my bones; I'm a master at impersonation. They'll likely scatter to the four winds.

Suddenly upbeat, I plough on towards the heper village. Gradually, the mud huts begin to take shape, growing in size and detail. Then I see the hepers, a group of stick figures moving slowly around the pond, stopping, moving, stopping. The sight of them both excites and unnerves me. There are five of them. They haven't noticed me yet, nor would they have: nobody has ever approached them during the day.

When I am about a hundred yards away, they see me. One of them, crouching by the pond, shoots straight up, his arm jacking forward like a switchblade sprung out, pointing at me. The others turn quickly, heads pivoting towards me. Their reaction is instant: they turn and flee, bolting inside mud huts. I see windows shuttered closed, doors slammed shut. Within a few scant moments, they've all vacated the pond, leaving upturned pots and pails around the pond in their wake. Just what I was hoping for.

Nothing stirs. Not an opened shutter or a cracked door. I break into a trot, my dried-out bones dangling in my body, snapping with every jarring step. My gaze, fixed on the pond, thirstily draws water out with the bucket of my eyes. I am getting closer, fifty yards out.

A door to one of the mud huts opens.

A female, *that* female heper, steps out. A look of rage on its face, but fear, too. It grips a spear in its right hand. Hanging off its hip is a simple flat slab of dark hide leather, almost like a wide belt. A deadly row of daggers lies strapped in taut against the leather, their blades strangely curved at the hilt.

I raise my hands with wide-open palms. I'm not sure how much it comprehends, so I use simple words. "No hurt! No hurt!" I shout, but what ekes out instead are hoarse, indecipherable sounds. I try to push the words out again, but I can't gather enough saliva in my mouth to lubricate my throat.

The setting sun, directly behind me, douses the heper village with colour, like bright easel paint dripping onto drab leather shoes. My shadow extends long and preternaturally thin before me, a long, gnarled finger reaching out to that girl heper. I'm nothing but a silhouette to it. No; I'm more. I'm the enemy, the predator, the hunter: that's why the other hepers fled. But I'm also something else: a mystery. A confounding contradiction, because although I am in the sunlight, I am not disintegrating. And that is why the female heper has not fled but stands in front of me, puzzled, curious.

But not for long. With a primal scream, it strides towards me, its body at a slant, one arm extended backward. It flings its arm forward in a violent blur.

It takes a moment before I realise what's going on. And by then it's too late. I hear a whistling sound as the spear cuts through air, can even see the wooden length vibrating slightly from side to side as the spear slices towards me. Right at me. In the end, I'm just lucky. I don't move to avoid the spear – there's no time – and it whizzes through the space between my head and left shoulder. I hear *and* feel the *whoosh* by my left ear.

And then the heper is reaching down to its dagger strap; in less than a second, it's unstrapped a dagger and is instantaneously flinging it with a rapid sidearm motion. The dagger shoots out of its hand, flashing in the sunlight. But way off. *Way* off. Like a mile off – the dagger sails harmlessly away.

Figures, I think. *These hepers are nothing more than—*

But then the gleaming dagger begins to curve back towards me, its trajectory that of a boomerang, blinking wickedly fast in the light. As if winking with mischief. And before I know it, it's coming *right* at me. I dive to my right, hit the ground. The dagger *swoosh*es past my head, giving off the harmonic overtone of a singing bowl. I land ungracefully, get the air knocked out of me. The ground is hard, despite the layer of sand and grit.

This heper girl – it knows what it's doing. This is not just for show. It really means to maim me, if not kill me.

I leap up, hands raised high, palms opened emphatically. It is already reaching down towards the strap, where three more daggers lie taut against the leather. Like hunting hounds pulling restlessly on a leash. In the blink of an eye, the heper has unstrapped a dagger and is already drawing back its arm. To unleash the next throw. It will not miss this time.

"Stop! Please!" I yell, and for the first time, the words come out clearly. It pauses midthrow.

I waste little time. I start walking towards the heper again, pulling off my shirt as I do. It needs to see my skin, the sun on the skin, see that I present no danger. I toss the shirt to the side. I'm close enough to see its eyes follow the shirt, then shoot back at me.

It is squinting; I stop in my tracks. I've never seen anyone squint. It is so . . . *expressive*. The eclipsed half closing of the eyelids, the wrinkles coming off the corners of the eyes like a delta, the brows contracted together, even the mouth frozen in a snarl of confusion. It is a strange expression, it is a lovely expression. It pulls its arm back again, the dagger glinting in the sun.

"Wait!" I shout with a craggy croak. It halts, its fingers whitening as they grip the blade tighter. I undo the buttons of my trousers, take them off. My socks, my shoes, everything off. Just my briefs left on.

I stand like that before it, then slowly move forward.

"Water," I say, gesturing at the pond. "Water." I make a cup motion with my hand.

It moves its eyes up and down my body, unsure and suspicious, emotions sweeping off its face, naked and primal.

Eyes fixed on each other, I walk past, giving it a wide arc, and head to the pond. It's more like a swimming pool, the way it is rimmed with a metallic border, perfectly circular. Before I know it, I'm on my knees, my cupped hands pushing through the plane of water. The water, when it flows down my throat, is heaven's wet cool on hell's coaled fire. My hands spring back into the water, ready to cup more into my mouth; and then I'm done with formalities. I plunge my head into the water, gulping down the blissful sweet cool wetness, the water reaching up to my ears.

I come up for air. The heper hasn't moved, but its confusion is carved even deeper into its face. But it's no longer dangerous. Not right now. I throw my whole head back into the pond, my dry, coarse hair gulping up water like straws. The pores on the back of my neck flinch at first contact, then they open up, delighting in the cool aquatic contact.

When I come up for air the second time, the heper has made its way down to the pond. It sits in a crouched position, its arms placed flat atop its kneecaps, the way monkeys do. Figures. It is still half gripping a dagger strapped to its hip, but with less urgency now.

The water's effect on me is almost instant. Synapses in my brain start refiring; my head feels freed of cotton wool, more like a well-oiled machine. Things begin to dawn on me quickly. The dusk, for one, how it is so quickly ceding to the night. Very soon – within moments – the Dome is going to emerge from the ground.

I take off my underwear and leap into the pond.

The water is overpowering at first; the sudden cold pummels air out of me. But there's no time to dilly-dally. I submerge my whole body under water, the frigid liquidity a shock to my system. The water, even in the subdued light of disappearing dusk, is surprisingly clear.

I can stand. The bottom is a gentle decline, smooth and metallic to the touch. I don't waste any time. I scrub myself, my face, my underarm, all the crevices and nooks in my body. I am not gentle with myself: I scrub myself raw. I turn my fingers into pitchforks and rake my scalp, washing my hair as best and quickly as I can.

Then I feel it. A deep vibration coming from the bottom of the pond, weak at first but getting stronger quickly.

The heper stands up. It's looking at the perimeter of the village, then back at me. I understand immediately. The Dome is about to start closing. I need to get out now.

I run out of the pond, spraying up water with my thighs and knees. Hop over the edge, start sprinting.

The vibration is now a full-fledged thrumming that shakes the ground. Then a loud click, and the hum turns into a loud groan. A wall of glass emerges out of the ground, encircling me.

It ascends faster than I expect. Much faster. It is shin-high and then knee-high in a matter of seconds. I sprint to the glass wall, leaping up from a few yards away. My hands land on the top of the glass; they find a tenuous grip on the near corner of the smooth top. My legs scrabble and thrash on the glass walls for traction even as it continues to rise. But the glass is made slippery by the water dripping off my body. I'm about to slip off. If I fall now, there's no way I'd be able to mount it again. I'd be trapped inside.

I close my eyes, shout a silent scream, and heave my arm across the top of the glass width. My hand finds the outer edge, and from there it's easier. I pull myself up, roll over the top width, and fall on the other side of the Dome, on the outside.

It's not a graceful fall. I land on my side; my vision whites out momentarily. Already the wall is twice my height and still rising.

The heper girl is standing beside the pond. It picks up my briefs, holds them up for closer examination. Its nose crinkles – "crinkle" is this thing hepers do when they pull their facial skin together – in mild disgust. And another emotion crosses its face, an unfamiliar, nuanced one. It's disgust, but there is a hint of something else: laughter? No, that's too strong. A hint of a smile touches its lips and mouth, barely perceptible. As if the smile doesn't quite have enough energy to break the surface.

The heper girl impales my briefs on one of its flying daggers. One quick look at me, and it flings its arm. The dagger sails through the air, my briefs waving like a flag, arching just over the enclosing Dome. The dagger lands a few yards from me, my briefs draped over it like slain prey.

The Dome closes with surprising quietness.

I dislodge my briefs from the dagger. They *do* stink. In fact, now that I've washed myself, the briefs positively reek. And then I do something I've never done before. I crinkle my nose. Just for size, to see how it feels. It feels forced and alien on my face, as if something artificial were cinching my nose.

The heper girl walks over to the glass walls of the Dome. I can't see it too clearly; the purpling skies cast a reflective smear over its face. I walk over until we're standing only a few yards apart, separated by the glass wall. It stands close to the Dome, its breath frosting the glass. A small foggy circle that disappears as quickly as it appears.

There's fear on its face, there's anger, there's curiosity. And something else. I look into its eyes, and instead of the glossy plastic shine I'm used to in people's eyes, I see something different. Flecks dance in them, like the trapped flakes in a snow globe.

I turn and walk away. On the way back, I pick up my clothes, quickly put them on. I turn around to take one last look at the Dome. The heper hasn't moved; it stands stationary, watching me.

Hunt Minus Two Nights

"The events that transpired yesternight at the Introduction," the Director says, "were a tad on the aggressive side."

We are back in the lecture hall after a quick and sombre breakfast. Gaunt Man and Crimson Lips had sat nervously at their own table during breakfast while everyone else veered far away. By their look, neither one had slept a wink all day. A strange quietness hung over everything, the tables, the chairs, the soppy breakfast food, like the mist that hovers over a beaker of acid. And the dining hall was emptier than usual, the escorts oddly absent. We were half expecting staff officials to come trooping in during the meal to lead away Gaunt Man and Crimson Lips. But they never came. That seemed to set Gaunt Man and Crimson Lips at ease as we headed over to the lecture hall after breakfast.

I'm also relieved, but for a different reason: I don't smell anymore. At least, not enough to attract attention. The quick scrub down at the pond seems to have done the trick – nobody seems hot and bothered by any odour. Or perhaps after the heper killing at the

Introduction yesternight, everyone's become desensitised to smaller amounts of heper odour. Either way, I win.

The Director is anchored behind the lectern as he speaks. If anger brews within, he hides it well beneath his clinically precise articulation. His eyebrows do not arch, his head does not snap forward. He speaks with the disinterested emotion of one reading random epitaphs, without a hint of reproof for the very serious breach that was committed. His slender voice: the quietness of a razor blade sashaying from side to side, daring contact.

"You had your fun. But consequences . . . There are consequences to your actions." His eyes don't gaze anywhere close to Gaunt Man and Crimson Lips, who are now sitting especially rigid in their seats. "In society, the parameters are clear. It is a capital offence to hunt and kill a heper. Kill and be killed. However, yesternight's killing was not – shall we say, *technically* – an illegal hunt. It was part of the training of the Palace-endorsed Heper Hunt. As such, it falls under the overall auspices of the Hunt."

I see Gaunt Man and Crimson Lips relax a touch.

"But there are consequences. Because a heper, old and emaciated as it may have been, was killed. Gone. No more. Years of possible scientific research never brought to fruition. It will simply not do for its death to go unaccounted for. A crime against a heper is a crime against the Palace. And so there must be consequences for these dastardly acts. Punishment must be meted out."

Gaunt Man and Crimson Lips stiffen in their seats again. "Of course," the Director continues, his eyes drifting down and settling upon them, "nothing can be done against you."

Their heads cock to the side.

"We have invested too much in you," the Director continues. "To expel you and seek a replacement so late in the game, mere nights from the Hunt, is simply not a feasible option." His voice drops off as he gazes at the empty seats in the back row. "But punishment must be meted out. So nobody gets any notion that the government is getting soft. Because a capital offence demands a capital punishment. Or two. Or three. Or seven."

His next words are razor-sharp. "You will have noticed that the escorts are gone." It is an ambiguous statement. And then it is not. A chill runs down my spine. And he says nothing else as he walks slowly across the stage to another lectern, this one made of glass.

"So, with that unpleasantry out of the way, some good news to report. A rather pleasant surprise, in fact. The Palace has directed us to host a banquet Gala. Hundreds of dignitaries will be arriving, high-standing officials, men of influence, their wives and mistresses. It is very short notice, but we do have a smidge of a window tomorrow evening. This Institute used to host many a banquet Gala back in the day, so it's shovel-ready. The facility just needs a dusting up. It'll be ready. And so will you. We're cancelling all other training events. Who needs training, anyway, just chase down the damn things and eat them." He peels back his sleeve like a snake shedding skin and delicately scratches his bony wrist.

"And one more thing. The media will be covering the Gala. We want you looking your best. Tailors are arriving in a couple of hours to measure each of you. They'll be busy with you the rest of the night." He runs his hand back along the gelled arc of his hair. "Two nights after the banquet, the Hunt will begin. All guests to the banquet are required to stay for the start of the Hunt. And so you will have quite the send-off, what with the hundreds of spectators and media coverage. Should make for quite the spectacle."

He stares at us, then scratches his wrist. "My, my, my, don't you all look so petrified. You should see your silly, worried faces. I know exactly what your concern is: you're afraid the hundreds of guests will all rush out after the hepers. You needn't worry. This building will be locked down three hours before dusk on the night of the Hunt. A total lockdown. No one will be able to leave the building except the hunters."

Without saying more, the Director, as is his wont, recedes into the shadows; and in his place, as usual, emerges Frilly Dress. This has happened so many times, I'm beginning to wonder if it's not the same person. If their physiques weren't so different – his lithe, hers doughy – it really would have given me pause.

With the Director gone, the release of tension is almost palpable. Frilly Dress has a far less imposing presence and usually has so little of substance to say that it takes a moment before we realise she is saying something important.

". . . so it has fallen on me to give you some specifics about the Hunt. The dawn before the Hunt is to begin, the hepers will be informed by letter that the Dome has suffered a malfunction: the sensor has broken down and there is a good chance that the Dome will fail to arise at dusk. As a precautionary measure, the hepers will need to journey immediately to a temporary shelter as indicated on a map we'll provide them. The journey should take only eight hours, assuming they don't dilly-dally, allowing them to reach the shelter before dark. The shelter will provide them with food, water, and shutters. They are to return after a week. Questions?"

Phys Ed raises his arm. "I don't get it. If they get there before dark, they'll be safely holed up before we even get to start. This is supposed to be a Hunt, not a siege."

By the number of head jerks all around, it's clear that Phys Ed has struck a common nerve.

But Frilly Dress is unperturbed, slowly scratching her wrist. "My, my, a little antsy this evening, aren't we? One thing you have all forgotten is the sheer gullibility of the hepers. They'll believe anything we tell them. After all, we domesticated them, we know how to pull their strings." Her face suddenly turns stern. "There is no shelter. No building, no shutters, no walls, not even so much as a brick. The hepers will be completely exposed for you to hunt."

At this, a smacking of lips ensues, so loud that, again, we can barely hear Frilly Dress speaking.

". . . stash of weapons," she says, finishing her sentence.

Phys Ed raises his arm again. "What did you mean by 'a stash of weapons'?"

Frilly Dress scratches her wrist, obviously pleased with herself. She pauses, knowing she has our attention. "There is a very significant change from the previous Heper Hunts. We've decided to arm the hepers. With a stash of weapons. This will undoubtedly slow down the Hunt, make it more challenging, and help you derive greater enjoyment out of it. Raise the stakes, raise the pleasure."

"Arm them? With what kind of weapons?" asks Beefy, his voice gruff, more curious than alarmed.

An image of a spear and dagger is projected on the large screen. I recognise them as the ones the female heper had brandished – and thrown at me – the day before. "It was once hoped that the hepers would learn to use the spear and dagger as weapons. They did, but their lack of strength rendered these weapons as useless as toothpicks. Fortunately, however, our staffers here at the Institute have come up with some more robust weaponry, something with real zing. Something that can actually hurt. And possibly maim."

The wrist scratching that began with the images of the spear and dagger comes to a sudden stop. "What kind of weapons?" Beefy asks again, warily now.

Frilly Dress turns to him, and there is suddenly nothing frilly or dressy about her gaze. "This," she whispers, and another image is projected on the screen.

It looks like a rectangular cup, but instead of an opening on one end there is a glass encasing behind which three glassy bulbs point outward. The surface of the weapon is panelled with a highly reflective metal, mirror-like. A large chrome button sits atop the weapon on the other end.

"This is the three-bulb Flash Uniemitter, or simply FLUN for short. FLUNs can inflict devastating flashes of light. Push the button situated at the back, and out shoots a continuous ray of light – not mercuric, mind you – that lasts up to two seconds. The beam is quite powerful: at a luminous efficacy of about ninety-five lumens, it will singe your skin deeply and painfully on initial contact. If the beam is held for a second or longer, the ultraviolet resonance will cause vomiting and loss of consciousness. If you happen to look directly into the beam, you will be blinded, perhaps permanently."

It is, as the saying goes, quiet enough to hear a heper hair drop.

"That is the lowest setting."

Silence.

"How many settings are there?" Beefy asks.

After a dramatic pause, Frilly Dress says, "Five. At the highest setting, a single shot is powerful enough to burn a hole through you. It has five times the potency of the noon sun rays."

Ashley June's arm wisps up like a plume of smoke. "How many?"

Her question is vague, but Frilly Dress seems to understand perfectly. "There are five FLUNs in total. Each heper will be armed with one. Each FLUN shoots upward of three shots. It has a range of about thirty feet." She purses her lips as if sucking out stuck entrails from between her teeth.

It is very, very quiet. "Why?" asks Beefy.

This question is also ambiguous, but again Frilly Dress has no problem understanding it. "We're doing it for you, my dear. To make this Hunt truly memorable, to make it surpass the excitement of any previous Hunt."

Nobody is moving now, nobody seemingly breathing. Only her dress moves, swaying about her wide body, embroidered fronds and ferns and sunflowers spinning about her.

"In fact, not only do we want to increase the combativeness between the hunters and hepers, we want to increase the level of competition between the hunters as well." Her voice has taken on a robotic tone, as if she's spouting a script. "This will indubitably make the Hunt that much more interesting and ultimately enhance the winner's enjoyment."

"How are you going to increase it?" Ashley June asks, glancing at the others. Her voice is a whisper in the airy lecture hall. "The competition between us?"

"Sometime later tonight, you'll each be given a piece of equipment. Nothing that will help you actually kill the hepers, but it will make the chase to them more interesting. The equipment is designed to give you an advantage over your fellow hunters. Perhaps. They're all still in the prototype stage, so their ability to deliver as advertised is unproven."

"What kind of items?" Abs asks. She's leaning forward, intrigued.

"Well, some of you will be given shoes designed to give more bounce and speed. We estimate that it will make you about ten percent faster. Others will be given either a SunCloak or SunBlock Lotion. Worn and applied properly, they can be used to block the early-dawn and late-dusk sunlight. We think, anyway. You'll be able to leave perhaps ten minutes before the others, an eternity of difference in a race like this. Some of you will be given an adrenaline shot. You get the idea. Things that will give you minor advantages over the others in the chase. But again, let me emphasise: these products haven't been completely tested. You use and rely on them at your own risk."

"I was hoping for something more along the lines of a protective suit – against the FLUNs," Crimson Lips says.

"I wouldn't worry about the FLUNs," Gaunt Man says before Frilly Dress can respond. "Remember, they're animals. They won't even be able to figure out how to operate the FLUNs."

"Believe that if you will," Frilly Dress says, her voice even and cold. "If you think that gives you a competitive edge over the others, then think that. The others here will be only too glad to take advantage of your wilful ignorance."

"Hey, you can't talk to me that way—"

"Funny, that. I was just about to ask for a volunteer, thank you for offering."

"Volunteer? For what?"

"That's right, just make your way up to the stage." Frilly Dress takes out a pair of shades from her belt, puts them on. "I suggest you all put on your shades now. Except you," she says, looking at Gaunt Man.

Gaunt Man gets up slowly, his hand creeping up to pull his earlobes. He stops himself. "What's this? What's going on?"

"Nothing the escorts haven't already gone through this morning."

"What's this? I'm not getting out of my seat," he says, sitting back down now.

"That's not a problem." And then Frilly Dress takes out a secreted FLUN from beneath her dress. "Didn't I just tell you this thing has a range of thirty feet?"

Gaunt Man strains back against his chair. He's pinned, got nowhere to go.

"Consider yourself lucky. I've set it on the weakest setting. But I think you'll still be impressed."

"Wait!" Gaunt Man's head snaps forward, then to the side.

"The Director said punishment had already been meted out. Upon the escorts. There's nothing left—"

"But to show what you were so lucky to miss out on. Albeit a very watered-down demonstration, compared to what they had to face. You'll live."

There is a click as her thumb pushes down on the button. A sharp, clear beam shoots out of the FLUN. Arms raised before our eyes, we're all blinded by the flash. Except me, of course. I see the beam hit Gaunt Man on his chest. His arms fly to block it, but already there is black smoke shooting out of his chest. He falls to the ground as if toppled by a sledgehammer, his body writhing in pain. His mouth is wide open, but no sound emits. He turns to the side, his tongue thick and dry and protruding out of his mouth; a sludge of yellow vomit pours out.

Frilly Dress releases the button. "Oh, stop being such a drama queen," she says as she floats by him and out.

We're ushered out of the lecture hall and taken on another tour of the facilities, more empty classrooms and laboratories. After our face-to-face encounter with a live heper yesterday, looking at heper teeth and anatomical heper diagrams fails to arouse any excitement. The only area remotely interesting is the kitchen. Gaunt Man rejoins us there, having been given clearance from the doctors, looking even more bitter than usual. The chefs are busy in the kitchen preparing for dinner, carving up huge chunks of cow hide. The group stays around the main prep table, where the sight and scent of bloody meat draws them. Except Ashley June, who has meandered to a side table where an apprentice chef is at work. I walk over.

"Now that," I say, salivating at the fried potatoes and noodles, "is absolutely disgusting."

The apprentice chef, a small man with beady eyes, ignores me. He scoops out the food and slaps it into a large plastic container. He opens the door to an oven behind him, tosses in the container, and slams it shut. He pushes a button and walks away. "Heper food," he murmurs. After taking a quick look around to make sure no one except Ashley June is watching, I open the oven door. Except it's not an oven. The container's gone: down a long narrow tunnel, on a conveyor belt, into darkness.

Footsteps approach the group from behind. With a military cadence. It's a staffer, his face chiselled and serious. "Your presence is requested," he barks, his sharp chin pointing at Ashley June. "Immediately."

"What is this about?" she asks.

He ignores her question, turns to me. "And you too. Come with me now." He pivots around and walks out, not bothering to look back.

Something is off; I sense it as we follow the staffer outside and along the brick path towards the library. His pace is more than just brisk and urgent; there is *fear* propelling his boots forward. No one speaks.

Walking through the front doors and into the library feels like walking into the lion's den.

Inside, the first thing I sense are bodies. Lots of them, perhaps two dozen, staffers and sentries standing just inside the foyer. All of them are wearing shades, all off to the side, standing stiffly at attention.

Don't swivel your eyes back and forth. Don't.

Nobody moves. I let my eyes adjust to the darkness slowly, taking long, sustained breaths. It's cold inside.

Nothing good is going to come out of this. The only silver lining: they don't know yet. That I'm a heper. If they knew, I wouldn't still be standing here. They'd have pounced on me the second I entered.

I hear his voice before I see him.

"I trust you have found these accommodations to your satisfaction?" the Director says in a tempered tone. He is standing in the centre of the room, just off the side of a table, the right side of his face lit by a mercuric lamp, his left side blanketed in blackness. His lithe figure, cutting an inconspicuous line in the room, possesses the thinness of a slashing razor. As he speaks, even the books on the shelves seem to tilt slightly away from him.

"Yes, they have been wonderful. Thank you."

His head arcs upward as if following a flock of birds hastily taking flight. "We worried about the size of the sleep-holds. They weren't custom-fit for you. We apologise for that."

"They were a coincidentally good fit."

"Were they now?"

"Yes."

He gazes casually at me with seeming disinterest, but beneath his stare a keen coldness lingers. Without warning, his feet suddenly lift off the ground as he leaps towards the ceiling. His body spins upward, his feet a half second later locking into the sleep-holds, the very sleep-holds I have never used. Minutely, his body sways languorously, like the pendulum of an ancient grandfather clock. His eyes, upside down, are still locked coolly on mine.

"Amazing how different the world is from this position, when everything is turned on its head. Do you find that to be true?"

"Yes. I do," I answer.

"Makes you see things from a different perspective. And that's why I'm upside down, looking at you now."

"Sir?"

"Because I'm trying to see you in a different light. Trying to see what's so special about you. Trying to see why the Palace is singling you out, giving you the royal treatment. Because I just don't see anything about you that's distinguishing." He closes his eyes, luxuriating in a long, drawn-out blink.

"Royal treatment, sir?"

"Ah, playing dumb, I see."

I don't say anything.

"Take a look around," he whispers, "at this whole wide library that is yours alone. It's even bigger than *my* chambers! And you tell me the Palace is not giving you the royal treatment." He descends slowly from the sleep-holds and lands unnervingly close to me, an arm's length away.

I fight the urge to step back.

"You know, just a few minutes ago, I received yet another directive from the Palace. Concerning you. Again." He pauses, a glint in his eyes. "There are very few things in life that leave me at a loss. But this kind of attention from the Palace for someone as bland and insignificant as you . . . well, quite frankly, it's left me flummoxed."

"I confess I'm not sure what you're referring to. Another directive, sir?"

"No confessions, please." He takes a step back to a nearby desk, his finger trailing along the back of a chair. He pulls it out, sits down. And that's when I notice the two attaché cases. On the table, reflecting the faint gleam of the mercuric lights. They stand straight up like everyone else in the room, at attention. But with an ominous air.

"If there's one thing I disdain, it's being kept in the dark. It's a cold stiff arm of disrespect. And the Palace has been doing this repetitively over the past few weeks. To *me*. Random directives arriving on my desk daily, without explanation or rationale, last minute twists and turns regarding the Hunt. Fortunately, my bright intellect helps me see the method to all the madness of these directives." His lips downturn. "Except when it comes to you."

Standing off to my right, Ashley June hasn't moved. Her arms hang still by her sides, her face lost in the dark shadows.

"I've done my research on you. Apparently, you're quite an intellectual standout at school, not nearly as dumb as you've been pretending to be here. Quite the brains, so they say. A natural, despite your only moderately above par grades. How did the report put it? Ah, yes, that yours was a *stupendous* and *prodigious* intelligence not fully tapped. That's the intel on you, anyway." He pauses. "Could that be what garners all this attention, favouritism? Your so-called intelligence?" he says, staring condescendingly at me with the naked disdain of someone feeling threatened. "Tell me: what do you think this Hunt is about?"

He's testing me. Sizing me up. "Hunting hep—"

"And don't say 'hunting hepers'. Because it's never been about hunting or hepers or hunting hepers. So don't use any of those words separately or in combination."

"It's all about the Ruler," I answer, strangely emboldened.

His eyes snap to mine, but there is no menace in them. "Ah, the lad might have a mind, after all. Expound, then, if you will."

I pause. "I'd rather not, I think."

His head snaps back. "You'd rather so, I should think."

After a pause, I speak, in as even-keeled a voice as I can muster. "The Ruler knows that his popularity rating has been sagging recently. This is unfair because he is a truly dynamic leader, the best this land has ever known in all its storied and glorious past. But our Ruler is not so much interested in his popularity numbers as he is in the happiness of his people. And nothing else brings as much communal bliss and sense of societal camaraderie as a Heper Hunt. It is to that end that he plans and executes the Heper Hunt with such adroit skill. Of course, it is merely incidental that – as history bears out – nothing will help his numbers as much as a Heper Hunt."

"Bingo," the Director whispers, his eyes closing in ecstasy. "My, my, my. The boy wonder surprises after all." He scratches his wrist. "But that was an easy question. The warm-up."

A slight shake of the head and then he sets his eyes on mine, a hardness flitting across his face. "Explain to me . . . all of this," he says, his arms floating above him momentarily like a ballerina. "Explain the reason for this training orientation. After all, who needs training to hunt down hepers? Why the idiotic lectures, workshops, training sessions? And explain the festivities, the fanfare of the Gala, explain the reason for the media, reporters, and photographers flooding into this Institute as we speak. And explain why on earth we are arming the hepers with FLUNs."

"I'm sorry, I don't know."

"Don't say sorry," he says. And he waits.

"I don't know."

"Not so smart after all. Are you?" His upper lip snarls up reproachfully, exposing the lower half of his fangs. "Fact is, you're just like everyone else around here, all the incompetent staff who need to be hand-fed intelligence, my intelligence. Clueless. Brainless. Empty-headed." His eyes stare out at me, flaring down his nose and upturned chin. "Empty as this Institute," he says, bitterness souring his words. "Empty as this Institute," he says again, quieter.

He turns his back to me, stares out of the window. When he speaks, the cratered emptiness of his voice surprises me. "It wasn't always this way. The hallways used to hum with foot traffic; classrooms spilled over with the very brightest first-rate minds; laboratories were hives of activity, brimming with experiments conducted by top-notch scientists. And the heper pens! They were filled, from top to bottom, with dozens of hepers, young to old. Our breeding programme – *my* breeding programme – was about to really take off. There was energy about this place, a spark running along the walls. We had purpose, recognition, admiration, respect, even envy. We had everything." He stops speaking, stops moving, his chest so still, it is as if he has stopped breathing. "Everything but self-control."

And then his eyes turn to the sentries and staff standing stiffly around us, his icy stare pinning each of them like moths to the board.

"Until one day, we had virtually no hepers left," he continues, turning to face me. "This will be the very last Heper Hunt. The Ruler knows this. But he is most unwilling to have what's been a popularity cow for him come to an end. So he has devised a way to keep feeding off this Hunt for years to come, in perpetuity, even."

Ashley June, off to my right, hasn't moved. Not a sound out of her.

"A book. A non-fiction account of this Hunt. The public has always been insanely curious about the Hunt. The good citizens, who salivate over every detail of the Heper Hunt, will keep this book on the best-seller list for decades. And this book will not be a dry journalistic work. No; rather – and here is the stroke of genius – it will be a memoir penned by the winner. The winner of *this* Hunt."

He strokes his cheek with the backs of his fingers, up and down, up and down. "Do you see how everything fits together now? Do you see why we have a training period? the Gala? the media flooding the Institute?"

And I see it. It all makes sense now. "It's all for the book," I whisper. "To draw out the Hunt, stretch it out to a week-long event, to provide material for the book. To make it all the more exciting. To make the stakes that much higher. The experience of the Hunt all the more enhanced, the victory all the more rapturous."

The Director nods me on.

"I mean, the training period alone will take up five chapters. And it'll be a chance to flesh out the hunters. The competitiveness between us, the conflicts within, all that will only be grist for the mill. It'll build up anticipation, leading up to the Gala, then, to the climax, the Hunt itself. The book will practically write itself."

The Director's eyes shine with reluctant approval. "And the FLUNs? Why arm the hepers with FLUNs? Go on, go on, you're doing well so far."

"For excitement. No, more than that." I pause, thinking. "To slow the Hunt down. Because these are the very last hepers in existence. What a waste to devour them into extinction in mere seconds. Chomp, chomp, gone, scarfed down in a frantic feeding frenzy. It'll be almost anticlimactic. No, better to draw out the experience, to kill off the hepers slowly, one at a time. One chapter stretched into three." I fight the urge to furrow my brow. "But that's possible only if the Hunt is slowed down – *by arming the hepers*. It'll increase the drama, the excitement, the pay-off for the eventual winner. And then the last chapter will be amazing. Drama to the hilt as the winning hunter drinks down the very last drops of heper blood. Down, down his throat . . . into oblivion." I look at Ashley June, then at the Director, understanding at last. "Everything is for the book. For the Ruler."

The Director is staring with a look of genuine surprise, his eyes wide, his jaw drooped and slack. Then his head snaps forward, then back again, a sharp staccato movement that cracks his neck. "Well done," he says. "You really are quite the surprise." His neck cracks loudly one more time, a bone-snapping *clap* that ricochets down the library.

Then he pauses: his eyes suddenly narrow into a dark and intense disdain. "And so that brings us back to you. The one thing I cannot figure out. How do you fit into all of this? And why the directive I received just a few minutes ago, again concerning you?"

"What directive, sir?"

"Why is the Palace so interested in you?" he asks, ignoring my question. "Everything else, I've figured out." And every last vestige of brightness in his eyes is flung away. Only razors of darkness stand in his eyes now, so keen on mine, I feel them slicing into my eyeballs.

"I don't know."

"You're lying," he says, caressing his forearm with the backs of his fingers as if stroking a hairless kitten. "Tell me. Now. Tell me what's going on. The Palace thinks it's so smart with these random directives, thinks it can keep me in the dark. Every other day comes some new directive willy-nilly, some new twist on this Hunt. They want to keep me on my toes, they want to keep me in the dark. But I have my ways of finding out." His words drop out of his mouth, sharp icicles falling into a dark canyon. "And of coercing it out, if necessary."

My fingers, hung by my side, begin to tremble. I press them against the side of my leg. "I don't—"

"Tell me!" His voice booms off the walls. Even as his words echo down the length of the floor, I see the anger rising in his eyes. He begins to move towards me—

"I know why," Ashley June suddenly whispers.

The Director stops. Everyone turns to look at her.

She looks at me briefly, as if about to commit an unforgivable betrayal, then says: "It's because" – her voice lowers even more – "he's different."

"What do you mean?" the Director asks.

She is standing in the shadows; now she steps forward, into a splash of moonlight. "He's exactly what the Palace is looking for."

Hesitation. Then: "Explain."

"You said the winner will pen this book. So they need someone who can write. And with the media here, there're going to be magazine interviews, TV talk show appearances, radio interviews after the Hunt. So they need someone well-spoken. But Heper Hunt winners have typically been loutish brutes, masters of physicality but not exactly the most articulate or cerebral of people. The Palace needs someone who is well-spoken, thoughtful, restrained, detail-oriented." She flicks her chin in my direction. "And with him, you've got all that. I know: I've been his classmate for years. He's always been an academic star, unwittingly. His intelligence is effortless. He'll be terrific. In press interviews, in front of the camera, penning the memoir. And the Palace knows this; it sounds like they've thoroughly vetted him. Of all the hunters here, he's by far the most media-ready."

The Director turns his eyes on me, scrutinising me as if from a newly discovered angle.

"He might be a bit on the shy, quiet side," Ashley June continues, "but even that's a plus: it's a quietness that's compelling and attractive. Girls love it." She pauses. "Trust me on that one."

The Director shifts his stare away to look outside, a flicker of annoyance flitting across his face. "Who's been giving you all this intel?"

"Nobody. It's just guesswork, that's all." Alertness shines in her eyes. "Nothing you haven't already thought of, I'm sure."

"I see." His left hand, glowing with a suffused paleness, strokes one of the attaché cases. His bony fingers lilt on the handle, brushing it with fear and disdain. "So you're just guessing – you could be way off base."

"Maybe. But I don't think so." She pauses. "But what about me? Why am I here?"

The Director raises his eyes to her and scratches his wrist in long, lethargic strokes. His pleasure is easily evident. "You are what we would call Plan B."

"I'm not sure I follow."

"Pity that. And to think you'd been doing so well." The Director sniffs. "Evidently, you're just like everyone else, always needing me to spell things out for them. An hour ago, I received yet another directive. Concerning both you and him. You are Plan B. In case Plan A – him – fails to pan out, in case he fails to execute, you're the safety net. Something goes wrong during the Hunt, he fails to deliver or is taken out of the action, you're there to win the Hunt. You're the insurance policy, the understudy winner."

"I don't think it'll work."

"But of course it will!" he says, mild irritation seeping into his voice. "You're every bit the package he is. Smart – though I'm beginning to have my doubts; verbose – though a little too much, I'm coming to think; and very knowledgeable about hepers. They've told me about you, little girl, about all the heper clubs and societies you've been involved in over the years. Your heper knowledge will come in handy during post-Hunt interviews and whatnot. And besides, you're quite the eye candy. You'd look good on camera, in photographs. Your pretty face would grace the covers of instant best sellers quite well. Yes, I can see it now."

"You need to think about the bigger picture of the Hunt," Ashley June says, her voice steely.

"I need to think? . . ."

Ashley June is silent: the silence of regret.

"You think you know better than me?" The words pepper her like pellets out of a shotgun, rancid with scorn. "Don't tell me what I need to think, little girl."

The Director closes his eyelids, his long eyelashes delicately interlacing. And with that, the temperature in the library, already low, plummets. Beams of moonlight freeze into pillars of transparent grey ice. I shoot a look at her. She knows she's crossed a line – her skin is even paler than before, and her eyelids are fluttering.

The Director's eyes draw down to the two attaché cases. He pulls them closer. "One of you'll need to win the Heper Hunt for this plan to succeed. That's what you wanted to tell me, isn't it, little girl? Please. Don't presume to share with me your pedestrian ideas. Because I already knew that. In order for you to grace the covers of magazines, to appear on talk shows, to be the talk of the town, one of you must win. Because yes, I'm well aware that there're other hunters, many of whom are not only as desirous to win, but far more capable of doing so."

He presses a button and the attaché cases open with a snap. He spins them around for us to see inside. A FLUN inside each case. The Director takes one out. "Nobody knows what really happens out there in the Vast during the Hunt, how dirty it can get. For one, the Hunt has never been videotaped: videocameras are too heavy, and besides, cameramen will simply throw the cameras down and join in the Hunt, unable to resist. And nobody really cares how . . . unsportsmanlike things can degenerate. Hunters have been known to . . . well, resort to dirty tricks. It's a dog-eat-dog world out there, and the more dog it is, the more interesting it'll be to read about later. Use these FLUNs on the other hunters. Everyone will think it was just the hepers who shot them. Somewhere in the Vast when you're far removed from the Institute. One FLUN for each of you, three shots in each. Should be enough, no?"

"And what if we take out all the other hunters?" Ashley June asks. Her voice is quiet but not hesitant. "And it's only the two of us left? What should we do?"

The Director's reaction is almost violent. His hands cross together at the wrists, and he scratches deep white lines into the soft give of his wrists, his head snapping back like a sideways pogo stick. "What do I really care?" Beads of delirious light shoot out of his eyes. "What do I really care so long as one of you wins? Oh, you silly girl!" He suddenly stops moving as if remembering something; he looks at both of us sternly. "Only know this: I want a clear winner. It's always better that way. No ties. The public does not like ambiguity. If it comes down to just the two of you . . . well . . . there can be only one. You will know what to do. Correct?"

Neither Ashley June nor I answer.

And he starts scratching again, long, slow strokes. "I see. I see. I see that I have not made myself clear. That I have not fully conveyed to you just how vested I am in the success of this Hunt. That I have not made clear how important this is to me, how one of you – and only one – must win the Hunt." He places the tips of his forefingers on each eyebrow, runs them down their thin, soft arches. "Many people think I have a dream job here at the Institute. To be able to work in such proximity to the hepers. Those people are ignorant fools. This place is hell."

His face turns graven, darkness shadowing over him. "A successful Hunt would give me a chance to leave this place," he whispers. "This purgatory where heaven is only a glass wall away; but that glass is as thick as a thousand universes laid side by side. You can only take it for so long, to be tantalised with the sight and smell of hepers, yet to be deprived of it at every turn. It is its own type of hell, to be so teasingly close yet so impossibly far. To get away from this faux heaven . . . and be promoted to work where heaven is real – the Ruler's Palace. To finally be promoted to Minister of Science."

Another long pause pregnant with angst. "Have you ever . . . no, of course you haven't. But I was there for a day. The Ruler's Palace. When I was officially appointed to this position. There, in all its glory and grandeur. The reality surpassed even the loftiest of my expectations. Towering sphinxes of hyenas and jackals, slippery-smooth marble edifices, the endless, elegant retinue of cupbearers, scribes, harpists, pages, message runners, court soothers, guardsmen, the silky-robed harem of virgins. But that was not even the best of it. Have you any idea what that might be?"

I do not say anything.

"You might think it is the elegant pools lined with waterfalls, or the grottoes, or the symphonic hall with the petal-cupped mercuric chandelier. But no, you would be wrong. Or the aquarium filled with oysters and clams and squid and octopus that you can simply pluck out like a dandelion and devour. But you would be wrong again. Or the paintings, or the royal stable with rows of regal stallions as far as the naked eye can take you. But again, you would be wrong."

He lifts his index finger weighed down by a heavy emerald-cut inset ring. Immediately, the staffers and sentries about-turn and walk out.

When the front doors close, he wets his lips and continues. "It's the food. The most exotic yet fattiest of meats, the choicest and bloodiest parts to sink your teeth into even as the animal's heart pumps. Pump-pump, pump-pump, just like that, as you chew on its liver and kidney and brain. Of dogs, of cats. And that's just the appetiser. After that, the main course." Out of the dark, I hear his lips quiver wetly. "Heper meat," he hisses.

I stare blankly, a horror dawning on me. *Don't widen your eyes,* my father's voice bellows, *don't widen your eyes!*

"Suppose I tell you there's a secret stash," he whispers. "That somewhere on the Palace grounds is a top-secret heper farm. Just supposing, of course. Because everyone knows that the last hepers on the face of the planet are in that Dome outside. But now, suppose that heper farm is underground, kept from view, spanning the whole length and width of the Palace grounds. Just supposing, of course. How many hepers? you might be asking. Who can say? But during the one night I stayed there, I could hear their howls and cries at night. Sounded like there were dozens, possibly hundreds." He strokes his cheek. "Perhaps – just supposing – enough to provide the Ruler a heper meal for the rest of his life. Just supposing, of course."

He looks at us in turn. "So now you know, yes? I am firmly committed to this Hunt's success. Meaning one of you – and only one! – will come out the winner. You do not want to know the consequences of failure." He stands up. "Trust me on this one. So you will give me this. One of you will win. That is all. I have made myself clear." He brushes by me and exits the room. The door closes behind him.

I let out my breath, and it's a long time before I inhale again.

Afterwards, Ashley June is sent back to her room to be measured. A team of tailors – sombre with hangdog faces – later arrives at the library to take my measurements for the tuxedo, their voices hushed in the airy library. It's a stressful experience for me, especially when the tailors lean in a little too close for comfort. I see their nostrils flaring; one of them even shoots me a curious look. I shoot him down quickly enough, but he gives me another odd look as the team packs up and leaves.

I head outside, wanting to be in open space. The last few hours have been intensely stressful. And it's a beautiful night, perfect for calming my nerves. The sky is sprinkled with pretty sparkles of starlight; the crescent moon hovers high, layering the snow-capped eastern mountains with a film of crusted silver. Soft gusts of air sigh across the plains, lifting the tension from my shoulders.

I hear footsteps behind me, the soft kick of sand.

It's Ashley June, walking towards me, her eyes tentatively on mine. When our eyes meet, her eyes fall shyly. She's wearing a new outfit: a black satin camisole, hung low and tight. Her long pale arms glide down her sides, shimmering under the moonlight, slippery marble columns. The sand shifts and swirls under me, dizzying me, disorienting me.

"I walk all the way back here, the least you can do is say hi," she says. She stands in front of me. "Oh, I see, you're not even talking to me now."

"No, it's not that. I'm sorry."

A breeze billows her hair with soft undulations, exposing the skin of her neck. "Look, I'm not your enemy here. Yet." She scratches her wrist. "I guess we're supposed to wait until the Hunt for that."

And I find myself scratching my wrist in return. "Do me a favour," I say. "If it comes down to only you and me in the Hunt, just shoot me in the pinkie toe, OK? No need to take me out with a shot through my eye."

"Right pinkie or left?"

I scratch my wrist. "I'll take the left. Just aim carefully, OK? It's a small toe."

"Deal," she says.

High above us, the shape of a large bird sails across the night sky. Its wings span disproportionately large, unwieldy, and stiff. It circles around us, then dissolves in the distance.

"I came here to ask you something," she says.

"No, you can't have my FLUN."

She doesn't say anything. I turn to look at her, and she's waiting with those emerald green eyes of hers, quietly, hopefully. As if she's been waiting for this moment for a long time: when I'm really alone with her, not distracted, our eyes finally meeting and merging.

"Take me to the Gala." Her voice is soft and even.

I start lifting my wrist to scratch it. But her arms dangle by her side, stationary. "For real?" I ask.

"Yes."

"I don't even know if it's . . . it's not like a school prom, you know. It's the Gala. A splashy government affair. It's a whole other thing."

"I know," she says. "It won't be like a prom at all. It will be a thousand times more special."

"I don't . . . I don't know."

"It'll mean a lot to me."

I glance over her shoulder, scan the horizon. "Look, I don't know how to say this. I know the Gala will be special and classy because of the music, the media, the red carpet, the dancing, the food—"

"It will be special because of you. Because you've asked me to be with you."

I look away. "I don't know."

And she moves suddenly towards me, swiftly closing the distance between us. She takes my elbow in her hand. The touch of her skin on mine jolts me. "Is it so hard to like me?" she asks, whispering, her eyes searching mine. "Is it really that hard?"

I don't say anything.

"Can you just pretend, can you just put on a mask, then?" And something about those words – or maybe it's the way she says them – makes me look into her eyes, longer than I ever have with anyone but my father. "Because you're really ripping me apart inside."

"It's not you—"

"Just pretend," she whispers, "that you're really into me. That you like the shape of my lips, the softness of my skin, the scent of my breath, the colour of my eyes. And pretend that you can even see past all that, the surface, that you know me deeper than that. The hidden beneath. And that you are still drawn to me, except even more so. Imagine there is nothing else right now but me standing before you, that no one else in the world exists. Not the other hunters, not the staffers, not the hepers. Not even the moon or the stars or the mountains. And that you have longed for me for a long time, and I am here now, right before you. Pretend all that, just for one night." Her free hand reaches to my back and pulls me closer to her. We're only inches away now. A gust blows; strands of my hair fall into my eyes.

And she reaches up and brushes aside my bangs, her fingers trailing slowly along the side of my head, above my ear, and down the side of my neck.

Years of resolve to freeze my heart and cauterise my feelings for her, and this one act is the first personable and genuine touch I have felt in years of living alone and living lonely. It triggers something in me. A seismic shifting within, an eruption of what has lain only frailly dormant. Her eyes lock on mine, their touch as tangible as the feel of her hand on my elbow, but deeper, more probing. I feel the yearning of emotions I thought were long dead. An unravelling in me.

"Please?" she pleads. "Take me?"

And I surprise myself by nodding my head. She shakes with delight as she grips my elbow harder, her long, thin bicep flexing, dissolving, flexing, dissolving. I take her elbow in my hand now, the etiquette of an invitation accepted. She tilts her head backward and closes her eyes slightly, eyelids fluttering, lips parted. But then her upper lip quivers into a shaky snarl, and two fangs jut out, wetly white and razor-sharp. Fangs that would, in five seconds flat, rip into my chest, pummel through my rib cage, and tear out my still-beating heart.

Why have I let myself forget, why, in a moment of weakness, did I give in? I can never forget that her beauty is laced with poison, that her lips veil twin rows of knives, that her heart is enclosed by a razor-sharp rib cage. She is impossible to me, untouchable, unreachable.

My hand on her elbow clamps down hard, with anger, with loathing, sinking deep into her bloodless flesh. But she misinterprets the force of my emotions and lifts her face to the night sky, shaking more fervently. And I realise how, from the outside, on the other side of the mask, how easy it is for loathing to be mistaken for longing.

With dawn soon approaching, I walk Ashley June back to her room. We make arrangements to meet tomorrow after dusk – she wants to come down and get dressed in the library so we can head to the Gala together, linked arm in arm. "It's going to be so amazing," she gushes as I leave.

I head back to the library. Within minutes, the shutters come down. I wait a while longer to be safe, then head outside. I'm thirsty again and in need of another wash. Stepping outside under the brightening skies, I glance at the main building to make sure the shutters are down. And then I'm making for the Dome, double time. This time I have three empty plastic bottles, tied together with a short length of twine, slung over my shoulder. The bottles bump against one another, making random hollow sounds like the thumps of a drunken drummer. The Dome hasn't descended yet; I keep saying *now* and pointing at the Dome. *Now.* It doesn't move. *Now.* Still doesn't heed my command; the glass walls don't budge.

Halfway there, a hum vibrates in the ground, barely discernible at first, then unmistakable. The Dome walls descend, the circular opening at the top widening as the glass wall sinks into the ground. Dawn light plays off the moving glass, swirling like ribbons around the plains in a menagerie of colour. And then the lights tail off, the humming stops. The Dome is gone.

I stand about a hundred yards from the pond and wait. It's better not to take any chances: despite what they must now know about me, they might still charge out of their mud huts (at least that heper girl, anyway) ready to spear me. That's the thing with these hepers: they can be so unpredictable, like zoo animals gone wild. The front door to a mud hut suddenly swings open. A male heper – young, about my age – stumbles out, bed-headed, legs rickety and stiff as it makes its way to the pond. It doesn't see me; it's squinting against the harsh morning light.

It's not until the heper splashes water on its face and is gulping water from cupped hands that its eyes drift up at me. Its hands instantly drop to its sides, water falling down to its feet. It beats a hasty retreat towards the mud huts, then suddenly stops as if catching itself. Glances back. Sees I'm still standing, that I haven't moved at all.

I raise my hands, palms facing forward, hoping to convey: *I mean no harm.*

It turns tail and begins to flee.

"Wait! Stop!"

And it does. Over its shoulder, eyes wide, face ridden with fear. But with curiosity as well. As with the heper girl yesterday, feelings pour off its face without restraint, like a zoo animal shamelessly scratching its behind before a crowd of derisive spectators. These expressions: so extreme, flowing like a waterfall. It stares at me with wide eyes.

"Sissy!" it yells, and it's my turn to take a few steps back. In shock. The thing talks. "Sissy!" it says louder, the inflections coming out clearly even in that short word.

"No, I—" I stammer, uncertain what to say. *Sissy?* Why is it calling me a sissy?

"Sissy," it shouts urgently, but its tone is bereft of ridicule. It's a neutral tone, but with a hint of urgency, as if calling for help.

"I don't understand," I say because, well, I don't understand. "I just want water." I gesture towards the pond. "Wa-ter."

"Sissy," it shouts again, and a door to a mud hut flies open. It's the heper girl, slightly dishevelled, its eyes grabbing at alertness, flicking off sleepiness. It surveys the scene quickly, soaking in the scene. Its eyes land on mine for a second, flick behind me, then return to me again.

"It's OK, David," it says to the first heper. "Remember what I told you yesterday. He won't hurt us. He's like us."

I'm thunderstruck. These hepers speak. They are intelligent, not savages.

The heper girl walks towards me, strides long and confident. As it walks past mud huts, doors open and more hepers come out, following the heper girl. It stops in front of the pond. "Right?" it asks, staring at me.

All I can do is stare at it.

"Right?" it asks again, and for the first time I realise it's wielding a long axe in its left hand.

"Right," I say.

We stare at each other for a long time.

"Have you come back for more water?" it asks.

"Yes."

A group of four other hepers – all male – are gathered behind the heper girl, peering at me. I see one whisper to another, then a nod in agreement.

"Help yourself," the heper girl says.

My thirst urges me along. I kneel by the edge of the pond and drink with cupped hands, keeping them all, especially the heper girl, in my vision. Then I fill the bottles with water, cap them off. I hesitate.

"Are you going to undress again?" it asks. This seems to relax the group behind it; they smile, look knowingly at one another. "If so, don't forget to take your undies with you this time."

Over the years, I trained myself not to blush. But there's no stopping this one. A surge of heat hits my face, heat humming off it in droves.

The hepers see it, and they suddenly become quiet. Then the heper girl steps forward, and the group follows closely behind. It steps right up to me, an arm's length away, close enough for me to see the faint freckles sprinkled across the bridge of its nose. Its hand touches my face, pressing down on my cheek; even the tips of its fingers are callused. It nods and beckons the others to approach. They do, slowly, encircling me. I don't move. They reach out to me, their hands extending towards my face, then touch my cheek, my neck, poking, probing. I let them.

Then they step back. The heper girl is still standing in front of me, the knife no longer in hand. And for the first time, I see something that is not fear or curiosity in its expression. I don't know what it is. Not exactly. But the small fires burning in her eyes are gentle and warm, like embers of a fireplace.

"My name's Sissy. What's yours?"

I look at her blankly. "What's a 'name'?" I ask.

"You don't know what your name is?" a heper at the back asks. It's the youngest of the lot, a short boy, maybe ten years old, puckish. "My name's Ben. How can you not have a name?"

"He didn't say he doesn't know his name. He said he doesn't know what a name is." The heper who says this stands off to the side alone. Its mouth is skewed at a slant on one side, as if inadvertently caught by a fishhook. It towers above the others, as skinny as it is tall, as if, in the aging process, its limbs were merely stretched without addition of muscle or fat.

The short heper boy turns to me. "What do people call you?"

"Call me? It depends."

"Depends?"

"Depends on where I am. Teachers call me one thing, my coach calls me another. Depends."

The girl heper grabs the nearest heper by the arm, brings him forward. "This is Jacob." It strides over to the next. "This one next to him is David, the one who saw you first this morning. Standing off on his own there is Epaphroditus. We call him 'Epap'."

I run those sounds in my head: *David, Jacob, Epap*. Odd sounds, foreign. David and Jacob look young, maybe eleven or twelve years old. Epap is older, maybe seventeen.

"You mean *designation*. What's my designation?"

"No," the heper girls says, shaking her head. "What does your family call you?"

I'm about to tell her that I don't have a family, that they never called me by any "name" . . . when I stop. A memory suddenly surfaces, faint and crackly in my mind. The voice of my mother, singing, in broken, eclipsed fragments: just a melody at first, the exact words indecipherable. But then a surfacing takes place, her words taking shape, a phrase here and there, still obscure, but—

Gene.

"My name is Gene," I say, and it is as much a revelation to me as an introduction to them.

They show me around the village. They've made the best of their lot. A small vegetable farm round the back, fruit trees dotted around the grounds. Laundry lines hung by a training ground, spears and knives and daggers littered about the sandy lot. Inside the mud huts, I'm surprised by the amount of sunlight pouring in. The roofs are punctured by large holes like a sieve. So strange, the absence of a barrier between them and the sky. A cool breeze blows through the huts.

"We only get the breeze in the daytime," the heper girl says, noticing my enjoyment. "Once the Dome goes up, the air goes still."

Each of the mud huts is only sparsely decorated, drawings and paintings tacked on to walls, a few bookshelves lined with a collection of threadbare books. But it's what sits in the middle of each of the huts that is most startling, almost brazen in its derring-do. A "bed". Not just some blankets tossed to the ground, but a solid wooden structure with legs and a foundation. Not a sleep-hold in sight.

Outside, beyond the perimeter of the Dome, sits a box structure made of metal, about the size of a small carriage. A green light is blinking from a small lamp sitting atop it. "What's that?" I ask, indicating.

"The Umbilical," David says.

"The what?"

"C'mon, might as well head over. Looks like something's arrived."

"What?" I ask.

"Come. You'll see."

On the side of the Umbilical is a wide slot door with hinges on the bottom that pulls open and flat. Jacob peers in, takes out a large Tupperware container that I recognise. I smell the potatoes and noodles.

"Breakfast," says David.

The green light stops blinking, turns to red.

I bend down, curious, sticking my head through the opening. A long, narrow tunnel – no wider than my head – runs underground, leading towards the Institute. This is the other end of the tunnel – the Umbilical, I guess – I saw in the kitchen.

"That's how we get our food," Jacob says. "After we finish eating, we send all the dirty dishes right back. Every so often, they'll send us clothes. Sometimes, on one of our birthdays, they'll send us a treat. Birthday cake, paper and crayons, books, board games."

"Why is it so far away from everything else?" I guesstimate the distance. "It's outside the perimeter of the Dome, isn't it? When the Dome comes up, the Umbilical is outside the glass wall, right?"

They nod. "That was intentional. They were afraid that someone small would attempt to squeeze his way down the tunnel to get to us. At night, obviously. So they placed the Umbilical opening outside the Dome perimeter. That way, even if the small person was able to burrow his way through at night, he'd still end up outside the walls."

"And nobody would ever do it during the day," says Ben. "For obvious reasons."

"Recently, they've been sending us textbooks," the heper named David adds. "Books on self-defence, the art of war. We don't get it. And then one night a few months ago, they left spears and daggers and knives right outside the Dome for us to collect in the morning. We've been messing around with them – Sissy's really good with the flying daggers – but we're not really sure why we have them. I mean, it's not as if there's game to hunt around here."

"And then yesterday, we get these metallic cases," Ben jumps in excitedly. "Five of them, one for each of us. But the letter instructs us not to open them until further notification. So Sissy won't let us even touch them."

I look at Sissy.

"I don't know what they're for," Sissy says. "Do you?"

I glance down. "No idea."

"But anyway," Ben goes on, thankfully, "we have all these weapons. We've been practising with them, the spears and axes and daggers, anyway. Sissy's the best, but we've run out of targets."

"Until you came along."

I don't need to turn around to know the heper named Epap said that.

"In fact, why did you come here?" it continues. I turn around. The expression on its face is unmistakably hostile and cagey. They're like open books, these hepers, with naked emotions swimming off their faces.

"He came here for water," Sissy says before I can answer. "Leave him alone, OK?"

The Epap heper circles around until it's standing directly in front of me. Up close, it seems even more gangly. "Before we start giving out food to him," it says, "before we start showing him around like he's nothing more than a cute stray puppy, he's got some answering to do."

Nobody says anything.

"Like how he's survived out there for so long. Like how he's survived living with them for so long. And what exactly is it that's he's doing here. He's got some talking to do."

I look at the heper girl. "What's its problem?" I ask, pointing at Epap.

The heper girl stares intently at me. "What did you say?"

"What's its problem? Why is it so worked up over—"

The heper girl steps up to me until it's less than a yard away. Before I realise it, its arm blurs towards me, smacking me on the side of my head.

"Hey—"

"Don't."

"Don't what?" I say, feeling the side of my head. No blood, just the sting of humiliation.

"Don't call him *it*." She bends down and grabs a fistful of dirt. "This ground is an *it*. That tree over there is an *it*. That vegetable is an *it*. That building is an *it*. Don't call us *it*, that's just insulting. What's your problem, anyway? What makes you so high and mighty? If you think we're a bunch of *its,* you can just walk on out and never think about coming back here. Besides, if you think we're nothing but *its,* then you're as much an *it* as we are."

"Fair enough," I say, the side of my face still smarting. "I apologise."

But in my mind, there is a huge difference between them and me. They are savages, undomesticated, uneducated. I am none of those. I'm a survivor, self-made, civilised, educated. Next to me, though we might look the same, they are nothing like me. But as long as I need them to survive, I'll play along as necessary. "Wasn't really thinking, no harm meant at all. Look, I'm sorry, Sissy. Epap, I'm sorry."

She stares at me, unmoved. "You're so full of it." The moment grows tense as the other hepers, taking their cue from Sissy and Epap, look back at me with suspicion.

It's little Ben who breaks the tension. "Come here, I'll show you my favourite fruit!" He then runs to grab me, pulling me along by my arm to a nearby tree.

"Ben, don't—" Epap cries after us, but we're already gone.

"Come on," he says, leaping up to grab a low-hanging red fruit. "The apples from this tree are the best. The south tree has apples, too, but not nearly as good as these ones. Love them."

So strange, I think, to use the word *love* so openly. And for a fruit to boot.

Before I know it, an apple is sitting plump in my hand. Ben is already tearing into the apple he's plucked for himself. I rip into the apple, the juices bursting into my mouth. I hear footsteps behind us. The group has caught up. Maybe it's the sight of me enjoying the fruit with such kidlike joy, but they don't seem quite as hostile as before. With the exception of Epap, of course. He's still glaring at me.

"Aren't these fruit the best? Wait till you try the bananas from—"

Sissy places a gentle hand on Ben's shoulder. He quiets immediately and turns his head to look at her. She nods softly, then turns to me. It's with the same look she just gave Ben: reassuring, but with a strange command, a gentle insistence. "Actually, we would like to know. Why you are here. Do tell."

After a long moment, I speak. "I'll tell you," I say, my voice hitching for some reason. "I'll tell you. But can we move inside?"

"Just tell us here," Epap snaps back. "It's nice right where we are now and—"

"Inside is fine," Sissy says. She sees Epap about to cut in again and quickly says to me: "The sun can't be comfortable for you.

You're not used to it." She is already beginning to walk towards the nearest hut, not bothering to see if the others follow.

Gradually, one by one, they do. And last to go is me, trailing all of them into the opening of a mud hut.

What I tell them is almost the truth. That's not as good as the complete truth, I know; but I like to think I don't so much lie as neglect to disclose certain parts. Still, as my second-grade teacher used to say, the almost-truth is the same as an outright lie. But I do it – lying – with aplomb: easy to do when your whole life is essentially a lie, easy to deceive when your whole identity has been built on deception.

There are many of us on the outside, I lie. In every sector of community, at every level of society, hepers abound. Our existence is as widespread and diverse as snowflakes during a night storm. And yet, like snowflakes in the night, our existence is unseen. We are joined by our shared lives of secrecy, of passing ourselves off as normal to the general populace. We are scrupulous about shaving, fake fangs, maintaining a blank demeanour. We do not form underground societies but build small networks of three to five nuclear families. It is a dangerous existence, but an existence not without its joys and pleasures.

Like what?

Like the pleasures of family life, I say, continuing my lies, the freedom within our cloistered homes once the shutters have fallen at sunset. Foods we love to eat, songs we love to sing, laughter and smiles and (rarely, only when necessary) the crying of tears. The retention of tradition, the passing along of books and ancient tales. Then there are the very occasional secret meetings we have with other heper families in the bright of day while the rest of the city sleeps behind shuttered walls, oblivious. And as we get older, there are the possibilities of romance, the exhilaration of falling in love, the eventual beginnings of our own families.

Why are you here?

I was recently hired to be on staff at the Institute.

You replaced the Scientist?

Yes, I have replaced the Scientist, moved into his abode, am continuing his research. He was very diligent, extremely hardworking; it will take me months just to catch up.

And so you know about him.

Of course.

That he was a heper.

A pause. Yes, of course.

Where did he go? He just disappeared on us.

What? What did you say?

Where did he go?

Can I have some more water, please?

Where did he go? He told us he was going to get us out of here. To a land of milk and honey, fruit and sunshine. A new beginning, a new origin.

It is something you think about, getting out of here?

Of course. Every day. We have been here all our lives. Imprisoned by glass, imprisoned by the desert, imprisoned by fangs and claws. The Scientist told us he was going to get us out of here. But he never said how or to where. Do you know where?

I do.

Where?

I point to the eastern mountains. Over there. Over those mountains. Where we are originally from. Where there are thousands of our kind. A land of milk and honey, fruit and sunshine.

How? It is too far away. We will die.

I nod. Of thirst, of starvation.

But they shake their heads. No: we will be hunted down and killed before we get halfway there.

Of course. Of course.

How will we get out?

I answer without looking at them. The Scientist. He will get you out.

Sissy nods with excitement. That's what he said. That he would lead us away. That we should always trust him. Even when all hope seems gone, he told us never to give up, that he'd come through for us. And then he disappeared one day. It was hard for us; we almost gave up hope. And now you. You appearing out of nowhere after all this time. You can help us, right?

Give me time, give me time. The Scientist left me mountains of papers to get through.

Well, we have a lot of that. Time.

I wake with a start. It takes me a second to realise where I am. Still in the heper village, still in a mud hut. On the floor, lying down, head atop a soft sack. The sun shines through the sieve-like ceiling, leaving a patchwork of sunspots about me.

They are sitting in a semicircle around me. A few of them are lying down in a semi-doze.

"He's awake!" Ben says.

I leap to my feet, heart hammering. I've never woken up in a crowd. In my usual life, I'd be dead by now. But they're looking up at me with amused, harmless faces. I sit back down, unnerved.

Sissy tells Jacob to fetch some more water, David to see if bread has arrived in the Umbilical, and Ben to pick some more fruit and vegetables. The three scuttle off. Only the two oldest, Sissy and Epap, remain. Somehow, I don't think this is unintentional.

"How long have I been out?"

"Two hours. You were just talking, then next thing we know, you're knocked out cold," Sissy says.

"Snoring, too," Epap sneers.

Judging from the position of the sun, it's about midday. "This is my usual sleep time. And I've been really up and about the past couple of days. Sorry I crashed on you. But I'm that knackered."

"I was going to kick you awake," Epap says, "but she let you sleep."

"Thanks," I murmur, my voice hoarse with dryness, "and for the pillow, too."

"You looked like you could use some sleep. Here," she says, handing over a jug of water. "Sounds like you could use some more water, too."

I nod my appreciation. The water slides down my dry, sandy throat. I'm a bottomless bucket: no matter how much I drink, I can't seem to get enough.

"Thanks," I say, handing back the jug. Hung on the walls around me are brightly coloured paintings of rainbows and the mythical sea. On my right is a bookshelf filled with worn-out books and a few pottery figures.

"How did you learn to read?" I ask.

Epap looks down. "From our parents," Sissy answers.

I look at her.

"Some of us had both parents here. Most of us had only a father or a mother. None of us are siblings, in case you're wondering, except for Ben and me. We're half-siblings."

"How many parents?"

"Eight. They taught us everything. How to read and write, how to paint, how to grow vegetables. Passed down to us ancient traditional tales. Taught us to grow physically strong, to run long distances, swim. They didn't want us to get fat and lazy, just waiting for our food to appear every day. We had something called 'school' every day. You know what 'school' is?"

I nod.

"Our parents pressed us hard, made us learn quickly. As if they feared time was short. As if they believed they might one day be gone."

"And what happened to them?"

"One day they were gone," Epap says, an anger tingeing his words.

Sissy speaks, quieter. "About ten years ago. They were given maps describing the location of a fruit farm. We were suspicious, of course, but we hadn't been given any fruit or vegetables in weeks. Our lips and mouths were breaking out in painful blisters. As a precaution, our parents made us children stay behind. The parents left at the crack of dawn. They never came back."

"The five of you can't have been much more than toddlers yourselves," I say.

She pauses before answering. "Ben was only a few weeks old. He barely survived. And there were more than five of us. There were nine."

"The other four?"

She shakes her head, eyes downcast. "You have to understand. It was just Epap and me looking after everyone. We were, like, seven years old. When the Scientist came, he really helped us. Not only because of the extra food he'd smuggle in, the books, blankets, medicine when one of us would fall ill. But he was such a morale booster, a great storyteller, really encouraging. That's why it was so crushing when he flat-out disappeared on us." She looks at me. "And you're telling us he'll somehow lead us to the eastern mountains someday? The land of milk and honey, fruit and sunshine?"

I nod.

"You're lying," Epap says. "About the Scientist. And about the heper civilisation over the mountains. There's nothing beyond those mountains."

"I'm not."

"You and your damn poker face. Think you can hide behind that and fool us? Maybe the younger ones, but not us. Certainly not me."

"Tell us what you know, Gene," Sissy says gently, earnestness in her brown eyes. So strange to be called by that name. Her eyes, with the sunlight reflecting off the floor, are a shade lighter than I remember. "How do you know about the heper civilisation past the mountains?"

"It's in some of the Scientist's journals I've been reading. The Scientist made some entries. He had reason to believe there's a whole civilisation of our kind beyond those mountains. Where hundreds, maybe thousands of us live." The lies slip off my tongue smooth as silk.

"How did he come by this information?"

"Look, I don't know. But he seemed to believe so."

"Liar!" interjects Epap. "If there're so many of our kind, why haven't we seen any of them? Why haven't they ventured out here?"

"Would you?" I ask. "Knowing what you know, would you come out here and place yourself within reach of them?"

He doesn't say anything.

"It makes sense," Sissy says. "Any heper colony beyond the mountains would be safe from people. It would take – even with their quickness – at least eighteen hours just to reach the mountains. They'd never get there before sunrise. No cover at all out there – the sunlight would incinerate them all. The distance is the perfect moat of protection."

"You don't believe him, do you?" Epap asks incredulously. "We don't know anything about this guy. He just appears out of nowhere, saunters in with this know-it-all attitude."

"Epap," she says softly, a hand on his shoulder. That's all she has to say. Or do. Immediately, his irritation flutters off him in droves. "We know a lot. Gene's for real, there's no denying that. We've seen him in the sun, eat our fruit, sleep, just act, well, like us. You saw him blush. You can't fake that kind of stuff. So he's one of us. And we also know – whatever you might personally think of him – he's a survivor. He has learned how to live even in the midst of them. For years. He's valuable to us, to have someone like that on the outside."

"But how do we know he's *for* us? He might be one of us, but that doesn't necessarily make him *for* us! I agree that he's a survivor. But it's *his* survival he's good at, not ours."

Instead of disagreeing with him, Sissy looks at me. Her eyes betray wariness and suspicion. She knows. That I'm holding something back. But she has no idea just how much. Otherwise she'd never have said what she says next.

"I think we can trust him. I think he has goodness in him."

"Excuse me while I barf in my mouth," Epap says.

"Epap," she says with less patience now, "Gene's brought us more information than we've been able to cull together in years. In two minutes, he's told us two lifetimes' worth of info. That says something."

"Useless information," Epap spat out. "Even if it's true – about the colony beyond the mountains – it's useless. There's no way we can get to it, not even close. For us, the mountains are a two-week trek away. We'd be hunted down and killed within hours. Even if we leave as soon as the Dome opens at dawn and get an eight-hour jump on them, as soon as dusk hits, they'll be flying across the Vast and be on us within two hours. No, that kind of information is worse than useless: it's dangerous. It puts silly notions in our heads, a fanciful pipe dream that some of us might try to bring to fruition. Think of David, Jacob. Those two were never born to be encased. They've wanted out since they were born. Think you can restrain them if they set their minds on it?"

As Epap speaks, Sissy does something slightly odd with her lower lip. Nothing I've ever seen before, but I can't quite take my eyes off it. She's sinking her upper teeth (no fangs, so strange to see) into her full lower lip, taking a half bite so that her lips turn whitish. She's quiet for a long time. Then, as the sound of footsteps approach, she says, "Do me a favour? Let's not talk about this in front of the others again, OK?"

"Sure," I answer, and then David and Jacob walk in with more bread and fruit. I eat and drink to my fill, the conversation now turned lighter, the younger hepers happy to have a new face with whom to chatter. They tell me of their lives, the routine, the passing seasons, their love-hate relationship with the Dome: how it stifles air circulation and traps the musty heat on hot summer nights; but how it also traps warmth and keeps out cold rain and snow in the winter months. On those winter nights, they tell me, they like to watch snowflakes drift downward from the night sky, melting into dewy streaks upon landing on the Dome. Sometimes, when it is especially cold, they build a campfire, small enough that the smoke can escape through the pores at the top of the Dome. On those nights, gathered around the fire, snow falling harmlessly about them outside the

Dome, they can almost imagine that the normal orbit of the world occurs inside the Dome and that it is the vaster outside world that is fallen, dysfunctional, afraid.

Later in the day, they grant me privacy for the wash I need. And more: a towel, something called "soap", and a promise not to peek. This time when I strip off my clothes next to the pond, I feel a thousand times more self-conscious alone than when I threw off my briefs yesterday in front of Sissy. The very memory makes me cringe.

I wade into the pond and scrub myself. The soap thing produces miniature bubbles where it rubs against my body. It's scentless but removes body odour, they tell me. Perfect for my needs. Once in a while, I steal a furtive look at the mud hut they're all in. The doors and windows, as they've promised, remain closed. I listen in that direction, expecting to catch some derisive laughter. But it's quiet.

I'm scrubbing my hair underwater when I hear something peculiar. At first, I think it's just my submerged ears playing tricks on me, but when I surface the sound is clearer. A melody of voices, warbling out of the mud hut.

The sound is eerie yet beautiful. I stand captivated, water dripping off my hair into the pond, ripples breaking out in circular emanations around me. I wade out of the pond, towelling off even as I grab my clothes.

At first, they don't notice me. I peer through the front door, my damp hair dripping onto my hastily flung-on clothes. They are seated in a circle, Ben and Jacob partially facing me, their eyes closed as if in rapture. The warbling brings back memories of my mother. Times when she would sit on the edge of my bedding and stroke my hair, her face barely discernible in the grey darkness of the house. It's her voice I remember, more so than her face, lilted and unaffected by the sadness or despair that later hunched my father's shoulders down.

Still unseen, I move away from the entrance and sit outside, out of sight but with the front door cracked open so I can hear. With my back against the scrabbled wall of the mud hut, I let their voices wash over me, even as the warm rays of the descending sun flood over me. Everything about me feels warm and soft, as though the world has gone buttery.

The song ends and there is a short discussion about what next to sing. At least five suggestions – they must have dozens in their repertoire – are quickly made before they settle on a song titled "Up High". It begins slowly. At first, it's only Sissy's voice, undulating with the peaks and troughs of the melody.

The ground beneath your feet
hums with the heat of the day's sun
all alone, the heat trapped within your heartbeat
until the night falls and the sun is done.

The other voices join in the chorus, harmonising perfectly. They're so fluid and flawless, it's evident they've sung this song hundreds of times before. Imprisoned by glass and distance, they probably have nothing else to do to while away the endless days but sing. Singing gives them what they most need: an illusion of hope, a transportation to other places.

Sailing through the bluest sky
above the hawks that sigh
above the clouds that cry.

The song, though haunting in places, has an undeniable catchiness about it. At first, I just mouth the words. Then, almost unwittingly, I find myself pushing air through my larynx, formulating sounds. But it's not easy. It's all croaks coming out of my mouth.

Then something happens: it's as if a giant ball of phlegm in my throat is dislodged. For one verse, I hit the notes. For just those few moments, I'm completely lost in the rhythm of the song. I ride it, a kite flung in the air, catching the sweetest of winds.

The song ends, and there is laughter coming from inside. They burst out seconds later, Ben leading.

"I thought I heard an asthmatic dog wheezing to death out here," Jacob says, friendly laughter dancing in his eyes.

"Dog, whatever," David says, smiling. "That was more like an elephant."

"More like a herd of elephants," Ben says, so beside himself, he's hopping from one foot to the next. They're all laughing now, the sun playing off their hair, adding dots of light to their eyes. Sunshine glimmers off the hairs on their arms, little puffs of dust kick up at their feet, their carefree voices ring into the bright air.

"C'mon, it's funny, you have to admit it," Sissy says to me. Her face is all abandon and nakedness as she looks at me. There is a smile in her eyes, her nose, her mouth, her cheekbones, her forehead, all of it spilling so infectiously outward to me, past me, filling the world like the sun. She busts out with sweet laughter, her eyes closing in sheer delight.

And just like that, something trickles out of me I thought was long ago irretrievably lost. A laugh shakes out, guttural and coarse through disuse, bursting through my constricted vocal cords. And my face – there's no other way to describe this – rips apart like a cracked hard-boiled eggshell. A smile crinkles across my mouth, spreading along my face. I feel pieces of the mask falling off, like crusts of dried paint flaking off a wall. I laugh louder.

"What the heck was that?" Jacob says. "Did a gorilla just fart through its mouth?"

And they crack up even more, their laughter lifting into the air, joined only moments later by the sound of my own laughter, guttural and coarse, free and thoughtless.

I leave the Dome not because I want to but because I have to. Not that the Dome will be closing anytime soon – after yesterday's close call, I'm not taking any chances and I have at least fifteen minutes to spare. I have to get back for some serious shut-eye. All two hours of what's left of the day, anyway. I've been running on fumes the last few nights, and there's a real danger, not so much of dozing off during tonight's Gala, but of getting careless in front of all the guests and cameras: a yawn, a frown, an unsuppressed cough. I can't get sloppy at such a crucial time. Just a couple more nights to hang on; then, as long as I can pull off my broken-leg stunt, I'll be home free.

With food and water in me, the walk back to the library seems so much shorter. What before was a significant hike is now nothing more than a short stroll. Even with the added weight of three full bottles of water, I'm halfway there before—

Hello, what's this?

In the distance, a dot, moving. Directly in front of the Institute building – no, not a dot, but a dark smear running. Towards me.

I freeze. There's nowhere to hide. Not a boulder to crouch behind, not even a depression in the ground into which to slink. It's got to be an animal lost out in the Vast. But then again, it's rare to see wildlife out here; most animals have learned not to stray too close.

A horse, I think to myself, *it's got to be a horse, escaped out of the stable.* Then I remember what my escort previously told me: there are no horses at the Institute out of fear the hepers might use them to escape. On rare occasions, like tonight's Gala event, when guests arrive by horseback and carriages, the horses are kept under tight lock in the stable.

It runs closer, and I realise what it is. Not wildlife, not a horse. This is a person.

I don't think I've been spotted. Yet. I quickly prostrate myself, my chin jutting into the crusty desert soil.

It's one of the hunters, it has to be, testing out one of the accessories. Donning the SunCloak or the SunBlock Lotion. Judging from the bulbous hooded shape around the head, probably the SunCloak.

And then I realise its intent.

The hepers. It's making a break for the hepers, trying to get at them before the protective Dome emerges. And now, just minutes from the Dome's closing and with the sun rays less potent, is its chance.

Just then, a door on the ground floor of the Institute building swings open. And something – someone – shoots out like a racing horse out of the blocks. It moves with wicked speed, a blur. Moving straight towards the heper village. Or me. I'm lying in a direct line.

The cloaked figure is at a full sprint now – I can see arms pumping hard, legs pounding the ground. But it's the second figure that's just emerged that is far quicker. Already, it's covered half the distance between them. Within no more than ten seconds, both are close enough for me to recognise.

The cloaked figure is Ashley June, her pointed chin unmistakable under the hood. There's something off about her. But my attention is quickly diverted to the sprinting figure almost caught up to her now – Beefy. His appearance is bizarre and frightening. He's smeared over completely with the SunBlock Lotion, the rich yellow white cream lathered thickly over his torso like icing on cake. He's completely naked (for speed?) except for a pair of black goggles pulled tight over his eyes.

I leap up, dropping the bottles of water, and sprint. Not to the library – it's too far away. But to the Dome. I'll pretend to be joining the Hunt, make them think I'm running with the pack. That's the only way I can explain being outside. True, I have neither SunCloak nor SunBlock Lotion, but I'm hoping that detail will be forgotten in the excitement.

It works. Ashley June runs past me, labouring – the SunCloak is not working, the sunlight is getting to her. Seconds later, Beefy flashes by, the smell of the lotion overpowering. Nobody says anything: we're competition to one another; it's survival of the fittest, not friendliest.

Just then, the sun emerges from behind a cloud. Shafts of light blaze across the Vast, bringing a hazy quality to the air. But it's not haze to Ashley June and Beefy. It's a shower of concentrated acid. Ashley June falls to her knees, crumpling in a pile of clothes. Beefy seizes up, stumbling. In the dusk light, the cream on his body glows with an eerie yellow luminescence, jaundice on radiation steroids. Still he pushes on.

I give chase. I smell something else, the raw burn of flesh. The SunBlock Lotion is useless; the sun is penetrating right through it. Beefy's energy flags, I'm catching up, he's not going to make it. I glance back: Ashley June is nothing but a pile of clothes, the SunCloak useless.

Another cloud drifts across the sun. Ahead of me, Beefy regains his form. Ashley June remains behind, a discarded and motionless pile of clothes.

In the heper village, nothing moves. I'm close enough to see that all windows and doors have been shut closed. Then Sissy springs out, her hands quickly tying the dagger strap around her thin waist. Arms and hands from inside the mud hut reach out for her, trying to draw her back in, but she slaps them away. She races towards Beefy and me, her face a mixture of determination and fear, the flashing daggers in her hands pulsating rapidly like the hammering of her heart.

Her appearance rejuvenates Beefy. He picks up even more speed, starts racing towards the village. Even in his debilitated state, he must know. That he is fast approaching the point of no return. Even now, he can still turn around, make it back to the safety of the Institute, if not in one piece, then at least alive. But if he presses on towards the heper village, there's no going back anymore.

With kamikaze intent, Beefy's head snaps back, his legs pound the crusty ground, and he emits a snarled hiss from between fanged teeth. He is going for the hepers. Come what may, he is going to them. No matter the sun: he will bound into the village, tear down doors and windows, rip the hepers to shreds, sink his teeth into the soft give of their necks, even as the sun burns into his skin and melts it into wax, even as his eyeballs explode and ooze vitreous juice down his sliding face, nose, cheeks. None of it matters even as he succumbs to the rays, even as he dissolves into a puddle of pus, so long as he dies with hepers in his arms and heper juice in his system. What a way to go, not so gently into the night.

Sissy, too, has picked up her speed as she sprints towards us. No one is backing off from anyone. Without breaking pace, she flings a dagger to my left, a ferocious sidearm thrust. The dagger shoots out, twirling as it sails across the plains, blinking with reflected sunlight. Again, it looks as though she's missed the mark by a mile; but again, the dagger swings around in a wide arc, boomeranging towards us. With that dagger in midflight, Sissy, still charging towards us, flings another dagger, this time in the opposite direction to my right. My head tries to follow it. But within seconds, I've lost it. And not just that one. I've lost track of the other dagger as well. They've disappeared in the plains. But I can hear them: a gyrating whirr, growing louder, zeroing in on Beefy from both sides.

A second later, the flying daggers collide midair right in front of me. There's a metallic *clink* as blade hits blade, then a brief spray of sparks. Sissy has thrown the daggers with amazing accuracy, their joint flight trajectories forming a perfect circle. But not amazing enough. She's missed Beefy's head, her intended target; instead of striking the temples of his head, the daggers have clashed into each other and fallen to the ground three yards *behind* Beefy. She underestimated his speed, his desire.

If Beefy notices, he doesn't slow down. Instead, he strides harder, faster. But the sunlight is doing a number on him. His breathing is more laboured, and despite his greater effort, he's slowed down some. I'm catching up with him.

Then I hear another whirring sound. Sissy's thrown another dagger. But I have no idea from which direction it's coming, the left or the right. Panicked, I swing my head from side to side, a desperate effort to detect a flash of light. But I can't locate it, can only hear it, the whirr slicing through the air louder and louder.

The dagger hits Beefy smack in the thigh. Sissy threw this one straight as an arrow at Beefy, head-on. But if anything, the impact, instead of slowing him down, seems to give him strength. He picks up speed and, though limping, is now leaping towards the village. He'll be there within ten seconds.

But Sissy's not done. Still running at us, she takes out her last dagger, gripping it in hand by the blunt side of the blade. In one fluid motion, her arm shoots out from her waist, then up diagonally across her chest, hand facing downward, her wrist flicking upward with the rapid snap of a card dealer. It's a perfect under-handed throw, a reverse sidearm flick that propels the dagger with speed and aim. Right at us. I duck down.

Needlessly. The knife catches Beefy in front of me, impaling him square in the chest. Because of the liquefying effect of the sun on him, his body offers little resistance; the dagger disappears into it like a spoon into soup. For only the briefest of moments, he slows; but then he gives an ear-piercing scream and races towards Sissy with renewed vigour, the dagger lost somewhere in his body.

A glimmering halo suddenly forms around the village. The glass wall of the Dome. It's emerging. But too late. Beefy will easily clear the wall in a single leap. Once inside the Dome, he will have at it with the hepers, be given free rein. The Dome will become a sunny globe of death, a prison of violence for the hepers trapped inside and, soon after, for him. But he is beyond caring.

Beefy suddenly slows, screaming, a gurgling, swollen sound. The sun's getting to him. The gap between us closes. Just as he's collecting his legs under him to jump over the rising Dome wall, I leap at him. I sideswipe both his legs out from under him; my arm comes away sticky. He spills, crashing into the dirt in a heap.

His face, when he shoots me a look, is horrific. Pus oozes out from open sores in his skin, milky yellow emulsions that coagulate with the creamy SunBlock Lotion. His upper lip, melted away and detached on one side, hangs on one end, flapping against his cheek. Without the upper lip, his upper teeth are bared now in a perpetual snarl. He wastes little time on me. To him, I am just competition, another hunter to outrace and outeat. He smacks me with the backside of his hand, and I go flying backward. He is already on his feet, running to the closing Dome.

I'm collapsed on the ground, my head spinning, unable to find my legs.

He's much slower. The sun is melting away not only his flesh, but his muscles. His legs have become squishy bags of pus now, his calf and thigh muscles quickly disintegrating. With a cry, he leaps up at the closing glass wall.

He doesn't come close. His body slams against the glass no farther than halfway up. When he slides down the wall, his flesh sticks to the glass like melted pizza. Yellow, cheesy, fleshy. He picks himself up, delirious with desire at the sight of Sissy, delirious with anguish at her unreachability. "I can smell you!" he hisses, and takes a few steps back and charges at the wall again. Then he is sliding down again. He slaps his open palms on the glass, hoists his body along the glass. The sticky melt of skin gives him unexpected traction on the glass, and he is crawling up with surprising effect.

He's going to make it. The hole at the top of the Dome is closing too slowly. Once he drops down on the inside, he won't have a lot of time before the sun disintegrates him completely. But the sight and feel and taste of the hepers will give him an adrenaline boost that will let him get to at least a couple of them, if not all of them.

Sissy sees what's happening. She barks an order at the others, who scamper into the mud huts. Then she's spinning around, trying to find a weapon. But there is none, not that one would have helped at this point. But her shoulders don't slump; her arms tighten, readying for the fight she knows is coming. But her eyes: even from where I lie, I can see fear flood them. Her eyes find mine. For a moment, through the glass of the Dome, our eyes lock. I remember the first time I saw her, through the glass of my deskscreen. It's the same look. Defiant yet afraid.

Ben comes flying out of a hut, tears in his eyes, gripping an axe. Sissy takes the axe, barks him back inside. He stays, fists clenched.

Beefy is halfway up the closing Dome. He's going to make it, the Dome—

There's no time to think or reflect. I just react. I leap to my feet, run to the Dome in seconds. Only one way to catch up to him. I plant my hands and feet in the sticky patches of his skin left on the Dome. Rungs of a ladder made the texture of melted cheese. I scramble up, using the sticky goo for traction.

Above, at the cusp of the circular opening, he slips down a few yards. He regains his footing. Starts climbing again. My last chance. I leap up, stretching out with my right arm as far as I can. My hand lands on his shin. Quickly, I fasten my fingers into a vice around his ankle. I pull him down a few yards. Then my fingers squeeze *through* his ankle as if they're going through warm butter. And then I'm sliding down on the glass, a screeching sound that follows me all the way down.

My grab isn't enough to drag him down, but it slows him. Just. He scrambles up with a scream filled with lunacy and desperation, towards the closing hole, now no wider than the diameter of a street manhole. He gets one leg into it, is about to swing his body down through the hole, when—

He doesn't fit. He squirms his body, torquing it, trying to twist it into the closing hole, but it's no use. He's too big. And it closes in on him swiftly like a no-nonsense vice, entrapping him. There's nowhere to go. He sits atop the Dome, one leg dangling down into the interior, awash in the rays of sunlight.

The Dome closes completely, slicing off his spongy leg. The leg falls into the interior, exploding on the ground in a yellow spray. His screaming is horrible; silence arrives only after his vocal cords disintegrate into a viscous liquid. And then he is no more. All that remains are yolky streaks of liquid running down the Dome on all sides, like an egg dropped on a bald head.

I pick myself up. Need to get away. Running on unsteady legs, I suddenly collapse to my knees. I'm doubled over like a beggar doing penance. My insides heave. Then I'm vomiting, all the food and liquids I'd taken in with the hepers gushing out. I get to my feet even as I'm dry heaving. My feet zig and zag against each other, wobbling. One last look at the Dome: Sissy is hurrying into a mud hut, one arm draped across Ben's back.

Minutes later, walking to the library, I'm better. I pick up the bottles of water I'd discarded earlier, wash out the sticky grime from my hands. Splash water on my face.

Capping the bottle, I see the pile of clothes where Ashley June fell. She'd gambled, foolishly, coming out so early. The protective gear was meant for late dusk, not now when the sun still had two hours of life in it. I remember what my escort had told me days ago, how the sight and smells of hepers had driven some staffers to charge out at the Dome in the middle of the day. I'd found it hard to believe back then, but no more.

Strange, I think, looking at the pile of clothes. All I see on the ground is the SunCloak. No sign of her other clothes: shoes, socks, pants. Just the SunCloak. Maybe she was naked underneath the way Beefy was? I head over and kick at the cloak, expecting it to be sodden and sticky with yellow fluid and melted skin. But there's nothing at all. No sign of any yellow fluid. Then it hits me.

She's in the library. Somehow she was able to escape inside in time.

But when I spin around towards the library, I see something that—

My mouth drops. My eyes widen.

The rays of the descending sun saturate the outside of the library – the walls, the shutters, the brick pathway – in a sea of purple and orange. And standing in the midst of this colour is Ashley June. Colour radiates off her pale skin, mixing with the orange of her hair, the green of her eyes. Her mouth is slightly parted, full and whole. And she is not screaming, not disintegrating.

We stare at each other, speechless, my eyes helplessly agog.

She reaches into her mouth, tilts back her head, pulls something out.

A set of fake fangs.

She holds them out to me like a peace offering.

The first thing she asks for when we walk in is water.

"Of course," I tell her, remembering how parched I was a couple of days ago. "You've gone this whole time without water?"

She doesn't answer but downs a whole bottle of water. That's answer enough.

"That's why I collapsed outside," she says, eyeing my other bottle of water.

"You want more?"

"Yes, but not to drink." She grabs the bottle. "In case *you* haven't noticed – the others certainly have – I'm beginning to smell. Really bad."

"You should wash up inside. Sun'll give you a sunburn, your skin's so fair."

She shoots me a look as if to say, *Really? I haven't survived seventeen years by accident, buddy*.

"In the back," I say quickly. "There's a place with a drain in the floor." She walks around the circulation desk and disappears. Leaving me with my tangled, bewildered, searching thoughts.

When she comes back ten minutes later, I haven't moved. Her hair is slick wet and her face freshly scrubbed. She looks paler and drained, but her eyes are brighter. "I hope you don't mind," she says timidly.

"What?"

"I said I hope you don't mind. I had to put on your clothes. My own stuff is . . . there's too much of a smell in them."

"No," I say, eyes looking down, "it's OK. All that stuff they gave me are a few sizes too small. I've never worn that outfit before, it's yours now."

We stand at a slant, looking at everything but each other.

"I'm sorry for using up two bottles of water."

"It's OK. We still have a half bottle left."

As soon as I say the word *we,* it's as though something breaks in her. Her head turns to mine; when I meet her eyes, they've welled up. She snaps her eyelids shut, and when she opens them again, her eyes have dried. She's good, she's practised; just like me.

"Have you lived alone?" I ask her.

She pauses. "Yes," she answers gently, sadly. "For almost as long as I can remember."

Her story, told to me after we sit down, is not unlike mine.

She remembers a family: parents, an older brother. Cheerful conversation at home, laughter, feelings of safety once the shutters came down at dawn and the world was locked outside, meals around a table, warm bodies asleep around her. Then she remembers the day. She was bedridden with a fever and stayed home while her parents and brother hiked to get some fruit. They left ten minutes after dawn. She never saw them again.

One day in a family, the next day alone. Solitude and loneliness her constant companions, their presence so enervating and cold, like two damp socks worn on a winter day.

That was ten years ago. She was only seven. At first it was incredibly hard. To live. Not an hour went by that she did not consider giving herself up at school. It would be so easy. To succumb. Stand in the middle of the soccer field during recess, prick her finger, let a droplet of blood seep. Watch them come flying at her. The end would be brutal but swift. Death would be an escape from this unbearable loneliness.

But her parents had taught her two things. Ingrained them in her. The first was survival: not just the basics, but the nuances, the minutiae, every conceivable situation she might find herself in. The second was life, the importance of it, the preciousness of it, the duty to persevere and never let it end prematurely. She hated how clinically they indoctrinated her: by the time they were gone, she had become a reluctant expert at survival.

Her beauty was a curse, especially as she – and classmates around her – hit puberty. Attention, something she was repeatedly told by her parents to avoid, came her way with the force of a testosterone-filled tidal wave. Boys would write letters to her, stare at her, converse with her awkwardly, throw spitballs at her, join the same clubs she did. Girls, seeing the social advantages of befriending her, flocked around her. Nothing she did to minimise her beauty helped. Clunky, self-cut hair; an abrasive, caustic personality; aloofness; feigning disinterest in boys; even outright stupidity. But none of these helped. The attention kept coming.

One day, she realised her approach was all wrong. Her defence was too . . . defensive. It didn't fit her, and this kind of faux defensive life would eventually be her undoing. She saw that. And she decided the best defence was offence.

Instead of tamping down her beauty, she played it up. She threw off the meek, stupid persona and instead exuded confidence and poise. It was an easy act mostly because it didn't feel like one. More than anything, it gave her power. She controlled the pieces, and instead of being pushed about by the horses and knights and queens about her, she turned them all into pawns. She grew her hair long and in a way that complimented her svelte figure. She'd stare down the boys who gazed at her, grab the social knives meant to backstab her and use them to cut down her competition. She was ruthless until she was needed.

Eventually, it became clear she had to get a boyfriend. As long as she was unattached, the boys would continue clamouring after her like magnet maggots. And too many questions about her would arise if she didn't.

So she plucked the varsity quarterback, an obnoxious and surprisingly insecure senior who played it cool when with her in public but in private boiled like lava. Killing him turned out to be easier than she'd thought. For their one-month anniversary (teens can be so sappy), she suggested a picnic at a secluded spot a few hours away from the city limits. He was all over the idea. They brought wine and blankets. Once there, he drank too much – she kept pouring – until he passed out. She tied him to a tree that was, in the late autumn, stripped of leaves and would provide no shade once the sun rose. She left him passed out and walked home.

She never saw him again. When she went back to the tree the next day, there was only a pile of clothes hanging off limp lines of rope, slightly bleached by the toxicity of melted flesh. She took the clothes and rope and burned them.

As with most "disappearances", the subject was taboo and spoken of only in hushed whispers. A perfunctory search was conducted and then abandoned after only twelve hours; the matter was filed away as a DBS (disappearance by sunlight). She pretended to be devastated by this tragedy, her heart cracked by the loss of her "soul mate". At his funeral, she professed her undying devotion and love to him, promising that her soul was forever bonded with his.

It achieved everything she hoped it would. Boys largely left her alone; girls sympathised with her tragic loss, and her stock rose even higher. Nobody questioned her lack of a dating life even as the other girls in the Desirables necked, armpitted, and otherwise hooked up at parties. She was the tragic figure in need of time and space. Give her a few years, she'd eventually come around, her friends thought.

She continued to build the deception. She joined the HiSS (Heper Search Society), a group that operated under the theory that hepers were still at large and had infiltrated society. The members of the HiSS sought to flush out these heper infiltrators.

"Why put yourself in the midst of the very people most keen to sniff you out?" I ask.

Because, she answers, the HiSS was the one place no one would ever suspect you. Membership in that club was the eye of the storm, where neither suspicion nor accusation would blow your way. And there was an added benefit: she would be the first to know about another suspected heper. Her plan was simple: first confirm that that person was a heper, then snuff out the suspicion as baseless.

"Then what?"

She turns to look at me, her mouth fashioning words and then stopping. "Establish contact," she finally says. She sits on one end of the sofa, a leg bent under her, half turned towards me.

"You were good," I say. "I never suspected. Not for a second."

"You weren't so good."

"What?"

"You slipped a few times. I'd see emotions breaking out on your face. Or falling asleep in class. Granted, it was only for a split second – but the slight head nod of sleep was unmistakable." Her eyes light up, remembering something. "I saved your butt more than once. Like in trig class a few nights ago, when you couldn't read the board. Even last night, here in the library with the Director. Your hands started to tremble."

"I remember that." Then something occurs to me. "Why didn't you ever approach me? At school. And here. When you had me all figured out? Just tell me you knew what I was."

"Because it could have all been a ruse. You might have just been trying to bait other hepers into coming out. It was a real possibility. So I just kept watching you. Even snooped around your house during the day."

"So there *was* someone outside!"

Her shoulders slumped forward. "You should have come out. I was hoping you would. I stood waiting, hoping you'd open the door, step out into the sunshine. See me, standing right there in the sun with you. All mystery gone, everything out in the open, just like that." She pauses. "Just think how things would be so different. If that really did happen back then instead of just now."

I pick up the bottle at my feet, uncap it, and hand it to her. She nods her thanks. I watch her mouth as she tilts the bottle towards her, her upper lip pressing into the opening as her lips slowly part. Water pours out; a thin trail snakes down her neck and gathers behind her collarbone.

"Well," she says, recapping the bottle, "here we are."

I shift my legs under me. "You have a plan," I say. "I saw you up to something in the Control Centre, snooping around, asking questions."

"What *was* a plan," she says with mild frustration. "It wasn't going to work, I quickly saw that."

"Which was?"

"I knew going in that I couldn't let the Hunt take place. It would completely expose me – there's no way I can keep up with the pace, the running. And even if I could, I'd be breathless and sweaty by the time we reached the hepers. And even if I weren't hot and sweaty – and I most definitely would be – there's no way I could eat the hepers. Kill them, yes, I could do that, but eating them? No way."

I nod. That's exactly how I see things.

She continues. "So then I thought: what if I could somehow sabotage the whole Hunt? What if I could find a way to lower the walls of the Dome at night? The hepers would be left out there exposed and for the taking. Everyone would be flying out there, hunters and staffers within seconds. Just like that, in one fell swoop, and no Hunt anymore."

"Except?"

"Except there's no way to lower the Dome walls. No button to push, no lever to pull, no combination of buttons to press. It's all automated by sunlight sensors." Her voice, which has been rising, suddenly stops. Then quieter: "So that took me to Plan B. That was what happened today. Except it turned out more like Plan B Fail."

"You used the sun protection equipment," I say quietly, finally understanding why she and Beefy ran outside. "You used them to convince him. That with the equipment, he could get to the heper village even in the daytime. Where he'd have the hepers all to himself."

She nods. "That's what I told him. That's what I was hoping for. I knew the equipment wouldn't work for long, not against the afternoon sun. But if it got him halfway there, close enough to see and smell the hepers, it wouldn't matter anymore. His desire for heper flesh would take over, he'd choose the taste of heper even if it meant dying in the sun."

"You were right. That's what happened. He totally lost it."

"He wouldn't believe me at first. But then I told him I didn't care what he believed, *I* was going out to get the hepers all for myself, he could stay inside and eat leftover pasteurised blood and processed meats for all I cared. He saw me flying out with the protective blanket, saw how the equipment seemed to be really working. So then he came out himself."

"It almost worked," I say quietly.

"How close did he get to them?"

"You didn't see?"

She shakes her head. "I fainted, completely blacked out. When I came to, you were walking back already, the Dome closed. I mean, I could see he didn't make it."

I'm glad she didn't see. She would be asking me why I tried to stop Beefy. And I wouldn't be able to answer her. Because even I don't know. "Do you have a Plan C?" I ask.

She scratches her wrist. "How about I tell you after you tell me *your* Plan A?"

I pause. "Break my leg."

"Excuse me?"

"Hours before the Hunt begins, fall down a flight of stairs."

"For real?"

"Yes."

"That's pretty lame. There are so many holes in that, I can't even begin."

"Like what?"

"Well, for starters, breaking a leg without spilling blood is possible, perhaps, but I wouldn't want to stake my life on those chances. For starters."

I don't say anything.

"Any other plan?"

"Well, I just thought of another one. We have FLUNs now. We can just take out the other hunters."

She stares incredulously at me.

"What?" I ask.

"You're not serious?"

"What? What's wrong with that plan?"

"Where do I start? Ten seconds into the race, they'll be out of range. Leaving us behind. With the hundreds of spectators gawking at us, wondering why we're so slow. We'll be barely out of the gate before we're mauled to death."

I raise my hand, then stop. Ever so slowly, it falls back down.

"Should I go on?" she asks, a friendly smirk on her face.

"No, it's OK—"

"My Plan C, then," she says. "I also only recently thought of it" – a flash of humour in her eyes – "so we'll need to work out the kinks. But do you remember when the Director was telling us about the start of the Hunt? How an hour before dusk, the building will be locked down to prevent any bandit hunters? Well, that got me thinking. What if we were somehow able to disengage the lock-down? With all the hundreds of guests already here for the Gala, there's—"

"Going to be a chaotic free-for-all," I say, nodding. "Disengage the lockdown, and suddenly everyone's going to be tearing out of this building, hunting down the hepers. Sheer pandemonium as all the guests and staffers rush out into the Vast. Nobody's going to even notice our absence."

"And two hours later and all the hepers are dead. Hunt over. We survive. Us," she whispers. And her eyes hook into mine. Something stirs in me.

I stare at her, nodding slowly. Then I stop, shake my head. "There's one flaw."

"Which is?"

"We don't know how to disengage the lockdown."

Her eyes twinkle. "Yes, we do. And it's easy. For us, anyway.

The other day, when we were visiting the Control Centre, I was snooping around. A guy started telling me about how the lockdown works. Can you believe it's a button? Push the button down, and lockdown is set for an hour before dusk; push the same button again and the setting is cancelled."

"No way. Can't be that simple. For security, they'd have to—"

"And they already have a fail-safe system. The sun. They don't close the shutters in the Control Centre in the daytime, remember? To keep people out. So that means the only time you can cancel the lockdown setting – before dusk – sunlight is pouring in. You can't get to it. *They* can't get to it. More effective than if that button were surrounded by laser beams and a moat of acid. It's genius."

"And so is our plan."

"My plan," she adds quickly, the suggestion of a smile on her lips.

"It really might work," I say, excitement uncharacteristically slipping into my voice. "That really might work." We rack our brains, trying to find weaknesses in the plan. By our silence, I know we can't find any.

"I need to wash up. Shave."

The water feels good on my face. I scrub my neck, my armpits, and then there's no water left. I take out the blade, graze my skin just so. My nails are chipped in a few places, but nothing to worry about. Just a few more nights, then I get to go home. That's the plan, so it seems.

When I walk back, she's gone. I glance up at the clock. Just past six, ten more minutes of daylight.

Only she hasn't left. She's in the reference section, where the sunbeam is. She's holding a book up in the air, her back to me. The beam of light is hitting her square in the chest.

"So you found the beam."

She spins around and the sight of her face – haloed by the light – stills me. There's a gentle smile on her face, a daring display of emotion. I feel walls between us crashing down, dirt bricks and cement chunks hitting the ground, the feel of fresh air and gentle sunshine on pale, deprived skin.

"Hi." Her voice is tentative but friendly, like shy arms extended, hopeful for but uncertain of an embrace.

We look at each other. I try not to stare, but my eyes keep snapping back towards her. "You found the beam."

"Hard to miss. But what's it all about?"

"You don't know the half of it. So much more than meets the eye." I walk over to where she's standing. "At just the right time of day, the beam shines at the far wall" – I walk her over – "then reflects off this small mirror, creating a second beam that shoots off to another mirror over there. It then hits this spot right around here, on this bookshelf right at this journal—"

It's gone.

"Oh, you mean this journal?" she asks, holding it up in her hands.

"How did you—"

"It was the only book not shelved, just lying here on this table. It's been here for a while, even back to when the Director met us here. So I put two and two together. You must have forgotten to put it back."

"Have you looked inside it? The Scientist guy, he wrote a whole bunch of stuff in it. Pretty out there." I look at her. "He was just like us, you know."

"How so?"

"You know." My eyes look down.

"Oh," she says quietly. "No way."

I nod. "But he was really strange. Must have spent months just writing up that journal, copying excerpts into it. Everything from textbooks to scientific treatises to ancient religious texts. And then there's this really weird blank page—"

"You mean this one," she says, opening the book to the blank page. And before I can say anything, she continues, "The page that reveals a map when you hold it up to the sunbeam?"

I pause. *A map?* "Exactly," I say in a low voice. "That's exactly the page I was talking about."

She stares at me, a smile cracking through her face. "Liar," she says. "You *so* didn't know about the map."

"OK, you're right," I say to her broadening smile. "I didn't know about the map. But give me a look-see. Hold up that page to the beam. Sun's going down, we don't have much time."

Sure enough, once she holds it up to the sunbeam, a map bleeds out of the page. But more: not just the outline of a map, but a tapestry of rich colours splashing across the page like a painting.

"You should have seen this map five minutes ago when the sunbeam was stronger. The colours were flying off the page, they burned into your eyes."

The vista depicted on the map is detailed and comprehensive. In the bottom left corner, I see the grey slab building of the Heper Institute. Right next to it is the Dome disproportionately large and sparkling. The rest of the map captures the land to the north and east, the stale brown of the Vast transforming into the lush green of the eastern mountains. Most curious of all is a large river flowing south to north, painted in a verdant deep blue. My finger trails along it.

"The Nede River," Ashley June says.

"Thought it was just a myth."

"Not according to this map."

My finger pauses. "Hello, what's this?"

Where the Nede River slants towards the eastern mountains, a brown raft-like boat is drawn. It's anchored beside a small dock. Also noticeable is a thick arrow drawn from the boat and up along the river channel, towards the eastern mountains.

"I know, I was confused when I saw that, too. It's as if it's saying that the boat is meant to journey down the Nede River. Towards the eastern mountains."

"Doesn't make sense. Rivers flow from mountains, never up them."

"Do you think" – her voice lights up – "it was his escape route? The Scientist's?" She sees my confusion. "Everyone says he got burned up by the sun. But if he really was a heper like you say, there has to be another explanation for his disappearance. Maybe he got away. By boat. This boat."

Possibly, I think. But then I shake my head. "Why would he leave a record of his escape route? Doesn't make sense."

"I suppose. But one thing's for sure."

"What is?"

"This map is for only hepers to see. Nobody else would be able to see this, even accidentally. Not as long as you need sunlight to view it."

I bend over to study the map more closely. The amount of detail is astonishing the closer you get. Fauna and flora reveal themselves with surprising specificity. "What does this all mean?" I ask.

"I don't know."

"We'll figure it out," I say.

She's quiet, and when I look up, her eyes are shiny with wetness. She's smiling. "I like it," she says, "when you say *we*."

My eyes linger on the small creases at the ends of her lips. I want to extend my hand, trace those small creases with my fingertips. I look into her eyes and smile in return.

She peers at my face as if it were a page, like a toddler learning how to read, enunciating in her mind the syllables of emotion on my face.

I'm unsure of what to do or say next; uncertainty floods the moment. So I turn my stare down, pretend to study the map. "Where do you think they'll be sending the hepers?"

"Could be anywhere. It really doesn't matter, they could practically place an X anywhere on the map as long as it's eight hours out. Not west, is my guess. They wouldn't want the hepers getting too close to the Palace. On a windy day, their scent might be picked up by the Palace staff. They wouldn't want to run the risk of Palace staffers sabotaging the Hunt."

She's doesn't say anything for a long time. When I look up, she's rubbing her bare arms.

"The other night," she says quietly. "When the Director was here. Do you remember how he went on about the heper farms at the Palace?" She shakes her head. "He was just kidding, right? The whole thing about heper farms, the hundreds of hepers? That was just a figment of his sick fantasy, right?"

"I don't know. Maybe. I couldn't get a read on him."

She keeps rubbing her arms. "It's so freaky, just thinking about it. I've got goose pimples all over my arms." She looks at me. "Do you get goose pimples, too?"

I walk over and stand close, looking at the tiny bumps on her arms. "I do get them. But I call them 'goose bumps', not 'goose pimples'."

"'Goose bumps'." she repeats. "I like that better. Doesn't sound as nasty as 'goose *pimples*'."

Before I can stop myself, I reach out and touch her arm. With my fingertips. Her skin, so soft, shivers under my touch. She draws back.

"I'm sorry," we both say simultaneously.

"No, I am, I shouldn't have," I start apologising.

"No, I – I – it wasn't a flinch. Like, I wasn't drawing back in disgust or anything like that . . . it's hard to explain." And then she suddenly grabs my hand and places it, open palmed, on her forearm.

A jolt shoots up my arm, a skein of heat and electricity. I draw back my hand, but her eyes are filled with invitation and longing.

"I just . . ." she starts.

The goose bumps on her arms pop up even more. This time, when the palm of my hand sinks into the soft give of her arm, she doesn't flinch back and I don't remove my hand. We look at each other, the tears in her eyes a reflection of the wetness in my own.

A short time later, she falls asleep on the sofa. It's a total collapse. Her body folds up like a failed origami piece, her head twisted to the side against the top of the sofa. Her mouth is slightly open, small puffs of breath pulsing out. The way her body's torqued, she's going to wake up with a sore neck. I reach out to centre her head on the armrest. In her slumber she complies, shifting her head at the gentle urging of my hands. So strange to be touching someone else.

I sit on the other end of the sofa, my body heavy but relaxed. Above us, the sleep-holds hover on the ceiling, two unblinking ovals staring down like all-knowing eyes, leering at me with mocking accusation. They have taunted me all my life, those sleep-holds. There was a time when I harboured a fantasy. In that fantasy, I live the normal life of a normal person. Every night, I take to the sleep-holds, my baby twins – in my mind, always girls – asleep in the next room, their cherubic faces made chubbier as they hang upside down. And my wife sleeps, hanging next to me, her face pale yet luminescent in the mercuric night light, her long hair spilling down to just touch the floor, her feet graceful even in the straps of the sleep-holds. And in my fantasy, there is no pulsating push-push of blood into my upside-down face; no pain from the sleep-holds tearing into the skin of my feet; no drip of tears falling to the ground beneath me. Only calm and coldness and stillness. All is normal. Including me.

I glance over at Ashley June, so wonderfully drooped on the sofa, her chest rising and falling, rising and falling. Beneath closed eyelids, slight bulges of her eyes move side to side. A spittle of saliva sits at the corner of her open mouth. I finally let my eyes close, sleep tugging me into a deep, blissful well. It is new, this sensation. Of falling asleep, lying down next to someone. I drift asleep, as intimate and daring and trusting an act as I've ever risked.

Hunt Minus One Night

At first, no one is particularly alarmed when Beefy fails to show for breakfast. He's notoriously difficult to rouse from sleep, something his now departed escort often complained about. Only after the dishes have been cleared from the table and we're all moving to the lecture hall is a staffer sent scurrying to his room to check on him.

There is surprise, but not sorrow, when news of his disappearance breaks out. We're in the lecture hall by this point, listening to a senior staffer drone on about upcoming weather conditions (heavy rain and windy) and how they might affect the Hunt tomorrow night, when another staffer pigeon walks into the hall. He whispers something to his superior; the superior stands up and walks out, leaving the junior staffer at the lectern.

"One of the hunters has disappeared," he says. He pauses, at a loss for what to say next. "Teams are now scouring this building in an effort to find him. Another search team is surveying the grounds outside. There's a possibility of a sunlight disappearance. But there's no need to be worried."

Not that anyone is. No tears lost here: it only means less

competition for the rest of us. But no cause for outright jubilation, either – it's not as if Beefy were ever a contender. If either Phys Ed or Abs had been missing, there'd be an all-out celebration right now.

"I'm sorry to have to say this," he continues, "but with all staffers preoccupied at this moment with the search, the lectures for the early evening are cancelled. You are free to do as you wish. Be mindful that the Gala begins in three hours at high moon, midnight on the dot. May I suggest you use this time to get some beauty sleep? You do want to look your resplendent best for the cameras and guests."

Gaunt Man walks up to me as we're all leaving. "Did you see the lectures that were cancelled?" He bends down to read the pamphlet in hand. "'*Taking Advantage of the Fauna and Flora of the Vast*' and '*The Sociological Heper Tendencies in an Environment of Fear: How Best to Leverage Gain*'. Remember how I said all this was a crock, that these lectures, this orientation, even the Hunt, was just a show?"

I nod, making sure to hide my irritation. I'm hoping to leave, but he's planted himself firmly in front of me without the slightest inclination of letting me go. Once he gets going, Gaunt Man can go on for a while. From across the hall, Ashley June shoots me a knowing look. She leans back against the wall, settling in.

"Need any more proof?" Gaunt Man says. "They're admitting this is all a sham by how easily they cancel the lectures. Without even batting an eyelash. It's all just a joke." His tongue slips out, wet and oily, lubricating his lips. "Release the hepers already. Just let us have at them."

"What do you think happened to him?" I ask, trying to change the topic.

"The big guy? He's a fool. He was trying to imitate me. Went out there trying to show ingenuity and nerve the way I did. But what an idiot. Probably went out there with his SunBlock Lotion foolishly thinking it'd help. For my money, the search teams should start looking for him outside – what remains of him, anyway – somewhere between here and the Dome."

"Maybe," I say non-committally. I pause, waiting for him to go away. But he doesn't. "What do they have you wearing?" I ask. Gaunt Man has shown such a disdain for the event, perhaps any topic related to it will cause him to pick up and leave.

"For the Gala?" He humphs. "A traditional, boring tuxedo that has 'Irrelevant Old Guy' written all over it. What about you? Something high-end and splashy, I'd expect."

"Why do you say that?"

"Media's been arriving in droves since yesternight. Reporters, photographers, journalists. This Hunt's becoming more and more a media event by the hour. Heard they're jockeying for post-Hunt interviews," he says irritably. "And for the Gala, they're gonna want to front the good-looking hunters. Including you, pretty boy; they probably have you in one of those dapper suits."

"Hardly," I say. But he's right. My suit, Super 220 with worsted cloth and full silk linings with my name sewn into the inseam, felt like a regal carpet when it was fitted on me yesternight.

"So I've been hearing something about you."

"What's that?"

"You have a partner in crime. That the two of you'll be going out in force during the Hunt. The dynamic duo, you and the pretty one."

"The pretty one?"

"Right there," he says, pointing at Ashley June, still waiting for me across the hall. "That's the word on the street, anyway."

"Where are you hearing all of this?"

"I have my sources," he says. "So what's your strategy?" His voice takes on an edgier tone. Now I know why he's approached me: to talk about this. "Cut out fast, make us chase you both? Or start with the pack, beat us out with a gradual but methodical increase in pace?"

"Well, you know we—"

"Separate the heper pack into two groups, then divide and conquer? Or keep them together, play to their group hysteria?"

"It's really something I can't get into right now."

He's quiet, as if mulling this over. "Say," he whispers, "got any room for an old geezer like me? In your alliance, I mean. I may not have the brawn, but I've got the brains. Not saying you and her ain't brainy, but I've got street smarts only experience gives. Maybe I can help."

"You know, we prefer to work in just a small group. Just the two of us, actually."

"What is it they say? 'Though one may be overpowered, and two can defend themselves, a cord of three is not quickly broken.' "

"Look, I don't know."

He stares at me, his gaze turning cold. "I see." He begins to walk away, stops, half turns towards me.

"Things I know about you," he says. "Don't think I didn't notice heper smells coming off of you the other day. Don't think I'm unaware that you've somehow got access to heper flesh. Really, just what is going on in that library during the day when you're all alone? What kind of access to heper meat do you have in there? Is there a secret bootleg stash you've discovered? Information like this could come out to harm you." He sniffs viciously, his nostrils shrinking inward. "I *still* smell it."

A staffer approaches; Gaunt Man shoots him a look, then walks away.

"Yes?" I say to the staffer.

"Pardon me. I wanted to let you know that your tuxedo is ready and has been delivered to your lodging. Also, the evening gown for your date tonight" – the staffer looks quickly at Ashley June – "has been delivered to your lodging. The Director approved her request to get dressed there."

"OK."

"Something else. When you walk to the Gala from the library, the media will be lined up along the brick walk, waiting for you."

"Is that really necessary?"

"The Director's orders. Once he realised the two of you were going as a couple, he decided you'd make an entrance of the first order."

"I see."

"One more thing."

"Yes?"

"You and the girl are not to spend the day in each other's rooms again."

"How do you—"

"How we know is irrelevant. But the Director is afraid of public perception. With the media here, he wants to avoid even a suggestion of impropriety among the hunters."

"You've got to be—"

"Make sure you wake up in your own rooms tomorrow."

"Listen, I—"

"The Director's orders," he says, and leaves. I watch him walk over to Ashley June. A short, clipped conversation later, he's walking out. I head towards Ashley June.

As I walk past Gaunt Man, now talking to Abs and Phys Ed, I hear him giving the same spiel about joining their alliance. He's desperate. Desperately hungry for heper flesh, desperately in need of help. He doesn't stand a chance of getting either. That's someone to keep an eye on. There's no telling what a person can become capable of once desperation takes hold of him. Can't put anything past him.

Back in the library, Ashley June and I get changed for the Gala, she in the periodical section, I by the front desk. My tuxedo, which I find hanging off the reserve shelf in plastic wrap, fits me to a tee. It comes with bells and whistles I could have done without: diamond-embedded cuff links, iron buttons embossed with the Ruler's face. Despite these, it's an impressive suit that compliments me well.

Ashley June, her voice travelling down the length of the library, keeps warning me not to sneak a peek until she's ready. And she takes her time, much more than I think necessary to simply take off clothes and throw on a fitted dress.

Before she's done, there's a knock on the door. A retinue of staffers walks in. Each carries a small case in tow. "Make-up," they say curtly, and I point them to Ashley June. To my surprise, one of them stays behind. "I'm going to do your face," she says.

"I don't think so," I reply. There's too much risk that she'll spot a stray hair follicle on my body or face or get close enough to smell my body odour.

"It's the Director's orders. Sit down now, lean your head back."

"No. It's not going to happen, trust me."

"It's just a touch-up job. It'll be barely noticeable."

"So don't do it. How can I make myself clearer?"

She glares at me. "You'll answer to the Director."

"Fine. Send him down here."

Anger boils in the staffer's half-closed eyes. She slams the kit shut and joins the others in the periodical section. There's not a chance she'll report this to the Director. She's all too aware of what happened to the escorts. Punishment will be meted out for indiscretions, but not to the hunters, who apparently have immunity.

From the back of the library, I hear Ashley June objecting to the make-up. But with less success. They are having their way with her.

I barge in, ready to parlay my hunter immunity card. They're grouped tightly around Ashley June, badgering her with their demands to sit back! pull your hair back! stop scrunching your face! All I can see of Ashley June are her knuckles, pressed white against the armrests of her leather chair.

"Get out." My voice is steady and quiet.

They spin around, surprise and annoyance written on their faces.

"This is not up to her. Or you."

"Get out."

"You'll answer to—"

"The Director? Sorry, but I've already heard this speech. Now get out." I see the smallest and youngest of them, a girl no older than me, clutching her make-up bag. She's afraid, and for an instant I feel a stab of sorrow for her. "Look, don't worry. Leave a make-up kit and a mirror here; we can put it on ourselves. Now get out."

They offer little resistance after that.

"That was close," Ashley June says after the front doors close. A look of horror suddenly crosses her face. "Get out!"

"What?"

"Get out!"

I spin around, expecting to see one of the staffers still lurking.

"No, you! Close your eyes. Close them, I said! Now get out!"

"What's going on?"

"You're not supposed to see me yet. Not until I'm completely ready. Go, already!"

I blink. Ashley June: such a romantic at heart. Even in the moments after imminent death, apparently.

One *hour* later, she's ready. I busy myself during that time taking out the FLUNs and familiarising myself with them. They're simple to operate: a safety on the underside that's easy to disengage and a large trigger button on top. I don't fire off any practice shots. With only three rounds in each gun, I don't want to waste even a single one.

As I look at the FLUNs, my thoughts drift to the hepers. I quickly try to think of something else, but my mind keeps boomeranging back to them. I see them walking in the middle of the Vast, map in hand, eyes swivelling around, trying frantically to find a shelter that does not exist. A dawning realization, then a sense of inevitability when they see the dust clouds in the distance, the hunters bearing down on them. Then the arrival of claws and nails and fangs flooding over them in a sea of ardent desire.

I wish I'd never met them, never talked to them; that they'd remained crude savages in my mind, incapable of the speech or intelligence or humanity that I'd thought separated me from them.

The appearance of Ashley June in her dress and fully made up quickly banishes these morbid thoughts. She's – in a word – resplendent. They've cut no corners on her dress. A tank-style silk chiffon gown, blazing lava red, fronted with ornate crystals. A tasteful touch of plumage. But it's her face that's the true marvel. Soft and graceful, without compromising the fine angles of her jawline. And her eyes. They cast a spell, those hazel green eyes, they really do.

"I wish," she says a little shyly, "the dress were a little brighter.

With some green to match my eyes, and a lighter red to complement my hair."

"It's fine." I shake my head, knowing I can do better. "You look amazing. I really mean that."

"You're just saying so," she says, but I can tell even she doesn't believe that.

"It's all over for me now. You know that, don't you? All night, in front of everyone, I'm going to be ogling you with big eyes, sweaty palms, and a heart hammering, pounding away. You're the death of me, Ashley June, you really are."

She gives me a funny look, a frown creasing her smooth forehead.

"Sorry," I say, "was that overkill with the cheese?"

"No, it's not that. I liked it. But who's '*Ashley June*'?"

I stare at her. "You are."

The day my father and I burned the journals and books, we stole out of our home at noon, carrying heavy burlap sacks. I was just a young boy, and I cried the whole way there. Not loudly; not even sobs escaped me. But a trail of tears fell from the corner of each eye, and though the day was hot and the distance relatively long, those tears never dried.

We found a clearing in the woods. By then, our shoulders hurt from the weight of the sacks and we were glad to unburden ourselves of them. My father told me to gather some wood, small twigs and sticks, nothing too big. When I got back, he was hunched over on his knees, his face almost touching the ground as if in deep, penitent prayer. In his hand was a magnifying glass he was using to direct the sunbeam onto a pile of leaves. He told me not to move, and I stood where I was, absolutely still. Without fanfare, a wisp of smoke rose from the pile of leaves that grew thicker and darker. A flame suddenly burst out, devouring the leaves in its midst.

"The sticks," he said, stretching out his hand to me.

The fire grew. Every once in a while, he'd hunch down and blow into the fire. It'd rear up in anger and surprise, venting sparks. He placed two shorn branches into the fire and sat back. The fire roared with a ferocity that frightened me. He told me to fetch the books and journals, and I brought them over to him.

For a long time, they lay next to him. He sat without moving until I realised he could not muster that last ounce of willpower for that final, irrevocable act. He asked me to come to him, and I did, sitting in the cosy warmth of his lap. I held a picture book, my sister's. I knew every drawing inside, the colour of every dog and cat and house and dress. He took a deep breath, and for a moment I thought he was going to explain again why we were burning the books. But instead his whole upper body began to hitch, as if he were trying to contain loud hiccups. I put my hand on his broad hand, muscles and rocks under his coarse skin, and told him it was OK. Told him I understood why we were burning the books, that because Mommy and sister had disappeared, we could not keep anything in the house that would cause unexpected visitors to ask about them. I told him "it was too dangerous", reciting back words he'd earlier told me that I had not understood and still did not.

I think he meant to go through each book with me one last time. But for whatever reason, he did not. He simply took each book and threw it into the fire one after the other. I still remember the feel of my sister's picture book pulled away. I did not resist, but the feel of the journal against my fingertips as it was whisked away and tossed into the fire felt like something lost forever.

We left an hour later, when there was nothing left of the fire (or books) but dying embers and grey ash. Like my father, ashen and grey, his inner fire smothered out. Just before we crossed the clearing, I went back for the burlap sacks we'd forgotten to take with us. They were lying right beside the pile of ashes. As I bent to pick them up, something came over me: I blew softly into the embers the way I'd seen my father do. Fine ash kicked up into the air and into my eyes. But right before my eyes shut, watering against the sting, I saw the smallest glow in the midst of the black ashes. Red, orange, a resurgent spark of an ember. It was a drop of the June sun in a sea of grey ashes.

It was not until years later, in a schoolyard on a drab grey night, that I saw the colour of that red glow again. It was the colour of her hair, a girl I had never seen before but from whom I could not look away. When she turned to me, our eyes connecting even across the length of the schoolyard and through the kaleidoscope of criss-crossing students, I remembered that red ember glowing in the dark ashes like a June sun.

Her designation is Ashley June, I thought to myself.

Alone in the library, standing before her in the beams of the midnight moon, this is the memory I share with her.

The press are out in full force when we step out of the library. As far as the brick path extends to the main building, reporters and photographers are lined along each side. Mercuric flashlights pop everywhere, not that they bother us. An escort leads us at a maddeningly slow pace, stopping us every few steps to pose for a camera or to answer a few interview questions.

Ashley June's arm stays hooked in mine the whole time, her wrist bent at the crook of my elbow. It's an awesome feeling. Alone, I would have hated the fanfare and onslaught of media attention. But with her next to me, I'm comfortable and at ease, and I sense the same is true for her. The soft weight of her hand on my arm, the occasional moments when the side of her hip brushes lightly against mine, the sense of togetherness as we navigate down the path. I think it's because we're masters of this game of image projection and deception that we're so comfortable with the media. A pose, a sound bite, an image: right down our alley.

"How has your training gone? Do you feel prepared for the Hunt?"

"It's been great, and we're chomping at the bit to get on with it."

"Is it true that the two of you are an alliance?"

"It's no secret. We're together."

"Which of the hunters do you think will challenge you the most?"

And on and on went the questions.

The usually short walk takes us almost an hour, and there's no let-up of media and curious guests once we get to the main building. They're still arriving in droves, guests and media, in carriages of various shapes and sizes; the horses are sweaty and out of breath as they are led away to the stable out back.

Inside, there are even more media and onlookers. They're cordoned off behind velvet ropes, and our escort thankfully takes us past them without stopping. "To the main hall," he says, glancing quickly at his watch.

They've spared no expense in decorating the main banquet hall. Gold chandeliers descend from high ornate ceilings, casting a misty mercuric light over each table. Onyx-embedded table silver, porcelain plates commissioned during the neo-Gothic Ruler era, wineglasses encrusted with diamond shavings set on embroidered violet linen tablecloths. A flower basket sits centre on each table, double-layered jade stemming from the Selah dynasty. Tall windows with decorative swagged velvet curtains loom over and around us. Guests cluster at the windows facing east, gazing at the Dome. It sits like a sliced marble ball. At the far end of the banquet hall, the grand staircase ascends to the first floor, its perfectly centred red carpet bright and lush like a swollen tongue. In the centre of the hall is a large dance floor, gleaming under the mercuric lights.

The hunters are separated, each to his or her own assigned table. When Ashley June removes her arm from mine to be taken to her table, it feels like a tragic parting. High-standing Palace officials sit at my table, their spouses peppering me with nettlesome questions. The food comes out in waves, tuxedoed waiters and waitresses with ruffled front blouses balancing trays of dripping meat as they manoeuvre between tables. Large bibs are tied on us, draping over our tuxedos and gowns from our necks to knees. They quickly become splattered with droplets of blood as we eat. After days of eating endless plates of meat sopping in blood, I can barely stand the sight of more. I hardly touch my plate, citing overexcitement with the Hunt tomorrow night.

Throughout the endless courses of meat, I steal glances at Ashley June. She's in her element, engaging the guests at her table with charm. Even during the main course when the fattest portions of meat are served, she still has their rapt attention. This setting plays to her strength. It's how she's always lived her life of deception. *Offence is the best defence*. I recall her words.

After dessert – cakes and soufflés, for which I claim to have regained my appetite – a succession of speeches are made by a handful of top-ranking officials. I spend my time gazing at Ashley June, who's in my line of vision. Her slender arms flow gracefully out of her gown, the gleam of silvery light along her arm like the reflection of moonlight along a river. She gathers her hair from the back and with the expert sweep of one hand brushes it over her shoulder, exposing the sinuous nape of her neck. I wonder if she is thinking of me the way I am of her: incessantly, obsessively, helplessly.

I'm not the only one who's looking at her. Gaunt Man, two tables away, is staring at her, his eyes wide and bulging. He takes a sip from his wineglass. And another, his eyes never budging from her.

Last to speak is the Director. He's powdered his face, puffed up his hair, polished his nails a blood red. "Dear esteemed guests, I trust that you have found the Institute – with its unsullied reputation – to have met your high expectations tonight. The food, the décor, the grandeur of this ballroom – all, I do hope, to be pleasing to such regal guests as yourselves, who ordinarily wouldn't deign to travel so far for entertainment. But this is not an ordinary occasion, is it? For tomorrow night, the Heper Hunt begins!"

The guests, already with a few drinks in them, clink glasses, pound tabletops.

"Tonight is the night to celebrate the benevolent sovereignty of our beloved Ruler, under whose leadership the Heper Hunt was made possible. And celebrate we shall! Without restraint! For we will have plenty of time tomorrow daytime to sleep off tonight's excesses!" The rasping of wrists sounds across the hall.

The Director totters slightly; I realise that he's had a few too many drinks in him. "Now, just in case some of you are getting ideas, ideas about, hmm . . . shall we say, 'unofficially' joining this Hunt tomorrow, upon my shoulders falls the burden of dispelling any such hope. This building goes into lockdown mode an hour before dusk. You simply won't be able to leave this building for the duration of the Hunt."

He swirls the wine in his glass dramatically, gazing at it in the mercuric light. "Sometime before lockdown, the hunters will be taken to an undisclosed, secret location. At the cusp of dusk, as early as each shall dare, they will set off into the Vast after the hepers. And so," he says, his voice rising, "the most exciting, most scintillating, most extravagant, most bloody, most violent Heper Hunt ever shall begin!"

The banquet hall erupts into a spasm of hisses and bone cracks and wineglasses smashed.

After the speech, as the guests settle down, a string quartet assembles on the edge of the dance floor. The quartet plays the Baroque piece slowly and freely, a late-century arrangement. Gradually, couples make their way to the floor. Halfway through the first song, I catch sight of Gaunt Man rising from his chair. He has his eyes on Ashley June, and as he starts making his way towards her, his tongue sticks out, licks his lips. I push my chair back and walk swiftly towards Ashley June, outpacing Gaunt Man. She sits with her hands placed in her lap, her back straight, head up, expectantly.

As I draw closer to her, her head tilts up ever so, and she looks at me from the corner of her eye. Do I detect the faintest smile touch her lips, a brief emergence of her cheek dimple? I offer her my elbow and she takes it, rising gracefully from her chair with the slightest pull on my arm. We walk to the dance floor, past Gaunt Man, left standing stiffly and awkwardly by himself.

As if on cue, the quartet starts another song, this one softer and more romantic in tone. There are whispers and murmurings all around, and then the other couples on the dance floor slide away to the edge, surrendering the spotlight to Ashley June and me, the hunter couple. The floor is ours. And suddenly, unwittingly, all eyes in the ballroom are on us. A few photographers move into position, cameras at the ready. I turn to face Ashley June: a hint of dread in her eyes. Neither of us wants this attention. But it is too late for that. My shoulder squares with hers, so close I feel heat waves humming off her body. And despite everything, there is an almost audible *click* of rightness. A strong pull draws us closer, as if our hearts are powerful, insistent, opposite magnets.

Drumming up everything I learned in school, I fist both hands and interlace my knuckles with the knuckles of her fisted hands. Back at school, I dreaded dance classes, hating the proximity, fearing that I hadn't shaved the light hairs on my knuckles close enough. But with Ashley June now, I am free of fear. And free to feel: the texture of her skin, the musky proximity of her body, her breath delicately touching my neck. Her glistening green eyes look into mine. I wish I could whisper to her, but there are too many eyes upon us, the music too soft. But what I would say.

I'm so lost in the moment that I almost forget we actually have to dance. I press my knuckles deeper into hers to let her know I'm about to start. A slight push back in acknowledgement, and then we begin. For two people who've never danced together, we're surprisingly adept. Our bodies move in fluid synchrony, the distance between us constant and close. Other than a few minor brushes, our legs are harmonised and rhythmic, our feet falling within inches of one another, never closer. In my school dance class, dancing was never more than a bullet-point progression to follow, a checklist to complete in sequence. But with Ashley June it is a flow, a matter of simply hoisting a sail and allowing yourself to be caught up. At the end of the piece, I let her loose for the three-step spin, and her long, slim arms raise above her head like a whirling dervish. She teases out of her spin, hair spilling seductively across her face, her green eyes puncturing me deep inside. I hear a few gasps coming from the tables.

"Wow," I mouth to her.

The next piece begins. Ashley June and I separate. Now begins the obligatory dances with the wives of the officials, all streaming their way over to me, their high-official husbands too disinterested in dancing or their wives (or both) to bother rising from their tables. It's taxing, the endless dancing and perfunctory small talking, and after a number of dances, a film of sweat starts forming on my forehead. I need to take a break, but there are simply too many women waiting in line.

"Do you smell something?" asks the woman in front of me. I've been dancing with her for the past minute, but it's only when she asks that question that I really see her for the first time.

"No, not really."

"Smell of heper is so strong. Don't know how you can all concentrate with that odour around. So distracting. I know they say you get used to it after a while, but it's so potent it's like it's right in front of me."

"Sometimes when there's a westerly wind blowing, the odour blows inside from the Dome," I say.

"Didn't seem to be much of a breeze tonight," she says, glancing out of the opened windows.

The next woman is even more direct. "I say," she declares, "there's a heper in this hall somewhere. Smell's quite pungent."

I tell her about the westerly wind.

"No, no," she says, "it's so strong it's like you're the heper!"

I scratch my wrist; she follows suit. Fortunately.

After the song ends, she curtsies and I bow; the next woman in line is already heading over. There's a swift movement, and someone else cuts in. It's Ashley June. Looking in her eyes, I can tell she knows exactly what's going on and she's worried. The other woman is upset and about to complain until she realises who it is. She backs away. Ashley June and I begin to dance. Some cameras start clicking again.

This time, the dance lacks enjoyment. We're too conscious of the people around, too fearful of a sheen of sweat that might appear on my face any moment, of the odour I'm emitting. I've danced too hard. When the number ends, I say (loudly, so others can hear) to Ashley June that I need to use the restroom. I'm not sure what good that'll do me, but I can't exert any more energy dancing. Got to get away, give my body a chance to cool down. She tells me she'll wait for me.

I'm cooling down and doing my business at the urinal when somebody walks in. He stands at the urinal next to mine even though the whole row is otherwise unused. The whole restroom is empty, in fact.

"How long you going to last?" he asks.

"Excuse me?"

"Simple enough question. How long are you going to last?" He's a tall and imposing man, broad-shouldered. A prissy pair of glasses sits on his nose, completely at odds with the burly brawn of his body. The tuxedo is ill-fitting, a few sizes too small and bunched under his arms.

I decide to ignore him, instead focusing on hitting the target sticker in the urinal. That's what you have to hit, supposedly the lowest splash zone that gives optimum drainage. In most places, the sticker is of a fly or bee or soccer ball. Here, it's a picture of the Dome.

"Long or short?" the man says.

"What?"

"Long time or short time?"

"Look, I still don't know what you're talking about."

The man sniffs. "I predict short. Maybe thirty minutes. Soon as you hunters are out of sight, that's when the other hunters take you out. You and the girl both."

A reporter. Probably a paparazzi hack who's snuck in using fake credentials, jonesing for an inside scoop. This is how they work: throw out an outrageous story to get a reaction, then report on the reaction. The best thing to do is ignore him.

I zip up and walk over to the paper towel dispenser by the door.

He zips up and pulls up next to me, hand under the dispenser, blocking my way out. The dispenser spits a short towel into his hand.

"Use the FLUNs, that's all I'm telling you," he says, crumpling the towel in hand. "Use them early, use them without hesitation. The hunters, especially the collegiate kids, will want to take you out early in the game. Be very careful." Not once does he look at me as he speaks, just at the dispenser as if it's a teleprompter.

"Who are you?" I ask. *And how does he know about the FLUNs?*

"Word to the wise?" he says. "Things are not as they appear. Take tonight, for example. Look at the glamour of this banquet. What did they tell you? That it was a last minute decision to host it? Look at the food, the wine, the décor, the number of guests, and you tell me if this looks like something slapped together quickly. And think about the so-called lottery – as manipulatable a scheme as they come. Think you're here by chance? Things are not as they appear." He puts his hand on the doorknob, about to leave. Then he turns back to me.

"And the girl. The pretty one you were just dancing with. Be careful about her." His eyes flick to me for the first time. I expect to find sternness in them, and it's there. But the hint of kindness, I did not. "You need to watch out. She's not who you think she is. Don't let her lead you astray." And with that, he brushes open the door and disappears.

Freakin' weirdo, I think to myself. I grab a paper towel and am about to scrub my armpits when a party of four or five come boisterously in. They're loud, unsteady, and clearly inebriated. I step out. I scan quickly for the paparazzi guy, but he's nowhere to be seen.

"Come with me." It's Ashley June materialising out of nowhere, whispering at my side. "We've done our due diligence. Everyone's so hammered, they won't notice we've gone. Come," she says, and I do.

She leads me out of the hall, her slim figure weaving right through the dance floor, between dark moving shapes. Outside the banquet hall, the corridors are empty and the music grows dimmer the farther we walk away. I think we're heading to her room, but on the stairwell we walk past the second floor and continue heading up until there are no more flights of stairs to climb. At the very top, she pushes open a door on the landing, and a burst of starlight falls on us.

"I've been up here a few times. Nobody ever comes," she says softly. The Vast lies spread before us like a frozen sea, its plates calm and smooth. And above us a slew of stars, shimmering slightly, suggestive of an even deeper emptiness.

She leads me to the centre of the roof, the small pebbles beneath our feet shifting as we step. She stops and faces me.

I am right behind her. Our shoulders touch as she turns, and she does not pull away. She is so close, I can feel her breath on my lips. When she looks up at me, I see the reflection of the stars in her eyes, wet as with the evening dew.

"Did your parents ever give you a designation?" she asks.

I nod. "They did. But then they just stopped using it one day."

"Do you remember what it was?"

"Gene."

She is silent for a few moments; I see her lips gently mouthing the word, as if trying it on for size.

"What about you?" I ask.

"I don't remember," she says quietly. "But we shouldn't be calling each other by our family designations anyway. We might get careless and inadvertently call each other by our designations in front of others. It might draw unnecessary—"

"Attention," I finish for her.

For a moment, we suppress the smile spreading on both our faces, as if my lips and hers are two sides of the same mouth. We stop ourselves, as we always have, and start scratching our wrists. "My father used to tell me that all the time. Don't draw unnecessary attention to yourself. All the time. Guess yours did, too."

She nods, a sadness crossing her face. Together, we look out at the Vast, at the Dome sitting small in the distance. From below us, we hear a group of partyers heading out, probably to the Dome, their drunken voices slurred and garbled. Their voices grow dimmer, then fade out altogether.

"Hey, let me show you something," Ashley June says. "Can you do this funky thing? We need to sit down first." She then plants her right foot down on the ball of her foot and starts bouncing her leg up and down in a quick, vibrating motion. "When I'd get impatient or restless, I used to want to do this with my leg. My parents warned me against it, but I'd still do it when alone. Once your leg gets going, it goes on autopilot. Look, I'm not even consciously thinking about it, it moves on its own."

I try. It doesn't work.

"You're overthinking this," she says. "Just relax, don't think about it. Make quicker, shorter jerks."

On the fourth try, it happens. The leg just starts hopping on its own, a jackhammer bouncing away. "Whoa-ho!" I shout in surprise.

She smiles the widest I've seen; a small sound escapes her throat.

"That's called 'laughter'," I tell her.

"I know. Although sometimes my parents called it 'cracking up'. Ever heard that one?"

I shake my head. "It was just 'laughter' for us. And we didn't do it much. My dad – he was always worried I'd forget myself and slip up in public."

"Yeah, mine too."

"Every morning, he'd remind me. Don't do this, don't do that. No laughing, no smiling, no sneezing, no frowning."

"But it got us here. Alive still, I mean."

"I suppose." I turn to her. "My dad had this one really odd saying. Maybe your parents used to say it to you as well? 'Never forget who you are.' "

" 'Never forget who you are'? Never heard that one."

"My dad would say it maybe once a year. I always thought it strange." I stare down at my feet.

"When did yours . . . you know?"

"My parents?"

She nods gently.

I stare at the eastern mountains. "My mother and my sister, years ago. I don't remember much about them. They just vanished one day. Then my father, about seven years ago. He got bitten."

We fall into a silence after that, comforting and shared. Music from the banquet hall comes at us muted and indifferent, a thousand miles away. Eventually, our eyes drift over to the Dome, tranquil and sparkling.

"Ignorance is bliss," she whispers. "Tonight, asleep, blissfully unaware of what awaits them tomorrow. The end of their lives. Poor things."

"There's something you should know," I say after a while.

"About what?"

"The hepers."

"What is it?"

I pause. "When I got water from the pond, I wasn't like in and out. I actually interacted with them. Spent time there. And you know, they speak. They even read. They're not the savages I thought they were, not even close."

"They speak? And read?" She looks incredulously at the Dome. Nothing moves inside.

"They love to. They have books in the mud huts. Shelves of them. And they're creative: they draw, paint."

She shakes her head. "I don't understand. I thought they were raised like barn animals. Why were they domesticated and trained?"

"No, I know this is hard to grasp, but it's not even about them being domesticated or trained like circus animals. They're beyond that. They're, like, normal. They think, they're rational, they joke around. Like you and me."

A frown creases her face. She is quiet, mulling something over. "So you haven't told them about the Hunt," she says matter-of-factly.

"They have no idea," I answer. "Sometimes ignorance *is* bliss."

"What did you tell them about yourself?"

"The Scientist's replacement." I hesitate. "It would have been too . . . awkward to say I was a heper hunter. Maybe I should have said something to them. Maybe I should have let them know about the Hunt."

"No, you did the right thing," she says. "What good would it have done? They'd still be as good as dead."

A zillion million thoughts plummet through my mind over the next few seconds. Then: "Think we should do something?"

She turns to me. "Pretty funny."

"No. I mean, seriously. Instead of our plan, should we do something to help them?"

Her eyes widen a smidge, then droop back down. "What do you mean?" she asks.

"Shouldn't we . . ."

"What?"

"Do something to help them?"

"Don't be ridiculous."

"I'm not. They're us. We're them."

Deep surprise sets in her eyes. "No, they're not. They're way different from us. I don't care if they can speak, they're still glorified cattle." She grips my hand tighter. "Gene, I don't mean to come over as cold-hearted. But there's nothing we can do for them. They're going to die during the Hunt whether or not we use it to our advantage."

"We could, I don't know, we could tell them not to leave the Dome. That the letter informing them about the Dome malfunctioning is all a hoax." I run my hand through my hair, gripping it hard. "This is really hard, Ashley June."

When she speaks again, her voice is softer. "If they die tonight according to our plan, then at least their deaths give us a chance of a real life. But if we just sit on our hands, their deaths are not only meaningless, but will ensure our deaths. We can make their deaths meaningful, giving us a chance of a real life, Gene." Her eyes are wide and pleading. "*Our* new life, Gene. Together. Is that so bad, to make something good come out of this?"

I don't say anything.

Tears start to well in her eyes, and perhaps for the first time in her life, she doesn't hold them back. They stream out and trail down her cheeks. I reach out with my arm, meaning to wipe them away with my sleeve; but she grabs my hand and places it on her cheek, palm pressed right atop the trail of tears. Her soft skin, the wetness of her tears, tingling my open palm. My heart, melting everywhere now, her tears intermingling.

"Please?" she whispers, and the plea in her voice breaks me inside.

Our shoulders touch. When I turn, she has already turned to face me. So close, I can see a tiny mole at the corner of her eye. I brush it lightly with my fingertips, back and forth.

"It's a mole. No amount of rubbing will wipe it away," she whispers.

"I'm not trying to wipe it away." I don't know what I'm doing. All I know is that my heart is bursting out and overflowing, and I don't know what to do with myself.

She lifts her sleeveless arm slightly. Her eyes are wide, inviting. The skin of her armpit is exposed, and she is waiting. She gazes at my elbow, then at me.

As gently as I can, I reach out and lower her arm. "Please," I say softly, a whisper's whisper, "don't misunderstand. But . . . I never . . . it's never done anything for me."

Instead of hurt in her eyes, relief and emotion flood them. She lowers her arm. "It's the same for me. I've always faked how much I enjoyed it." She turns her head the other direction. "The times with the boyfriend, the one time with you in the closet. I felt like something was wrong with me." She sighs with a shudder. "Of course something was wrong with me," she says, her voice hitching. "I'm not normal. I'm a heper." The last word comes out like a release, the final plea of guilt.

Hardly knowing what I'm doing, I grab her hand with my open palm placed on top of the back of her hand. I feel the small ripple of bones, the slight startle in her fingers. I pull my hand away, but she reaches for it. And places her open palm in my hand, the skin of her palm touching the skin of my palm, a full embrace. We stare at each other, eyes wide. The sensation, unlike anything I've felt before, is overpowering. I don't dare to breathe. Her eyes close, her head tips upward. With that, her lips part, full and strangely beckoning.

And then her fingers interlace with mine. I've never seen that before, never knew such a thing was even possible. But the soft skin on the sides of her fingers as they graze the sides of my fingers is like the nape of her neck, tender and smooth, sending a chill and a heat up and through my body.

"Ashley June," I whisper.

She doesn't say anything, just keeps her head tilted heavenward, eyes closed. "I know," she finally whispers, "I know."

Stars blinking down. Ashley June's head on my shoulder, her arm draped across my chest, still holding my hand. We haven't let go, even as we lay down and drifted to sleep. I hear small puffs of her even breathing, the faint thump of her heartbeat against my rib cage. My eyes close. I fall asleep again.

When I wake up, the sky has lightened, the muted stars receded into the grey sky. The scent of dawn hangs ripe in the air. Ashley June is gone from my side. I sit up, the pebbles shifting under me.

She's nowhere on the rooftop. I head over to the ledge, puzzled. I see her in the distance. Walking, deep in thought.

Minutes later, I'm outside on the brick path, hurrying towards her. Evidence of the evening's revelry is littered everywhere: paper plates, kebab skewers, wineglasses, empty bottles, strewn all along the path. Even puddles of vomit. As I draw closer to her, she senses me and turns around, waits for me to catch up.

"Hey," she says with a faint smile, and reaches for my hand. "Hope no one sees us."

"Nah, everyone's completely sloshed."

"Hope so. What are you doing?"

"Something was weighing on me. I had to take a walk to clear my mind." She squeezes my hand. "I'm glad you came. Come with me," she says, and we head towards the Dome.

Hand in hand, we walk under the brightening skies, our hands fitting perfectly, our arms intertwining with surprising ease, her skin soft against my own. Our bodies tilt towards each other intimately as we approach the Dome. It is easy to forget what this day is. A day that will end in the Hunt, in violence and death.

And then we stop in front of the Umbilical.

"Open it," she says.

Inside, sitting dead centre on the conveyor belt, is a large envelope. I look at Ashley June and she nods with her wide, penetrating eyes.

I take it out, feeling the large embossed lettering in all caps:

URGENT: OPEN IMMEDIATELY.

"I thought it would be here by now. It's the letter informing the hepers about the supposed Dome malfunction. It's what gets them out of the Dome, out into the Vast. It's what turns them from the protected into unwitting prey. It's what makes the Hunt possible. It's what kills the hepers."

I stare at her, then back down at the letter. "Why are you showing this to me?" I ask.

"Because I wasn't fair to you before, Gene." I try to interrupt, but she shakes her head. "No, this is important, so let me speak. I feel like I may have forced you to agree to something you'll later regret."

"That's not—"

"No, Gene, listen! I don't want you to feel you were coaxed into something. So I want to give you one more chance. To really think about it, and make up your own mind about what you want to do."

"What are you talking about?"

"If you put that letter back into the Umbilical, then the Hunt happens. *We* happen. But you can also not put it back; you can rip it to shreds. Then the hepers live. It's up to you. It really is up to you, I mean that."

"If I rip it up, the Hunt gets delayed. Maybe by a few days, possibly as long as a week. I won't last that long. I'll be found out well before then."

"I know," she says.

"Why are you doing this?"

"Because," she says, her voice wavering, "I can see how something like this might eat you up. I couldn't live with myself knowing I did this to you. But now, look, it's in your hands now, literally. You choose."

I stare at the envelope in my hands, square and fat. I shake my head. I cannot decide.

"Don't do this," I say, but she looks away from me, biting her lower lip, her eyes shining with a new wetness. I look at the Dome, the mud huts inside, doors and windows still closed. I think of the hepers inside, asleep in their beds, chests rising, falling, eyes closed, skin pulsing delicately with the pulse of blood.

The dawn sun peeks over the crest of the eastern mountains. A slate of pink orange radiates across the Vast, hitting the top of the

Dome; the refracted rays bounce inside, shimmering the pond underneath with a reflected glow. Dawn has come.

Ashley June cannot look at me. Her eyes dart left and right over my shoulder. I stare at her, waiting for her eyes to finally come to a rest on mine. Sunrise orange lights a fire in her auburn hair. And finally, her green eyes, sparkling with diamond intensity behind the screen of tears, find mine.

That is all it takes, apparently. To fully convert me, to slay me. The warm glow of dawn's light, the most beautiful girl I've ever known, the possibility of joining her in a life I've never even dared wish for.

"OK," I whisper. I open the slot door and place the letter back into the Umbilical. The slot door clangs shut with finality.

We leave quickly after that, not wanting to be seen by any early-rising heper. Despite our longing to be together, we decide it's best if we separate to our respective abodes. The Director's order that we sleep separately – or, technically, awaken separately – seems pretty charged; and even though no one's awake to notice, it's probably best not to risk drawing his negative attention at this point. Plus, we need to have our wits about us tonight when the Heper Hunt starts, and some shut-eye – which we're not likely to get much of if together – will only help.

"We're doing the right thing," she says reassuringly outside the doors to the Institute.

"I know," I tell her, I tell myself, "I know."

"You don't have to take me up to my room. I can make it from here. Sun's out now, we shouldn't open and close these doors more than we have to."

"OK."

"I'll see you in a few hours. We'll join up with the hunters for the start of the Hunt. By that time, people will start realising that the lockdown failed. The mass stampede will begin. We'll find a place to hide."

"OK." I frown.

"What is it?"

"Just wondering where all the hunters are. The staffers should have let us know where we need to be gathering for the start of the Hunt by now."

"Don't worry. I'm sure they'll let us know."

"OK."

"Oh," she says, "if you come to my room and I'm not there, check the Control Centre. I'll be there, disengaging the lockdown. And I want to check out the monitors, find the best place to hide out during the stampede."

We embrace, long and tight, our bodies tired but hearts aflame. She opens the door a sliver, slips in. The door closes quickly, quietly.

Minutes later, I'm back in the library. The door clicks shut behind me. Darkness inside broods, saturates everything; I need to give my eyes time to adjust. I walk slowly into the heart of the library, the darkness no different were my eyes closed, until I see a distant dot of light in the main section of the library. It's the drilled hole in the shutter. No beam of light yet; it will be hours before the sun swings into position on that side of the library. For now, it's merely a faint dot of light, like an eye staring at me.

Fatigue hits me like a waterfall. I lurch towards a nearby sofa chair. It doesn't take long to fall asleep. Even as my body plummets into the sofa cushioning, even as my eyelids collapse down like velvet theatre curtains, I'm already tumbling headlong into sleep. And in that last moment before I succumb completely to slumber, a little thought raises its hand like a splinter, that something is amiss, something not altogether *right*. But by then it is too late and I am fast asleep.

I wake up, my heart racing. Even without opening my eyes, I sense *wrongness*. My muscles are tense, my back stiff. Slowly, I crack open my eyes. For a moment, all I can see is a splotch of light on the other side of the room, spouting out of the hole in the shutter, languidly, but solidifying by the second. And even now, as I watch, I see a beam start to form, angled and hazy, but lengthening like the stigma of a flower.

Judging from its intensity and columned angle, hours have passed since I collapsed asleep.

And still that feeling that something is awry permeates the air, only heightened now. I stand up very slowly, fear and thirst creaking my bones. The hazy light is cratered and splintered, like the fragmented face of the moon seen through the bare branches of a winter forest.

I make my way towards it, arms stretched forward, drowsiness still lingering despite the fear.

And then.

Long strands of hair brush against my face, a sickeningly intimate caress. A small, involuntary shriek slips out of my mouth. Like walking into a spiderweb, but so much worse; strands of hair that don't dissipate on contact but drag upward along my face, across my cheekbones, along the sides of my nose, intertwining with my eyelashes and eyebrows, wispy fingers feeling my face like a blind person reading Braille.

It takes everything in me not to flail away at the hair. I drop to the floor and look up. Someone is asleep at the sleep-holds. Abs. Her long black hair flows down like a waterfall of disease, her white face looming above it like a sickened moon. The rest of her body is hidden over in the ceiling shadows, creating the illusion of a hovering, decapitated head.

I shut my eyes, count the seconds, willing her not to stir. I listen. Nothing but a faint, short creak of wood from across the room. I open my eyes, see the books on the floor, hundreds of them shoved roughly off the shelves, piled up at the bottom of the bookshelves like the canted slope of snow after an avalanche.

Phys Ed is dangling upside down on a bookshelf, asleep. His legs are tucked into the top shelf, his shoes wedged into a small opening to support him. He has found sleep in this shelf-turned-cot.

And not just him. As the room brightens, I see Crimson Lips a few shelves down, also hanging off the top shelf. And there is Gaunt Man, his belt looped around an air duct, dangling from the ceiling. Frilly Dress is tied to the centre chandelier; she rotates in a slow spin, the chandelier pulled askew by her weight. All the hunters. They came here last night. I'm not sure why.

I was sleeping this whole time in the hornets' nest.

Trying not to panic, I survey the room. The room is turning from black to grey by the second, the columned light concentrating into a sharper, longer beam. And then I see the pile of equipment by the circulation desk, SunCloaks, pairs of shoes, packs of SunBlock Lotion, and syringes filled with adrenaline boosters. Equipment and accessories for the Hunt.

They're here for the Hunt. To sleep during the day. To be safely away from the Institute as it goes into lockdown. The library is the starting point.

But of course it is. How could I not have realised this before?

The sunbeam intensifies and lengthens; a dread sense of inevitability encloses around me like a noose tightening around my neck. And then, just like that, I realise what will happen in the next few moments.

First, the slumbering hunters will feel a slight burn, an irritation that will intensify as the light begins to singe their eyelids. Perhaps the effects of the light is already upon them, a nausea taking over their insides, a burn on their skin. They will awaken and flee from the light, frothing at the mouth. They will run screaming and hissing to the other end of the library, far from that light.

And there they will remain, cowering from the still bothersome sunbeam. They will wonder – for they will have hours to talk among themselves before nightfall – about the young male hunter who lodged in here, how he was able to survive. The young hunter who never complained about his lodging, about any problems with the lighting, who always seemed to carry about him the odour of the hepers, come to think of it.

I shake my head, snapping myself out of my morbid thoughts. Because there's still time for action. I just need to plug up the hole. And quickly. I step carefully away from Abs' dangling body, walk down the length of the room.

"Ah, there you are."

I spin around. The Director is gazing at me, dangling upside down, halfway down an aisle. "We were looking for you earlier. Couldn't find you. Or the lovely girl. Needed to let you know that the hunters were assembling in the library for the Hunt. Anyway, looks like someone was able to tell you."

"We were—"

"No, no, no need to explain to me. Just glad you were able to get in here before dawn." He stares at me, then behind me, gazing around. Bemusement creeps into his eyes. "Did you leave the door open? Awfully bright in here."

"No, I—"

"You seem nervous. What's the matter?"

"No, no. It's not nervousness. I'm just excited, is all. It's the Hunt, after all. Starts in just a few hours. Five, six hours? Not sure what time it is."

"More like four hours. Heard that a vicious storm's coming. Will be darkening earlier than usual." He looks at me. "Don't lose your head. Keep your wits about you."

"I know. But it's hard not to get excited. People would kill to be in my spot."

"Would they now?"

"Yes. I suppose they would."

"Good," he says, nodding. "That's the mind-set you need." His eyes flick downward to my left. "The FLUNs are under me. Thought it best to keep them away from the others."

"Of course." The attaché cases sit a couple of feet away. Next to them, the Scientist's journal.

"Couldn't sleep earlier. So I started to read that journal I found on a table." His eyes pour into mine. "Tell me, one thing I don't understand—"

Right at that moment, a feline howl shatters the quiet. It's Abs. The beam has suddenly sharpened with a violent purity, striking her dangling hand and gouging a hole in her palm. The smell of burning flesh, then an eruption of full-throated screams and howls around me as the others awaken. Abs' eyes are snapped open in raw pain. I turn around. The Director is still dangling, his eyes looking right at me. His eyes flick to the side; he sees the beam shooting straight and pure behind me, and me standing right in front of it, unfazed. Something else enters his eyes besides searing pain: a suspicion, a realisation, an accusation.

I've been found out, by this beam of light. Of all the things I imagined would be my undoing, never would I have thought it'd be a light beam. I always felt it would be a sneeze or a yawn or a cough that would inevitably expose me. Something beyond my control, a bodily betrayal.

But not this: not something so simple, so pure, beautiful even. Funny how that is, how it's the beautiful things in life that betray you in the end.

I pedal backward; my feet hit up against the FLUNs, and I trip over them, sending them careening across the floor. I glance up. The Director is gone. More screams, the heavy thumps of bodies landing, furniture scraped roughly aside, the scrabbling of nails and claws on the wooden floor. Then silence.

I pause, waiting for some noise. Then I hear it: a long, meandering howl. From the east wing. They've all fled there, away from the beam. Then the sound of whispers, collective and intense, accusatory. A single pitched wail, now brimming not with fear but with craving, fused with a charged desire. It's quickly joined by a chorus of others. Panic grips my heart, even as I start sprinting. They're regrouping; they're realising. I have to move.

I leap to my feet. The beam is now full strength, a tightrope stretching to the far wall.

Something moves towards me – a flash of movement – leapfrogging over furniture and shelves. Just a blur, then it pounces from the top of a shelf with shocking speed. Abs, flying through the air with hideous speed. At me.

I close my eyes. I am dead.

Then a dreadful scream explodes out, followed by the sound of sizzling, the singe of smoke. The sunbeam. She landed right on top of it, and it's burned a deep canyon across her chest. She's on the floor, on the other side of the beam, arm pressed against her eyes, her mouth torqued in a twisted cry of agony, her upper lip writhing atop her lower lip.

I scurry to my feet, scrambling across the floor. An upended table trips me; even as I fall, I catch from the corner of my eye the hazy shapes of others running down the hallway towards me, arms clamped over their eyes, their speed almost obscene. Their yelping, hissing screams stroke against my eardrums like razor-sharp fingernails.

I hit the floor, my head knocking against something hard and metallic. Blood pours out; instantly the snarls ratchet up to the level of the insane.

They leap at me, strangely synchronised, left arms splayed across their faces, right arms pointing at me, razor nails first. And still synchronised together, their snarls turn to screams as they fall into the beam. As one, they are propelled backward.

An awful, fetid smell of rotting flesh and burned skin hits my senses. I think to move, but I'm blinded by the blood pouring into my right eye from the cut above my eyebrow. I swipe away the blood with my sleeve; and as I do, I see the hunters getting back to their feet, their actions herky-jerky with desire. My blood; they're driven mad by the fresh, overpowering scent of my blood. They come at me again, but wiser now. Instead of trying to punch through the beam, they're scaling up the walls and crossing the room by way of the ceiling.

That gets me moving, adrenaline surging through me so fast, I almost miss it. A FLUN attaché case. It's what I banged my head on. And under the case, the Scientist's journal. Without a thought, I grab it by its twine, the feel of it like the thin tail of an emaciated rat, and stuff it down my shirt. I can feel the wooden spine hubs jutting into my stomach. Then I grab the attaché case and start hauling, the case swinging in my hand. The howls and yips are breaking all around me now, those of pain and those of hot desire. I sprint for the doors, through the narrow corridor leading into the foyer.

And then.

One of them – Phys Ed – drops right in front of me, a fallen icicle of black ice. I pummel through him a millisecond later, catching him by surprise. He reaches for me as I sprint past and brushes my shoulder (did he cut me? did he cut me?), spinning me around. And he comes at me even as I'm still midair, my arms flailing, attaché case still in hand.

The attaché case catches him flush, breaking his face as it snaps open, the FLUN inside flying through the air. The FLUN skitters across the floor.

The impact dazes him momentarily. I dive for the FLUN, grabbing it even as he grabs me by the ankle and starts pulling me in, with enough force to almost wrench my leg out of the hip socket. I feel his nails puncturing through my jeans, piercing my skin.

"Gah!" I scream, hardly conscious that I'm unlocking the safety switch.

He yanks me towards him, has my leg pulled up to his face, his mouth opening, fangs bared.

I pull the trigger and the light beam hits me right in the foot.

It's enough, though, for him to drop me. He cowers back momentarily, then flings himself at me.

This time, I hit him square between the eyes. He falls back as if sledgehammered in the face.

Behind him, the others are sprinting towards me.

Phys Ed, screaming in pain, leaps back on his feet. Creamy pus gushes out of his forehead. The FLUN needs to be turned up to its highest setting. But there's no time to fidget with the settings now: the moment I do, they'll be on me.

Crimson Lips, screaming like a hyena, flies at me.

I fire off the last round, hitting her in the chest. She falls back, clutching her chest, yelping in pain. But then she's back on her feet, her face twisted awfully in pain and lust.

"Who wants more?!" I yell. *"Who wants more?!"*

They stop in their tracks, their fangs connecting to the ground by a waterfall of drool. Uncertainty in their eyes, mixed with keen lust. Their heads flick sharply back and forth, their teeth snapping and grinding.

"Who wants more?!" It's all empty bravado. I've fired off the third and last round already. All that is left is to bluff.

"You?" I yell, pointing the FLUN at Gaunt Man inching towards me. "How 'bout you?!" I shout as I swing the gun around to the other side at Frilly Dress. I'm stepping backward, towards the front doors.

For every foot I retreat, they advance a yard. Their chortling grows louder, more slippery, individual desire beginning to trump their collective fear. Phys Ed in the front crouches low, readying to pounce. They're not going to let me retreat much farther.

"You're the animals! You're the hepers!" I yell as I spin around, throwing the discharged FLUN at them.

They scream as one, members of an insane choir.

In the end, what saves me is the very thing that threatens to kill me: their insatiable lust for my blood. As Phys Ed in the front leaps up for me, he is pulled down by the ones behind. They surge forward, tripping over him. It gives me a two-second head start, and that is all I need.

I sprint towards the exit doors, and five yards out – even as I feel their hands grasping my back, their nails brushing the back of my neck – I leap for the handlebars on the door. The feel of the cool metal in my hand is something I will never forget. My momentum pushes the handlebar down, the door flies open, and a blinding whiteness fills my vision. The sting in my eyes is a beautiful pain.

Their screams, once charged with desire, are now suffused with pain and agony. I hear them beat a hasty retreat.

But I'm not done with them. Not by half. I reopen the door – I see a mad skittering away from the light like rats scampering – and prop it open with the attaché case. Enough light floods into the library, even to the far wings, to make the remainder of the day sleepless and painful for the hunters inside.

"Sweet dreams, you animals!" I shout as I begin to walk away.

But then I hear a voice, hoarse and brittle with rage, echoing down the foyer like rancid spit racing up a throat. Gaunt Man. "You think you're getting away?!" he yells from the darkness inside. "You think you've got us beat, you stupid heper? You think you're so smart? Hey, you sweaty, smelly, singing heper! We're only getting started! You better run! You hear me? Because come dusk, the Hunt starts. And we'll be pouring out of here to hunt you down, to rip into you, to shred you to pieces. You hear me? You came here for a Hunt?! Well, a Hunt is what you're going to get! You *get* me? *You're going to get a Hunt!*"

Everyone is still slumbering in the main building. My footsteps echo down the dark, empty hallways. I pass by the banquet hall. It's like a bat cave inside. Scores of people hang asleep off the main chandelier, their dark, dangling silhouettes like a putrid clump of clogged hair. Off to the side, hanging off some air ducts, is a group of reporters, their cameras still slung over their necks, almost touching the floor.

Ashley June doesn't answer when I knock. I push her door open. Her room is empty.

She's upstairs in the Control Centre, as she said she'd be, in front of the monitors, her head swivelling around.

"Hey," I say as I walk in, gently, not wanting to startle her. Sunshine pours inside in slanted beams, flooding the centre with brightness. I walk to her.

"Hey back. You're supposed to be sleeping." She turns around. "I think I found the ideal place to hide—"

"Ashley June."

"What's the matter?" She sees the look on my face.

I shake my head.

"Gene, what is it?!"

"I'm sorry."

She peers deeply into my eyes, studying me. "Tell me what's going on, Gene."

"Something really terrible."

She sits up, places a hand on my arm. "What happened?"

"It's over for me."

"What do you mean?"

I explain to her. The hunters in the library, the sunbeam, their discovery of what I am. Alarm ripples across her face. "It's over," I say. "They're on to me. Once the sun goes down, they'll hunt me down."

She stands up, walks a few paces away. Her arms stay rigid by her side, her head bent down, deep in thought. "We've got the FLUNs. We can go back to the library, take them down."

"Ashley—"

"No, listen, we can do this. Nobody else knows about you, it's only the hunters in the library."

"Ash—"

"If we take them out, no one will be any the wiser, your secret's still safe."

"It's a suicide mission—"

"We've got the FLUNs—"

"There's *one* FLUN left, I used the other up. And it's buried somewhere in the library, I don't know where it is. They outnumber us, they've got speed, power, fangs, claws—"

"We'll find it, then, put it at the highest setting, it's fatal—"

"We won't find it!"

"We can—"

"Ash—"

"What!" she screams, her voice suddenly catching. "What do you expect me to say, what other choice do we have?" She starts to sob uncontrollably.

I reach for her, gather her in my arms. Her body is cold; she's shivering. "We've got to try, we've got to keep coming up with answers," she urges.

"It's over. We tried our best. But there's nothing more that can be done."

"No! I refuse to believe that!" She pulls away with a cry. Her hands whiten into tight fists. Then her breathing steadies, her body reaches perfect stillness. The stillness of a person who's reached a decision.

"We can make a life for ourselves in the Dome," she says softly, still facing the windows, her back to me.

"What?"

"The Dome. We'll survive, just like the hepers have, for years."

"No way. I can't believe—"

"It'll work. The Dome runs on continuous autopilot. It comes up at dusk, descends at dawn. It'll always protect us."

I stare at her back. I can't take it anymore, seeing that back. I walk over, grab her arm, spin her around.

Her face betrays the steadiness of her voice and gait. Tears run down her cheeks.

"Ashley . . ."

"It's the only option left for *us*." She stares into my eyes. "And you know that, don't you?"

Us. The word resonates in my ears.

"I won't let you . . . it's just me they want right now," I tell her. "You can go on with your life."

"I hate that life! More than you do."

"No, you're good at it. I've seen you, you could go on—"

"No! I *hate* it with every fibre of my being. I could *never* go back to it alone. The fakery, the burying of desire." Her eyes take on a flash of raw emotion that at first I think is anger. But then her words: "You've done this thing to me, Gene. And now I can't go back to that, not alone, not without you." She sniffs. "The Dome. That's the only way we can be together now."

"The Dome's a prison. Out here, at least you'll be free."

"Out here, I'm a prisoner in my own skin. The restrained desires, the repressed smiles, the fake scratches, the fake fangs – these are the bars of a deeper prison."

My thoughts race in me, spiralling in a mad tailspin. But her eyes slow everything down, anchor me. And I move towards her, helpless to do otherwise, cupping her face. My hands on her cheeks, my fingers on her jawline, her cheekbones, wiping at her small mole, wet with tears.

"OK," I say, smiling despite the situation, "OK, let's do this."

She smiles back, squeezing her eyes shut; more tears flow out. She pulls my body against hers, holds me fiercely.

A loud, piercing scream suddenly screeches from outside. We look at each other. Then another, filled with pain and agony. Silence. Then another hellacious scream. We rush over to the window.

Somebody is making a break for it from the library. Phys Ed. He's holding above his head a SunCloak. But the SunCloak was never meant to be used in broad daylight, and the sun's impact is immediate and devastating. Phys Ed stumbles, then gets up on his feet, his legs pushing forward with a spongy propulsion. As he draws closer, I see his skin – shining with an almost radioactive paleness – start oozing under the strong sun, pus already leaking out of his eyeballs. He screams again, and again, even as his vocal cords start to disintegrate. But if the SunCloak is not perfect, it's good enough: he's going to make it to the main building. Where he can tell others about me, that I'm a heper in disguise, that I'm a heper in this building.

Ashley June reads the situation with chilling accuracy. "We might not have till dusk anymore." We watch in disbelief as Phys Ed pulls open the front doors and flings himself inside. He's in now. He's in.

I shake my head in denial. "You should go. It's just me they know about. You can't be found with me. That would implicate you, you'd be guilty by association."

"I'm staying with you, Gene."

"No. I'll make a break for the outside. I can make it if I'm quick enough. You come out when you can, if not today, then tomorrow. We'll meet up at the Dome. As long as they don't suspect you, you'll be fine. It's just me they're after."

A horrific howl rips up the hallway, a screech that rattles the building. A skittering of noises along the walls. Distant thumps. Another howl, softer but with more anguish.

She suddenly freezes up: I see a realization strike her dead cold. She stiffens up. With dread.

"What is it?"

Ashley June turns away from me. When she speaks, her voice is unsteady. She can't bring herself to look at me. "Gene," she says, "go to the back. Take a look at the surveillance monitors, see if you can see what's going on."

"What are you going to do?"

"I'll stay here," she says. A strange pitch to her voice, an oblique light in her eyes.

I head back towards the monitors, curious myself to see what is happening around the Institute. At first, the monitors indicate little movement. Everyone is still sleeping. It's all grey and still. But a monitor in the corner catches my eye. There's movement. In the foyer, where Phys Ed is writhing on the floor, his legs pedalling air. His mouth is stretched open, as if in a silent yawn. But I know it's not a yawn, nor is it silent. It's a spine-rattling scream. On the monitor of the banquet hall, snoozing people, still dangling off the chandelier, begin to stir. The chandelier is shaking now. On other monitors, people hanging off air ducts in the corridors are rousing, eyes beginning to pop open.

"I gotta go now!" I yell to Ashley June as I spin away from the monitors, making ready to run out.

But she's gone.

I don't know what to make of her sudden disappearance. *She listened to me*, I think, but somehow that doesn't ring true. Something else is going on.

I swing the door open, step away from the Control Centre. The corridor is empty. "Ashley June!" I yell at the top of my lungs, no longer caring if others hear me. The only answer is the sound of my echo reverberating back to me.

Not a second to waste. I sprint down the corridor, turn down another. After the brightness of the Control Centre, the corridor is the black of midnight. If I can get to Phys Ed in the foyer before anyone else, I can take him out. Literally and figuratively. That would silence him and buy me time, at least until dusk.

And suddenly I know that's where Ashley June is headed. To the foyer, to take Phys Ed out. She knows I'd never have let her go.

Frustration heated by a mad tenderness, I race down the second corridor, then push through an exit door leading to the stairwell. At the top, peering down the dark well, I hear the cries and screams and shouts. The pounding of boots, the slap-dash ricochet of bare feet scrabbling along walls and stairs. Doors bang open and shut. The sounds float up at me haphazardly, echoes bouncing up the walls and stairs from afar.

It's too late now.

They know. They all know now.

Then, like a cannon shot, doors explode open a few flights down. Manic skittering of feet on the chrome stairs, the click of long fingernails on the metal railings. Heading up. Towards me. A collective hissing, like a swarm of wasps, flies up towards me. Then a primal squeal screeches up the well, and just like that, they've sniffed me out. They're coming for me.

I turn on my heels and run. Back the way I came, back towards the Control Centre. They're coming in fast and furious, their screams bouncing off the walls around. Just two corridors to run down, just two.

I'm down the first corridor and just turning the corner when I hear the doors to the stairway bang open. *Faster, faster—*

The knob of the door to the Control Centre is in my hand. I

turn it. It slips in my grip, my palms and fingers too slick for traction. I take it in both hands and squeeze it like a vice. The door swings open and I fling my body through the gap, kicking the door shut as I fly through.

The door slams shut; a second later, a gigantic *boom!* sledgehammers the door from the other side. It's a race to the doorknob now. I leap up, push the lock button. A second later, from the other side, the knob turns, twisting in my hand, then stops against the lock. A terrific howl breaks out that rattles the door. Then another *boom!* They're body slamming the door.

I reel all the way to the back of the Control Centre. The door isn't going to hold for much longer. Maybe a dozen blows at the most. They'll burst through, a flood of alabaster white skin and glistening fangs and bulging eyes hot with mad desire. The sunlight won't be enough to hold them back. They'd gladly suffer skin boils and temporary blindness for even a droplet of heper blood.

The video monitors at the back that only moments ago displayed little movement are now a dizzying array of motion. On every monitor, people are leaping through the hallways in nightgowns and flannel pyjamas, eyes aglow. They all know. That I am up at the Control Centre.

Boom! The bang at the door is louder: more bodies, more force. Nails scratch on the other side, howls and cries. And panting, the chortling of the insane.

I grab a steel-framed office chair and heave it at the windows. It bounces uselessly off like a ping-pong ball. I spin around, looking for another exit. There is none.

Every monitor is now blurry with the energy of a collective beast awakened. All except one: on the third row of monitors, to the right. Something on it captures my attention, not for the action on it, but for the inaction. A solitary figure just standing, slightly bent over, writing something.

It's Ashley June. Relief, and an odd sense of pride, fills me: she got away. Judging from the pans and pots hanging behind her, she must be in the kitchen. Then I see her suddenly lift her head as if hearing something. I hear it, too. A blood-curdling squeal that vibrates the very walls of the building. Ashley June pauses, puts pen back on paper, starts writing. She suddenly stops, looks up, her mouth dropping.

She's realising something. A light turning on in her head.

She bends over the paper again, her hand a blur as she writes furiously across the page.

Loud screams and moans sound up and down the building.

She stops, her face grimacing with indecision. Shaking her head, she throws the pen aside angrily and hastily folds the piece of paper. She runs to a slot in the wall, pulls it open, places the paper inside. The oven? Then she punches at a large button. A light shoots out from the button, illuminating her face. Tears are streaking down her face. Her head tilts upward and a horror crosses her face. She's hearing it. The howl of desire streaming upward, towards me.

BOOM! This bang is the loudest, denting the door. The top hinge is snapped askew like a broken bone breaking skin. It won't withstand more than a few more hits.

This is how I will die, I decide. Facing away from the door as it explodes inward, my eyes fixed on the image of Ashley June on the monitor. Let that be my last vision. Let my death be quick, let my last thought and vision be of Ashley June.

On the monitor, she suddenly does something strange. She snatches a knife from a hanging knife rack, a long swirling blade. Places the blade in the palm of her left hand and, before I understand what she's doing, squeezes.

Her mouth widens in pain, stretches into a scream.

Then I understand. And I scream: "*Ashley June!*"

On the screen, she drops the knife and sprints away.

BOOM! The door bends inwardly but holds. Just barely. One more hit is all it will take.

Then, suddenly, a fever-pitched wail breaks out on the other side, and I hear a scrabbling of nails on the floor and walls and ceiling. Away from the door. Then silence. They're all gone.

I look at the monitor and see Ashley June flying down the stairwell, her hair flowing behind her. She's leaping from one landing to the next; barely after she's landed, she's already leaping for the next landing. She's headed down, all the way to the Introduction.

On the other monitors, I see hordes of people, in a synchronised stampede, racing down the stairs.

For the blood and flesh of a female virgin heper.

They move as one, wordlessly but ferociously, their blurred speed astonishing on the monitors. The pull of gravity gives them even more speed as they fly down the stairwell. Falling like black rain.

Ashley June races down, panic etched on her face. Each time her feet land, she grabs the rail with her left hand, pivots her body around quickly, and leaps down to the next landing.

The black rain continues to fall, continues to close in on her.

She reaches the bottom floor. Her face is flushed, sweat pouring off her and creating a damp ring of darkness around her neck. Strands of wet hair lie pressed against her face. Her breathing is ragged; she flies towards the doors leading into the Introduction.

They land behind her, a viscous black waterfall crashing down, spraying onto the walls and floor. They go right at her.

She squeezes through the tiny opening between the doors, miraculously opened. A half second later, a dozen of them jump that very spot. Their sheer mass jams them, prevents a single one from slipping through the doors. She has time, maybe a few more seconds of life.

I switch over to a different monitor. Now I see what she has planned all along. She's heading for the chamber where the old male heper lived. She sprints past one of the poles, past dark stains in the ground, and towards the manhole-shaped door of the chamber, tilted up and open. Three people – two men and a woman – have slipped through; stark naked, their clothes stripped during the chase, they're bounding right for her. Their mouths are hideously wide in a scream that, though silent to me through the monitor, must be ear-shattering for Ashley June. Yards out, Ashley June does a running slide right into the opening, her arm grasping the bar as she falls through, pulling it down. It falls with a thud, kicking up dust. The three of them slide right across it; they circle around, their muscles bunched, fingers jamming around the edges, trying to pry open the cover.

With horror, I see the cover start to rise. She hasn't been able to apply the locks yet. The steel door rises high enough for them to wrap their fingers around the bottom –

– when a galleon of bodies pummels into them, knocking them off. Naked bodies everywhere, elbows jockeying for position, arms striking randomly in the air. The cover falls back down. And this time, even with a dozen hands grabbing for the edges, the cover stays down. She's applied the locks.

Run! a voice in my head shouts. It's my own voice, barking at me. *Run!* But my feet are cemented to the ground, my eyes glued to the monitors. I need to be sure she's fine.

She's fine, my voice tells me again. *She's locked in, there's no way they can break in. Everyone knows this.*

Or will, and very soon. Will know there's no way to get to the virgin female heper.

And they will remember, very soon, something else: the virgin male heper still in the Control Centre. And that the male, unlike the female, is very accessible.

Run, Gene! And this time the voice is not my own, but Ashley June's. *Run! Now's your chance to get out!*

This is why she cut her palm. This is why she lured them all the way down to the Introduction. To give me the slimmest of windows through which to escape to the outside.

Run, Gene!

I run.

For the moment, the corridors are eerily quiet. Even the stairwell harbours only a faint murmuring, a backwater of hisses. I need to go down four flights, towards them, to get to the ground floor and then out.

I place my foot down on the first step . . . and it's as if I've inadvertently triggered a button. Instantly, a roar shrieks up the stairwell, a bellow of anger, frustration, realisation, lust. And then a grab bag of sounds: nails, teeth, hissing, clawing, bounding up the walls and stairs. Towards me.

So soon, and they're coming.

I leap down to the next landing – towards them – and the impact sends a reverberation shooting up my legs and along my spine. Ashley June made it look easy. I grab for the railing with my left hand and – imitating her – swing my body around, leaping for the next landing, my body still rattling.

From below, the bellow of shrieks intensifies. It's my fear, oozing off me in waves, they smell. I fling my body down another landing, just one more to go, even as they race up towards me. The impact is a sucker punch to my intestines. I collapse to my legs, cradling my midsection, doubled over in pain. My vision goes yellow, red, black.

I get up, gritting my teeth against the pain, and heave my body to the landing on the ground floor. I glance down the well just before I land: long-nailed hands on the railing, a flurry of bodies flashing by on the stairs, eyes glowing in the dark. Black oil gushing up at me, unleashed.

I burst through the doors on my left, get my legs working under me. Turn right, right, left, then I'll be in the foyer. Twenty seconds away.

They are five, ten seconds away.

With my legs filling with lactic acid, I push for the exit, ignoring the mathematical certainty of my own demise. That is the exact phrase as it enters my turbulent head: *the mathematical certainty of my own demise*.

I turn right, knowing I have at most only two seconds of life left.

Race down the corridor, my form all but forgotten, just a rag doll pulled along by fear, arms flailing out.

Five seconds later, as I turn down the last corridor into the foyer, I'm still alive. I'm almost blinking in surprise.

They must have shot past the ground-floor landing, thinking I was still up in the Control Centre. I'm safe, I'm going to make—

An explosive bang. They've burst through the doors on the ground floor, are already racing down the corridors towards me, fast and furious and desirous, panic now driving them, the panic that they might lose me to the sun outside. A dark sea, an incoming tide of black acid.

My feet sink into the cool Turkish-knotted royal carpet in the foyer. I turn to my left. There. The double-panelled front doors, thinly rimmed by the daylight outside. Twenty yards to freedom. I take off for them, every last ounce of energy long gone, somehow finding speed.

The deranged voices behind, the scrabble of nails on marble, skittering and slipping.

Ten yards away. My arms stretch forward, reaching for the door handle.

Something grabs my ankle.

It is warm and moist and sticky. But with enough solidity and strength to keep its hold on me, to bring me to the ground.

I crash with a thud, air pushed out like a bagpipe squashed.

It's Phys Ed, the spongy stickiness of what remains of him, anyway, holding my ankle, pulling himself towards me. Yellow pus runs down his pizza face. His mouth, partially toothless now (I see his fallen teeth scattered on his chest and the carpet), opens to hiss, but what comes out instead is a blubbering, sloppy mess of sounds.

I kick at him with my foot, but his grip around my ankle tightens. "Gah!" I shout. "*Gah!*" I strike out with my other foot, missing his hand but finding his face instead. My foot sinks in through the gooey stickiness – for one stomach-churning moment, I feel his eyeball pressed against the sole of my foot – before finding bone. What used to be bone. The head not so much explodes as *peels* off his neck.

No time to dwell. I'm on my feet, hand on the handle, pushing through the front doors. The brightness is blinding, but I don't stop. Not with the cries of anger and frustration baying right behind me. I run with squinting eyes, barely seeing, my feet slapping at the sand beneath me, intent only on creating more distance, more distance between me and the doors; and I don't stop, even when I know I'm far enough, but keep pounding the ground, and I'm shouting, "*Gah! Gah! Gah!*" not sure if this is because of anger or victory or defeat or love or fear. But I just keep shouting it over and over until I'm no longer shouting it but sobbing it, no longer running but face down in the sand, bent over with fatigue, my hands clenching and unclenching sand, sand in my fist, sand in my nostrils, sand in my mouth, throat, and the only sounds are my ragged breath and raspy sobs, my tears dripping down into the sand, bathed in the wonderful, painful, blinding light of day.

I am emptied of energy, thought, emotion, as I pick myself up and walk to the Dome. My bones are still jangling from the pounding they took on the stairwell. I examine my ankles: no swelling and, more important, no cuts or scratches on my left ankle where I was grabbed. It is quiet, not even the sound of wind blowing. I make a wide arc around the library; I'm not overly worried that any other hunter will charge out, especially with the SunCloak gone, but I'm not taking any chances. I think I hear a hissing, wet and slushy, coming from inside. But that recedes as I draw closer to the Dome.

And in the heper village, all is quiet.

"Hey!" Silence. "Hey!"

I walk into a mud hut. Empty, as expected. And the second mud hut is just as empty. Dust motes float in a beam of sunlight.

And everywhere I go, it's the same. Empty. Not a heper in sight. Not in the vegetable patch, not under the apple trees, not on their training ground, not in any of the mud huts.

They're gone. From what I can gather, they left in a hurry. Their breakfast sits half-eaten in the mess hall, slices of bread nibbled at, glasses half-full with milk. I scan the plains, looking for a moving dot or a cloud of dust. But they're nowhere to be seen.

The pond offers the reprieve I seek: water. And space and sunlight and silence. I take a long drink, then lie down next to the pond, dangling my right arm and leg into the cool water. In about four hours, the walls of the Dome will rise up, emptied of its former occupants. A new occupant will have taken their place – no, not an occupant, a prisoner. For that is what it is going to feel to me, alone within its glass walls. A prisoner as surely as Ashley June is a prisoner within the walls of the pit, down in the dark recesses of the earth.

How long can she last down there? The old male heper, they'd said, had stored enough food and water to last a month. But how long, alone in the darkness and cold, before you lost all hope? How long before your mind snapped under the constant scratching and tapping and pounding of the door above?

And why had she done it?

I know the answer, it's obvious, but I don't understand it.

She did it for me. She knew, as soon as she saw the SunCloaked man burst into the main building, that I'd be dead within minutes. She did the only thing that would save me.

I run my left hand along the gravel, letting the sharpness pierce my palm. I bite my lower lip, unable to shake a feeling that I'm missing something crucially important. An indelible sense that I'm loafing when I should be hustling. I should be doing something – but what? I slap at the pond in frustration, letting water splash onto my body, my face.

I sit up. What am I missing? I replay in my mind the last images of Ashley June in reverse order: jumping into the pit, rushing into the Introduction, flying down the stairs, in the kitchen writing a letter, throwing it into the oven—

I jolt up.

That wasn't an oven.

It was the Umbilical.

I leap to my feet and run over to it. Even yards away, I see a blinking green light, right above the slot, a steady pulsing. I'm there in seconds. I grab the slot, pull it open.

There. In the corner, a small folded piece of paper.

It crinkles lightly in my fingers as I unfold it. A short letter, written hurriedly, if not frantically.

Gene,

If you're reading this, you made it. Don't be mad at me. Or yourself. It was the only way.

~~*I'll be fine. You've given me something to remember; no matter how dark or lonely it gets down here, I'll always have the memories we share. Those few hours when we*~~

There's still time. Bring the hepers back. When you return, as everyone's rushing out at them, use that as cover to come get me.

I'm @ Intro. Will wait 4 U.

Be quick, stable

Never forget

And there the letter ends, seemingly in midsentence. She was rushed towards the end, her words screeching across the page, forfeiting grammar, scratches of her panic.

I read the letter over and over until the words are carved indelibly into my memory, until the impossibility of what she's asking sinks in.

Bring the hepers back. Those words speak to me, in Ashley June's voice, with a haunting realness. I hear the hushed, urgent inflections of her voice. But there's nothing I can do – she must know this. I can't bring them back. The hepers are gone, and I have no idea where they are. And I can't randomly set off into the Vast, hoping to run into them. That's tantamount to randomly plunging my hand into the desert sand in the wild hope of coming up with a long-lost coin. And when night falls and I'm still out there, it's over for me. They'll sniff me out, hunt me down, as surely as they will the hepers.

I open my eyes, let the sun rip into my eyeballs, hoping the bright glare will erase her words from my mind. I walk to the training ground, looking for something to vent my frustration on, a spear to snap in two or a dagger to thrust at the side of a mud hut. But I can't find anything. I kick at rocks on the ground, throw stones as far into the Vast as I can. And all the while, I have the gnawing sense that I'm missing something, not reading her letter right.

Bring the hepers back.

I ignore those words, pick up more stones and rocks. I'll head over to the apple tree to see if—

Bring the hepers back.

"How am I supposed to do that?" I shout into the air. "When I don't even know where they are!"

Be quick, stable.

I crumple the paper in both hands, fling it as far as possible.

Be quick, stable. Her voice is audible in my head.

After a few moments, I walk over and pick up the balled paper, put out by my own histrionics.

The paper is now more crinkled than a smashed mirror, the words and phrases hung up in it like insects caught in a spider's web. A crease runs from top to bottom, right between "be quick" and "stable".

My head shoots up, suddenly seeing, understanding.

Be quick, stable
Be ~~quick,~~ stable

Be stable.
~~Be~~ stable
stable

The stable is attached to the southern wing of the Institute. I stand outside the chrome-reinforced stable doors and listen carefully. Silence. No snarling, mewling, or hissing. My fingers drum against my legs, indecision halting me. I reach for the door handle, give it a pull. It doesn't budge. Solidly locked and fastened.

Then I hear it: the sound of a horse nickering. Oddly, it's coming from the outside, on the other side. I walk around: there's a parked brougham carriage, the jet black Arabian horse still harnessed to the frame. Probably belonging to a late guest who arrived after the stable hands had already retired and simply rushed off to join the festivities. Leaving behind the perfect gift.

I know better than to startle the horse by approaching from behind. I come at it on a diagonal, treading loudly on the ground. Its head perks up immediately as it swings its muzzle in my direction.

"Atta boy, nice and easy," I say as soothingly as possible.

It snorts, agitated, a spew of spit shooting out. Its large nostrils flare wet and wide, almost as if blinking in surprise. *A heper?* it seems to be asking.

That's a good thing. A horse that can sniff out hepers – exactly what I'm looking for.

I hold out my hand for it to sniff. Its whiskers brush against my fingers, prickly because they've been trimmed short. I stroke its neck, back and forth, not too light that I'm tickling it, but firm enough to be comforting and sure. The horse is well groomed and, with its high-carried tail, arched neck, and powerfully muscled hindquarters, clearly of good stock. And likely well trained.

Agitated at first, it calms quickly. When I sense it is ready, I unhook the rein from the hitching post and lead the horse away. Its hooves *clip-clop* noisily on the gravel, not that I care. Nobody's rushing out in the daylight after me.

"Good boy, you're a good boy, aren't you?" It turns to look at me with large, intelligent eyes.

The carriage is also in tiptop shape. Well oiled, the wheels turn smoothly and noiselessly. The horse snorts disagreeably. It thought I was taking it inside the stable to rest.

"Not yet, my boy. We still have some running to do today."

It snorts again, in protest. But when I stroke its muzzle along its star and strip, it quiets. I pull it forward, and it follows with only a little urging. A good horse. I've lucked out.

I climb into the carriage, place the Scientist's journal next to me, and grab the reins in the driver's seat. The horse should get some nourishment before we take off, but its food is probably in the locked stable. I can't take that risk. Or time.

"Ha!" I yell out, flicking the reins.

The horse doesn't move.

"Ha! *Ha!*" I yell louder. It stands stationary, unimpressed.

I'm not sure what to do. I've always ridden on horseback, never in a carriage. "Please," I say softly, "let's go."

And with a neigh, the horse trots out. Head held up high, confident and proud.

I could love this horse.

I stop by the Dome, letting the horse drink from the pond as I retrieve clothes – the hepers' – from the mud huts. When I get back, the horse is still drinking, its muzzle half-submerged in the water. It lifts his head, snorting in appreciation. Sensing it's in a cooperative mood, I lift up the clothes to its muzzle. It seems to understand; its nostrils press into the shirts and shorts, one at a time, sniffing deep and hard until sure of the scent. A pause; it snorts one more time, a mist of water and mucus spraying out. Then, like a wise sage, it gazes with its large, sad eyes at the horizon. Blinks once, twice. Then trots forward without further beckoning, not even waiting for me to hop back into the carriage. I grab hold of the rail, hoist myself up and onto the driver's bench.

Bring the hepers back.

Ashley June's handwritten words flash before me again. *I'm trying*, I want to tell her, *fast as I can.* There are so many things I wish I could tell her. That I'm alive. That her sacrifice wasn't in vain. That I got her letter. And that I'm now doing my best to save her. I want to send her my thoughts, across the stretch of land between us, through the cement and metal and trapdoors, right into her mind.

Be quick.

I don't know, I want to tell her. I don't know if there's time. I don't know if I'll ever find the hepers or convince them to come back with me. Don't know if they'll see right through my act, know that I'm just gaming them. That I mean to use them as bait, to bring them back here, into the hornets' nest, where they'll be so tantalisingly near that nobody – not the hunters, the guests, the staffers, the stable hands, sentries, escorts, kitchen help, the tailors, the reporters, the camera crew – will be able to resist. Certainly not once the blood of heper begins to flow and seep into the ground, the odour lifting and spreading into the air. And in that moment when not just dozens but *hundreds* of the disallowed and unauthorised join the feasting, that is when . . .

Even then, Ashley June, I don't know if I'll have time to slip in and rescue you.

Be quick.

"Tah!" I shout, snapping the reins harshly, more than the horse deserves. "*Tah!*" And the horse picks up speed – the ground becoming a blur beneath us – as ribbons of muscle ripple out of its haunches. The sudden pickup in speed is exhilarating, takes me out of myself; it *whoosh*es my breath away, making it hard to fill my lungs. And as the Institute falls away behind us, diminishing into a dot, as we begin to delve deeper into the unexplored Vast, something about the moment catches me. Perhaps it is the feel of wind in my hair, the sun splashing down on my face, the eastern mountains drifting ever so slowly closer, the brilliant black sheen of the horse, its mane flowing so freely behind. But it's more than just the beauty. It's the *contradiction* that does me in: how in this moment of unspeakable horror, I can be graced with this unexpected beauty. Of this place, of a horse. I tear up uncontrollably. I don't know how to handle this contradiction.

"Ha!" I yell out at the top of my voice. The dust kicked up by the horse makes my voice craggy and hoarse. "*Hah!*"

Bring the hepers back.

I'm coming, Ashley June. Coming.

The Heper Hunt

THE SAPPHIRE SKY spans high above as we ride deeper into the Vast. Isolated clouds blotch the sky like the untouched white spaces of a canvas otherwise painted deep blue. As the terrain gives way to a hard, shallow crust, the horse picks up speed, ploughing ahead with a relentless fury. So fast that when we hit larger bumps, I get bounced off my seat; for a few exhilarating seconds, I'm flying.

I scan the land as best I can. Other than the rare sighting of a Joshua tree, there is little that interrupts the barren monotony of coarse grass and coarser terrain. No wildlife at all, not a single hyena or wild dog. Only vultures circling in the sky, disconcertingly over me.

And after half an hour of hard riding, not a heper in sight.

"Whoa, boy, whoa," I shout, pulling hard on the reins. It slows to a trot, then stops. A sheen of sweat glistens on its black body, streaming down its barrel chest and haunches. "Gonna give you a little break, OK, horsey?"

I undo the twines of the journal and open to the blank page. In the sunlight, the colours and lines of the map bleed out onto the page. A fierce wind has picked up, and I have to clamp down the pages with my hands to stop them from fluttering. I find my location on the map, using a pile of large boulders on my right as a reference point. The detail of the map impresses me again, right down to not only the colour of the boulders (washed grey), but also the exact number (four).

Where are the hepers? They can't have walked this far out. Even if they'd run, I should have come upon them by now.

I grab the heper clothes out of the carriage and lift them to the horse to sniff. But it's having none of that. Globs of saliva stretch between its lips as hot air huffs out of its mouth. Not in the mood to smell, thank you very much.

"It's OK, boy, you've done well. We'll rest a bit more, OK?"

It stares at me with those intelligent eyes again, blinks, then stares off vacantly into the distance.

I climb back into the carriage and stand on the driver's seat, scanning the endless expanse. Rising in front, looming larger than I've ever seen them, the eastern mountains, snow-capped at the peak; to my left and right, nothing but the barren plains, the horizon bereft of any movement. I look down at the horse. Is it possible it's been taking me for a ride all this time? Perhaps it has no idea where it's been maniacally running, and I've mistaken the glint of insanity for the shine of sagacity.

As if overhearing my thoughts, it suddenly cocks its head, turning its left ear towards me. Then it points its muzzle into the air, sniffing. The wind is gusting about us now, kicking up sand. I see the horse's whiskers fluttering in the crosswinds. It nickers, and just like that, we're off again. I barely have time to jump off the seat and grab the reins before we're flying across the plains, in a more southerly direction this time. In a much more southerly direction, as in a ninety-degree turn.

Now I'm really questioning if this horse knows what it's doing. It's not running with conviction anymore, and every so often it'll slow down to a trot, muzzle in the air. Then, changing direction, it will charge off again. Maybe it's the wind that has really picked up, blowing every which way: one second blowing easterly, then shifting north, before heading south. That might explain why the horse is having a tough time following the scent.

The first time I see the black dot in the sky, I mistake it for a distant flock of vultures. Then it grows in size and darkness, and I realise that it's a dark cloud growing like an inkblot. A tide of clouds follows it, black as the horse.

Be quick.

Wind lashes at me; the pages of the journal whip to and fro, almost dog-eared by the sheer force and fickle direction of the wind.

"*Hah!*" I yell, snapping the reins. The horse understands; it pounds its legs harder, as if my growing panic has somehow been absorbed into its body. Drifts of sand blow across the plains with astonishing speed, yellow brown apparitions spiralling swiftly across the land.

Be quick.

More intensely than ever, I search the plains, hoping to find movement in the diminishing light. But there is nothing. It doesn't seem to matter how far we ride into the Vast, the blank slate of land is never-changing.

"Keep going, boy!" I shout. But it grows more frustrated, derailing, its breathing laboured, its gallop less fluid. It slows to a stop. I jump off the bench, grab the clothes. This time, it's even less receptive, pushing the clothes out of my hands with its muzzle. It stomps its hind hooves into the compacted earth, frustrated. The skies darken. Before too long, the clouds will cover the sun and the land will be plunged into darkness. It'll be even more difficult to spot the hepers.

"We've got to keep tryin—"

The horse lifts its head. A sudden movement; it's caught something. Its nostrils, strings of saliva hanging across them, are like dark eyes suddenly seeing. The horse lurches forward. Just in time, I grab a rail and swing back into the carriage, the heper clothes dropping to the ground.

Not that the horse needs them anymore. It gallops hard and straight, not a doubt left in its direction. Resolve and urgency thump in the pounding of its hooves, as if to make up for lost time, as if knowing thickening bands threaten to darken the skies.

Ten minutes later, I see them. A tiny line of dots, like ants. "Over there, horsey! Over there!" But its needs no encouragement or direction.

By the time we reach the hepers, they've clumped together defensively. I slow the horse, then get off some distance away. I don't want to come on them too hard or fast.

They look worn and fatigued, and their faces are lined with angst.

When they speak, it is to one another, not to me.

"I told you we should have checked the stable. A carriage would have helped, oh, I don't know, maybe about six hours ago," Epap says snidely.

"I did," Sissy says. "While you were busy gathering up all your precious drawings. The stable was locked. Like it always is."

"Well, *he* found a horse and carriage."

They are all staring at me now, Epap and Sissy with suspicion. Each of them is carrying a heavy knapsack, sheathed knives and spears tied to the side, water bottles slung over their shoulders. And attaché cases, five in all. Dust and sand cake their hair and faces and clothes.

"You must come with me," I say. My voice is high-pitched with the deceit that lies in my heart.

They stare wordlessly at me.

"Now," I urge. "There's little time to waste."

Epap steps forward. "Where?" he says, his voice barbed.

"Back. Back to the Dome."

Epap's mouth drops, then curls into a sneer. "This letter," he says, reaching into his back pocket, "we got it through the Umbilical this morning. It says that the Dome's malfunctioned. The light sensor's damaged. The Dome won't close at dusk."

"So they told you about a shelter. Gave you a map and told you to make haste. That it's about six hours away." I pause. "What if I tell you that's all a lie? The Dome's not broken. There is no sanctuary." It's easy to speak with conviction – everything I've said so far is true. And they sense it, too. Panic floods their eyes, tightens their shoulders. I see little Ben look with worry into the distance. No shelter in sight, although by now they should be on top of it. They all know it.

Sissy, who's been quiet up until now, speaks. "Why are they doing this?"

"Get in the carriage. I can tell you as we ride back. But we have to hurry."

"I'm not getting into that carriage – which might very well become a coffin – until you tell us what's going on," Epap snarls at me.

So I tell them. All about the Heper Hunt. Why they've been given weapons. The reason there's been so much activity over the past few days at the Institute.

"Bollocks," Epap says. "Would you listen to the nonsense this guy's spewing?"

Sissy, staring intently at me, says, "Go on."

"We have to go back to the Dome. It's not broken." And now

begins the lie. "You'll be safe there. We get there before sundown, the walls will come up. Imagine the surprise on their faces when they rush out for the Heper Hunt and you're all right there roasting marshmallows, safely cocooned inside the Dome."

Epap spins around at the others, looks at Sissy. "We can't believe him. If he's lying and we go back, then we're dead. The sun goes down, the Dome doesn't come up, we're toast."

"And if I'm telling the truth, and you don't go back, then you're dead out here."

"We can't trust him!"

"How do you think your parents died?" I explode. "It wasn't on a fruit expedition. It was the Heper Hunt, they were sent out to be hunted! Just like you're being sent out right now! Can't you see? Isn't it obvious? The very same thing is happening again. A letter sending you out into the Vast, out of the safety of the Dome. How can you be so gullible?"

Sissy's face is torn with conflict.

"Sissy, don't listen to him!" Epap cries. "He could have told us about this supposed Heper Hunt yesterday, but he didn't, did he? Why should we believe anything he's told us? I bet he's not even the Scientist's replacement!"

At the mention of the Scientist, an idea springs into my head. "Wait here." I run back to the carriage and fetch the journal. "This journal was written by the Scientist. It's all about the Heper Hunt. Now you tell me if I'm lying." I hand the journal to Sissy, who turns it over in her hands, shoots me a suspicious look, then opens to the first page. The others huddle around her.

They are quiet as they read, their bodies tensing as the minutes go by. Sissy's expression turns from horror to disbelief to anger.

"Now do you believe me?" I ask softly.

None of them speaks. Finally, David steps forward. "I don't know who to believe: you or this letter. But according to the map on the letter, the shelter is within reach; and now that we have a carriage, we'll be able to cover a lot more distance quickly. If we can't find it, then we'll head back to the Dome."

"That map's a crock. There is no shelter."

It darkens, suddenly. I spin around, look at the sun. A thin cloud, like intestinal entrails, drags across it.

Be quick.

"C'mon, let's go!" I say, my voice rising.

"No!" Epap says.

"Look at my map, then! In the journal. There's no sanctuary in there. It's got every flora and fauna and stone and rock, but doesn't it strike you as odd that he'd miss something as obvious as a shelter? You go if you want, I'm done arguing with you, that shelter is nothing more than a mirage." It's a total bluff – I need them to return with me – but I'm out of options at this point.

Sissy lifts her head from the journal map. "We do what David said. Go look for the sanctuary, then head back if we can't find it. That way—"

"There's no time!" I exclaim. "We have to make haste right now. Do you see those clouds? It's going to be as black as night within the hour. And you don't need me to spell out what that means." I'm not bluffing here. Ominous bands of dark clouds are racing across the sky, threatening to pull darkness down prematurely, hours before dusk.

"You shut up!" shouts Epap, his face red with fury. "You have no say here!" He steps towards me, his bony arms stiff and crooked at the elbows.

"Take it easy," I caution him.

But he keeps coming. "We don't even need you." He flashes a look back at the hepers, waves his arm beckoningly to them. "C'mon, let's just take the carriage for ourselves."

I reach out for his arm, but he brushes my arm aside.

"Stop it." Spoken quietly but with command. "We all stay together. Every one of us." Sissy is looking past us, west, back to where the Institute lies.

"We can't trust him," Epap says.

"We can and we will. He's right. There's no time. Those clouds mean business."

Epap spits into the ground. "Why are you so quick to believe him?"

She looks at him for a long time, as if giving him a chance to come up with the obvious answer on his own. "Because," she says, walking to the carriage, "he didn't have to come out here, did he?"

Ben sits next to me on the driver's seat. The other four squeeze into the carriage as we race back to the Institute. They are quiet in the back, gazing out of the windows. Sissy is nose-deep in the journal, studying it intensely.

"What's the horse's name?" Ben asks.

"I don't know."

"Maybe you and I can think of a name together."

"I don't think so. Let's just be quiet, OK?" I say tersely. I'm not in the mood to talk. Something about leading a boy to his death kills conversation.

He's quiet for only a little while. "So glad you came. As soon as I saw the dust cloud, I knew it had to be you. Everyone else was freaking out, they thought it was one of them. I knew it couldn't be, not with the sun out." He gazes awestruck at the horse. "So awesome that you came by horse. We've been trying forever to steal a horse from the stable."

Despite myself, I'm curious. "Why's that?"

"Sissy wants out. She hates the Dome. Calls it a prison."

"Why didn't you all just escape years ago? Dome walls come down, you get away, as far as you can."

Ben shakes his head with too much sadness for a boy his age. "Wouldn't be able to get far enough. Even in the summer, when the sun's out fourteen hours, we'd only be able to travel forty miles, tops. Once night comes, they'd only take three hours to cover that distance. Besides, there's nowhere to go. It's all just open land, endless."

The wind has picked up again, stirring the clouds into a more ominous hue. More plumes of sand sail across the plains, ghosts scurrying as if afraid of their own shadows. At times the wind catches the carriage at an angle, whistling through it with an eerie jubilation.

An unbroken swathe of clouds moves across the face of the sun. Sunshine peeks through the gauzy haze, then disappears altogether.

The Vast plummets into the grey darkness of a day gone dead.

Ben places his hand on my thigh, afraid.

I look down at his hand, chubby and guileless. We hit a bump and he scoots even closer to me.

"It's OK," I tell him.

"What?"

"It's OK," I shout, "everything's going to be OK."

He looks up at me, his lips drawn tight across his face, his eyes tearing up. Two streaks cut across his face, across the caked dirt. He nods once, twice, his eyes never leaving mine.

Something breaks inside me. I tear my eyes away.

Be quick.

It's one thing to plan for something like this, another to execute it.

Never forget.

I pull up on the reins, stopping the horse. Ben looks quizzically at me. "Hey," I say, staring straight ahead, "you need to go into the carriage."

"There's no room."

"Yes. There is. I need to be alone for this last bit, OK?"

"Why have we stopped?" Epap says, leaning out of the window.

"He's joining you all," I say matter-of-factly. "There's no room up here." I jump down, indicating to Ben to follow suit.

"There's no room in here," Epap replies. "Seems like you've done plenty fine so far."

"Why don't you shut your trap?" I yell.

They pour out of the carriage at that, tension filling the air between us. I look at David and Jacob standing by Epap. "Do you always need their help in your fights?" I ask.

"Shut up!" Epap yells.

"Easy, Epap," Sissy says, climbing out of the carriage, "he's just trying to provoke you."

"And do you always need her around telling you what to do?" I ask him.

He's gathering his body to throw himself at me – I see his legs bend, his mouth downturn – when a horn sounds across the plains. Coming west, from the direction of the Institute.

For a moment, we're so completely stunned that we simply stare at one another. Then, slowly, we turn our heads.

We see nothing across the plains. Just a grey band of darkness, sitting on the horizon.

Then another blast of the horn, a forlorn, meandering sound.

"What's happening?" Epap asks. "What's that sound?"

All eyes turn to me.

"The Hunt," I say. "It's begun. They're coming."

"It's just our ears playing tricks on us, wind hitting those boulders," Epap says, pointing to our left at five large boulders piled messily on one another.

Nobody responds.

"There," Ben says, standing on the driver's seat, his finger pointing out like a weather vane. Directly ahead of us, in the direction of the Institute. His voice is neutral, almost casual.

"I don't see anything, Ben," Sissy says.

"Over there!" he says, his voice getting more excited now, afraid.

And then we all see it. In the far distance, a cloud of dust, puffing upward.

I feel my internal organs falling through a trapdoor suddenly opened.

The hunters are coming. How fast.

I try not to think of Ashley June. Still in a dark, cold cell, holding out hope—

Somebody grabs me by the scruff of my neck. "You've got some explaining to do." Epap's voice. "What's going on?"

"Let go of me!" I shout, swinging my arm back. I connect with his cheekbone. His head goes flying back, then snaps forward, rage raving in his eyes. He smacks back, a stony fist surprising me with its bite. Before I can respond, he's pummelled me in my stomach, winding me. I double over, fall to my knees. But he's not done with me yet. He kicks me in the side of my ribs. A flash of white washes across my vision.

"You're just a wimp! You're just an emaciated, emollient fake! You couldn't blow the pods off a daffodil if your life depended on it."

Bring the hepers back.

"Tell us what's going on!" he yells.

I spit blood out on the ground. It splatters the dirt, splintered, like a pigeon's footprint. I close my eyes: everything's still a washed-out white.

"They're coming," I say.

"Who's coming?!"

"The hunters!"

There is a long silence. I can't lift my head to meet their eyes.

Then we hear it again. This time not just a solitary howl, but a chorus of them.

My blood. They've picked up the scent already.

"Now you've done it, you idiot," I say. "Now you've made it easier for them to find us."

"No. To find you, not us." Epap turns to the others. "I say we leave this guy here. We take off in the carriage. That will—"

"No," Sissy says.

"But Sissy, we—"

"No, Epap! You're right: we can't trust him. There's more going on than he's letting on. But that's exactly why we can't leave him. We need what he knows." She walks over, dirt kicking onto me. "He's a survivor," she says. "We know that much. If he can survive, then sticking around him will only increase our own chances of survival." Her eyes blaze into mine. "So start speaking. What do we do?"

I stand up, my crestfallen heart suddenly galvanising. "We go toe-to-toe with them and fight." I dust off sand from my clothes. "We surprise them by not fleeing. Because that would be the very last thing they'd expect from you. They think you're weak, cowardly, disorganised. But to stand toe-to-toe with them, go blow for blow. That would catch them by surprise."

Epap starts to interrupt: "We don't stand a chance—"

"Yes, we do! Look, I've seen the way you handle the flying daggers and spears. You could inflict real damage. They never expected you to become so adept – those weapons were only supposed to serve a cosmetic purpose. And look at us. We've got numbers on them. There's only three hunters left. And there's six of us. *And* we've got five freakin' FLUNs between us. We can do this. We can take them down. And then there'll be nothing between us and safety, the Dome."

"You're nuts, you know that?" Epap shouts. "You have no idea what they're capable of. One of them has the power and speed of ten of us. So we're actually outnumbered, you idiot, thirty to six. Outnumbered, outpowered, outsped. Fighting them is pure suicide."

Epap is right; I know that. There's not a chance of defeating the hunters. But the only hope I have of rescuing Ashley June is if the hepers and I can somehow pummel past the hunters and make it to the Institute. And for that to happen, I first need to convince the hepers to dig in their heels and fight rather than flee. We flee, Ashley June dies. It's as simple as that. But as long as we stay and fight, there's still a glimmer of hope for her, no matter how small.

Epap spins around to Sissy. "We need to run. Right now. We leave this guy behind, he'll buy us the time we need to get some distance between us and them."

I'm already shaking my head. "You just don't get it, do you? Running will buy you maybe twenty minutes, if that. Less. The horse is tired, it's been running all day. They'll overtake us, sooner than later."

They grow quiet at that. They know I'm right. On the carriage, Ben starts to cry. Even the horse, gazing at the cloud, starts to whinny.

Sissy takes two steps towards me. "What about the map?" she asks. I'm surprised by the softness in her voice, how quiet she is despite the situation.

"What about it?"

"It shows a boat to the north of us. Tied to a dock. If we can get there in time, there might be a chance."

"Are you nuts? You can't trust that map. The Scientist was crazy."

"Not to us. He seemed reasonable."

I stare north, in the direction of where the boat would be. "If the boat is real, why didn't he ever tell you about it?"

A frown creases her brow. "I don't know. But what I do know is that everything else in the map is accurate. The ridges, the mountains, everything is where it's depicted on the map. Even the boulders over there," she says, pointing at them. "And so why not the boat?"

I shake my head. "Look, even if it exists – and it doesn't – you'll never get to it in time."

"I'd rather die trying."

We can't flee, we must stay and fight, I remind myself. *The only chance of saving Ashley June is to fight back against the hunters.* I raise my voice: "And I'm telling you the only option for survival is to fight them head-on."

Epap lurches forward. "C'mon, Sissy. Let's go. Leave him here, already."

The hepers aren't stupid. They know a doomed fight when they see one, they know their chances are better if they flee. I need to come up with a plan. One that will convince them to stay and fight. I stare at the hepers. Fear has shrivelled their faces; they look tiny and vulnerable out here in the Vast, without the protection of the Dome around them. And then a thought occurs to me. The hunters don't even know I'm with the hepers. They must think I'm alone, separated from the hepers, a solo fugitive, and there's no reason for them to believe otherwise. And the smell of my blood, even across the miles of the Vast, now overpowers any trail of the hepers' odour.

I look at the hepers, their weapons, the FLUNs. And at the boulders toppled atop one another, high and encaving. I blink. And there it is. A plan.

Sissy steps forward, stands right in front of me with a look of curiosity. "What is it? You look like you thought of something."

I look at them in turn, locking in on each pair of eyes for a few seconds. "Tuck tail, run away if you're too scared. But if you want to join me and fight back, I have a plan," I finally say.

The night merges with black. Not a speck of light in the skies, the stars hidden by gargantuan dark clouds shifting above, bloated continents of brooding darkness. The eastern mountains are gone, their once silhouetted borders breached by blackness.

I am alone. Sitting on the ground, leaning back on a boulder. In my hand is a spear that Sissy gave me right before she disappeared into the darkness. I place the tip of the spear against the palm of my hand and pause. It is all emptiness before me, the Vast stretched in an endless grey that is not quite black yet. Only the boulder I lean back on keeps me company. Its surface is cold and brittle against my back, but in this endless sea of aqueous darkness, its solidity is strangely consoling.

I press the spear tip into my flesh and slice downward.

It leaves a small slash, and only a dribble of blood trickles out. But for the hunters chasing me down, that is more than enough; it is a lighthouse flashing in a sea of darkness.

And only a few seconds later, the cry of hunger slices across the Vast. Already so close, so much louder, the intonations of desire heightened. They will be here soon, in less than a minute.

I fist my hand and squeeze. More blood sluices out. Enough now to overwhelm their olfactory senses; not a chance they will be distracted by any faint heper odour. I feel the pulse of blood against the cut, a push-push of seepage, oddly unsynchronised with the rapid, frightful beating of my heart.

The hepers left me with this spear and nothing else.

A skittering sound, sand tossed harshly across the ground, whispery hisses lisp into my ears.

The hunters have arrived.

I stand up, my knees buckling.

A hazy flush of movement, darting from left to right. Then another in the opposite direction, just outside my cone of vision. Three shapes emerge from the darkness, faintly at first, then attaining definition.

Abs.

Crimson Lips.

Gaunt Man.

And then, solidifying out of the milky grey, two more shapes emerge, phantom-like at first, then all too horrifyingly real.

Frilly Dress.

The Director.

I expected only three of them, not five.

All five of them are gruesomely naked, SunBlock Lotion whipped over their bodies like buttercream frosting. Where the lotion has worn off, open sores gouge their skin like volcanic craters, glistening red raw even in the dark. The effects of a whole day in the library with sunlight pouring in. It is their eyes that are the most chilling, the naked anger bristling behind their eyeballs, raw hatred mixed with a pulsating lust for my blood.

"Aren't you a sight for sore eyes," I say.

They edge forward, snarling at me. Slowly, a few yards at a time, creeping towards me.

Something is wrong: this is not how I envisioned the scene

would play out. They are much too controlled; an unbridled feeding frenzy was what I imagined, bodies soaring at me, fangs bared, a race to get me, to tear through me. That I would be ripped into a dozen different pieces within seconds. But this seems too methodical.

"Did you not get your beauty sleep today?" I say. "Because you all look terrible."

They start to spread out in a wide arc.

My eyes are on all of them, but especially the Director, directly in front of me. He is the calmest of the lot, his breathing steady, his feet stepping with fastidiousness on the desert gravel. His long left arm is dangling down, his nails delicately tapping his kneecap, his right arm kept strangely behind his back.

"We've decided to play a game," he says.

"Do tell."

Gaunt Man is on my far left, hunkering lower even as he continues to move down an imaginary arc.

"I'm trying to decide what to call this game. The Sharing Game and the Savouring Game are probably the top contenders."

Frilly Dress is rolling on my right, slowly, like a guttered bowling ball, her eyes filled with wet anticipation. Her mounds of fat loll downward off her body, like pregnant water droplets about to drip off. Her teeth are bared, a faint hiss sluicing out. She continues to roll right until she hits up against the boulder.

As does Gaunt Man on my left. Each of the hunters holds position; they look at the Director as if for further instructions. Then they edge closer, the circle shortening, tightening.

"See, we need to make an example of you," the Director continues. "You've made a mockery of the Hunt, of the Institution, of the Ruler. And of me. My reputation has been irreparably damaged. What kind of heper expert wouldn't be able to detect a heper right under his nose?" And for the first time, his voice betrays emotion. A hitch. "It is not enough to simply devour you. That would be too quick – for us and for you. So, we have decided – my suggestion, of course – to *share* you, to *savour* you. Slowly. Luxuriantly. One piece at a time."

And still they inch forward, eyes swivelling back and forth, examining me, behind me.

Crimson Lips suddenly darts forward at me.

"*Stop!*" the Director yells, and Crimson Lips falls into a frozen crouch, her body erect, like a startled cat. And for the first time I see a FLUN in the Director's right hand, pointed at Crimson Lips. It must be Ashley June's FLUN, the one left behind in the library.

Crimson Lips retreats back into formation.

"It's hard to play this game, sometimes our excitement can get the better of us." He swivels his head about at each of the hunters. "Proceed," he says.

They creep closer, the circle enclosing, everyone staying in formation. Eyes constantly on the move, scrutinising me. "We will take you piece by piece, each of your limbs at a time," the Director says. "The two male hunters will rip off each of your arms, and the two ladies will rip off your legs, one by one. We'll space it out, maybe five minutes between limbs? We'll be sure to keep you alive through it all. It will play out *so* well for the book, see? Draw out this ending, really keep the readers on edge. A heart-thumping climax like no other." He stares at me, his eyes glistening wetly over as if drooling. "Last to go will be me. I get your head."

"And then what?"

The Director leans back like a wolf howling at the night sky, scratching his wrist with rabid delirium. "Did you really say, 'And then what?' What does it matter to you? You're dead!" He pauses, studying me. "Oh, are you concerned about your heper buddies?

Don't you worry about them. We'll get to them eventually. Even in this large desert, we'll find them."

They don't know where the other hepers are, I think.

"And then we go back to your girlfriend and tell her what we did to you!" Gaunt Man sneers, drool now leaking out of his mouth.

"We will do that," the Director cuts in, shooting a cold look at Gaunt Man with the irritated expression of a man deprived of the punch line he's been chomping at the bit to tell. "And, eventually, we will do the same to her. Limb by limb. The Savouring Game. Oh, I quite like that name, actually, I think that's the name that's going to stick."

The circle encloses on me even more. Their bodies percolate with ravenous excitement now, heads bobbing up and down, arms twitching at their side, weird nipping sounds escaping their lips.

"Who do you think will scream louder, you or her? She's got a lot of passion, that girl, so perhaps she'll scream louder. But then again, she's got quite a bit of spine, wouldn't you say, what with that stunt she pulled? Not at all like you, running away like a squirrel and leaving her all by her lonesome."

Abs cries out in frustration and impatience, "Enough talking, let us have at him already!" Her tongue darts across her scabbed lower lip, hard and insistent like a callus filer. "Let me in on him!" She crouches low, readying herself.

The Director lifts his head, scans the scenery, an establishing shot for the viewers back home. "Very well, then, remember to take only the left leg and nothing else. Everyone else stay in line," he says, tapping the FLUN. "You'll have your turn. And now, for the pleasure of the Most Excellent Ruler and for the delighting of his good citizens, I now—"

And even before he's finished speaking, Abs is bounding towards me, on all fours like a rabid hyena, her hair streaming behind her in impossibly straight lines. And though she is moving with lightning quickness, everything seems to slow down. I see everything: her lips pulled back, her face nothing more than a yawning black hole of sharp teeth, her eyes burnished with a red glow.

And I see the other hunters, a split second later, leaping forward as well, their bodies unable to resist, their back legs uncoiling like a cheetah's, propelling their streamlined bodies through the air, their nails and claws finding traction in the desert gravel as they land and then push off again, sailing towards me with a grace that belies their violent intentions.

I see the Director, his face bland but eyes filled with seething anger, lifting the FLUN at Crimson Lips and Abs, his hand shaking with rage and surprise.

And Abs launches herself at me for the final time, arms stretched out, soaring through the air, saliva and snot flailing behind her, her opened mouth turning sideways as it homes in on my Adam's apple.

A harsh beam of light, then a brief white blindness. A scream pierces the night. The stench of burning flesh fills my nose. A second later, I see Abs curled on the ground, screaming, a hole burning where her collarbone is. Used to be.

The Director, staring dumbly at his FLUN, does not understand.

Another beam of light shoots out, from *behind* and *above* me. From someone standing on the boulder. This one hits Crimson Lips in her upper thigh just as she is taking off for me. "*Cha!*" she yells, reaching down uselessly with her hand. Smoke shoots out from her thigh.

"*Gene! Get down!*" screams Sissy.

And I fall to my knees just as Frilly Dress soars towards me, her momentum carrying her over me, her nails ripping the back of my shirt. She lands on my other side with an efficient somersault, starts coming at me again instantly.

Another shot from above, this one wildly off target, hitting empty desert ground.

From the periphery of my vision, I see a dark shape – Gaunt Man – leaping up the boulders. "Jacob!" I shout. "Watch your side, he's flanking us on your side!"

Frilly Dress is leaping towards me, her snarling mouth like a smile.

Someone screams behind me – David? Ben? – naked fear ringing out.

Another beam shoots out, this one from the far side of the boulder, a complete misfire into the sky. I hear Epap – "Sissy! Help me over here" – his voice whittled with fear.

Then a series of flashes creates a strobe-light effect: Frilly Dress's lunge at me is staccato-like and jagged. And then she is suddenly flying above me, descending with her terrible size and weight. Her eyes are fixed on mine, intense and focused as a lover's.

A circle of light flashes from above; her head is instantly haloed by a nimbus of light. Halfway down, her body goes limp.

Her body crushes over mine, sagging. I pry her off, the smell of charred flesh rancid and nauseating. Smoke billows out from the back of her head. I glance up. Sissy stares down at me, then turns to Epap at the sound of his voice: "I'm out, Sissy, I'm out of the first FLUN!"

I spin around, scan the scene before me. Only Frilly Dress remains prostrate on the ground; Abs and Crimson Lips are leaping to their feet now, their bodies scorched with burns but adrenaline and anger and hunger propelling them off the ground. They're running to the boulder, launching themselves up.

Jacob, atop one of the boulders, is bent over his FLUN, uselessly pulling and pulling on the trigger. The safety switch, he's forgotten to disengage the safety. He hasn't fired off a single round; that's one reason the plan is failing so miserably. Yards away, Gaunt Man has crested the top of the boulder, is beginning to leap for Jacob.

Nothing is going as planned. Because of the hepers' inability to use the FLUNs, all advantage is gone: a crisp ambush from the hidden recesses of the boulders – gone; the element of surprise – gone; an overpowering, coordinated attack – gone. My plan is now torn to shreds. As we all likely will be soon, unless something is done. And quickly.

"Jacob!" I scream at him. "Throw me the FLUN!" He turns to me, fear in his eyes. From the other side of the boulders, panic-ridden beams flash uselessly in quick succession – it's Epap, senselessly wasting all the rounds in his second and last FLUN. In the flashes, I see tears streaking down Jacob's face, his mouth twisted in panic. "*Now,* Jacob, throw me the FLUN!"

He flings it to me; it's a perfect throw. It has to be. I disengage the safety, firing off a beam even as my arm is still swinging upward. It shoots out, hitting Gaunt Man square on the nose. But the FLUN is still set at its lowest setting. Gaunt Man is merely knocked off his feet, landing on his back, stunned. He's already getting up, coming again at Jacob.

I reset the FLUN to its highest setting, look up. Gaunt Man is almost on top of Jacob now. I fire off another round. The beam misses left of Gaunt Man by about a yard. He spins, snarls at me. I aim right between his eyes and shoot my last round. The beam flies just over his head, a few inches too high. But he's blinded momentarily. For a few seconds, anyway.

"Get off the boulders!" I yell, tossing away the expended FLUN. "Everyone, get off now. Regroup down here."

And I see the hepers tumbling down, their faces taut with fear.

Epap lands near me; I grab him by the collar, lifting him up. "Where're your FLUNs?" I ask.

He shakes his head grimly.

Sissy is right behind, leaping down from the top of the boulder, pulling Jacob roughly down with her. They land in a pile; Epap and I are already hauling them to their feet.

No one has a FLUN.

We start retreating immediately, away from the boulder. Epap grabs the spear I dropped from the ground, then we start sprinting from the boulders.

The hunters are leaping off the boulders now. Gaunt Man lands on the still-prostrate Frilly Dress, letting her motionless flaccid body cushion his fall. All three hunters are FLUN-wounded, but their pain only feeds into their blood thirst.

"*Now, David. We need you now!*" Sissy yells into the air.

The hunters stoop down, then start racing towards us with ear-piercing shrieks.

"Where is he!" Epap screams, running to the right, searching. "*David!*"

"We need FLUNs," I shout.

"Screw the FLUNs," Sissy yells, and reaches down to the dagger strap tied around her waist. In a heartbeat, she's slid out a dagger; in one motion she pushes me aside, whips her hand away from the strap, and flings her arm out, across her chest from left to right. Just as her arm reaches full stretch, the dagger flies out from under her hand, palm facing down. The dagger shoots out, a blur of light. She doesn't pause to see if she's hit the mark; instantly she's reaching down for another dagger, unstrapping and flinging, then unstrapping and flinging yet again. Three daggers in the air, slicing through the night towards the three hunters charging at us.

We need a FLUN, I think. *Daggers will do nothing—*

The first dagger hits Crimson Lips in the leg. To my surprise, she screams in pain, tumbling to the ground, clutching her thigh, the hilt of the dagger jutting out.

The second dagger catches Abs in the shoulder. She spins in the air as if by a violent whiplash, then crashes ungainly to the ground, squealing. The dagger has pierced right through her body, the blade slicing out of her back under her shoulder blade.

How is she doing this? How can the daggers be wreaking such devastating force?

And then I realise what Sissy has done. She has aimed at the very points on each hunter where the FLUNs have already inflicted significant damage. In the X mark of FLUN-punctured soggy flesh and disintegrating muscle and milky yellow discharge. In Abs' collarbone, in Crimson Lips' thigh. The only spots where a dagger could inflict real damage.

But the third dagger. It's headed straight for Gaunt Man's nose. And he's already seen what's happened to the other two hunters. He ducks down in the last millisecond; the dagger sails over his head. And without breaking stride, he still comes at us. Specifically, he's charging at Sissy, trying to reach her before she can throw another dagger.

And he's going to make it, by a long margin. Sissy is fluid and quick as she reaches down to her hip for a dagger, but not fast enough, not by half. She's unstrapping the dagger, has her fingers on the blade, when Gaunt Man leaps at us. Sissy looks up; her face falls. She knows she's too late.

And right then, off to the side, Epap heaves the spear.

It hums through the night air, an awesome throw bereft of hesitation. It bludgeons right into Gaunt Man's nose, dead-on.

A horrible squishing sound. Gaunt Man's head snaps back, his legs fly out from under him; flipped, he hangs frozen midair, his body parallel to the ground, then crashes down. The spear has impaled his face, ridiculous as the fabled Pinocchio nose.

I grab Jacob and Epap and start hauling them backward. Sissy has bought us a short reprieve, nothing more. She knows it, too.

"*David!*" she yells. "We need you *now*!"

And then we hear it, finally, the sound of hooves striking the ground, the carriage grinding towards us.

"What took you so long?!" Epap yells.

"The stupid horse," David says, his face petrified at the sight of the hunters sprawling on the ground, groaning. "It took off in the wrong direction, it was trying to get away."

"Let's go, please let's just go." It's Ben in the carriage, smeared tears glistening on his cheekbones.

"It's OK, we're going to leave now, OK, everything's fine," Epap says.

We're all piling in. Something is wrong, though, something I can't put my finger on.

"Wait," I shout. I grab Epap's shoulder to stop him from getting in. "Get out!"

"What is it?" His eyes aren't angry, as I thought they might be. Instead, fear dots his eyes.

I spin around again, trying to figure something out. My eyes catch Sissy's eyes. They're a reflection of my own: a sense of impending danger, that we've forgotten something—

Someone.

"The Director," I whisper.

I spin around again, eyes scanning the darkness. Nothing. "Nobody move," I whisper.

We all freeze, barely able to breathe. He's out there, behind the wall of darkness, watching us. I *know* it. Waiting for us to expend all our weapons, to tire ourselves out on the other hunters. Watching and waiting for us to crowd into the carriage; once we're packed in like sheep in a pen, he'll fly in for an enclosed orgy of frenzied feasting, his teeth and claws slashing wildly like razor blades, turning the carriage into a bloody coffin.

Sissy knows it, too. Without moving, she whispers, "David, give me the FLUN we left with you."

"It doesn't work," he says. "I tried to shoot it, but it wouldn't fire—"

"The safety," Sissy says. "Gene told you to disengage—"

"How?! I don't know how—"

The horse's head suddenly snaps to the left, its nose flaring in panic.

A black shape flows out of the darkness, unnervingly fast. The Director comes at us silently, bounding on all fours, twenty yards at a time, the speed pulling his cheeks back, peeling his lips away, leaving his teeth bared in what looks like a sickening, jovial smile. He flings his body upward, towards me. He is coming for me first.

I close my eyes to die.

Seconds later, I'm still alive; when I open my eyes, he's standing in front of us, ten yards away. He is not looking at me. Or at Sissy. He's looking behind us.

I turn. David is standing on the driver's seat, the FLUN pointing at the Director. Behind his hand, hidden from the Director, I see the safety switch. Still engaged.

"It's on the highest setting," David says, his voice sturdy. "Set to kill."

The Director scratches his wrist. "A little boy wants to play hero. So cute."

"The FLUN that's strapped on your back," David says, ignoring his words, "throw it over here."

"What's it to you? I can't possibly hurt you with it—"

"Just throw it now!" David yells, fear sparking off his words. His eyes flicker towards the boulders. Dark shapes are beginning to pick themselves up off the ground.

"Ahh, I see," the Director says, observing. "You're worried about the other hunters."

"No," David says. "Just you. You're the only one I'm worried about right now. And that's why I'm about to shoot you in three seconds unless you hand over the FLUN."

And there must be something about David's tone, because the Director does just that. The FLUN lands at Sissy's feet. She picks it up.

"Now what?" the Director asks. He studies David's face. "Are you really going to kill me? Why, I've known you since you were born. I've seen you grow up, from when you were just a little bay-be. I was the one who sent you all those gifts on your birthday, the books, the cake, do you remember that? Are you really—"

"Yes," Sissy says, and fires a round into his chest.

In a blur, the Director darts back. The beam grazes off his chest, superficial damage. But enough to slow him down. He flits away into the dark, retreating.

Sissy nods at us; everyone quickly piles into the carriage. I jump onto the driver's seat, grab the reins. Sissy sits next to me, her body twisted around, scanning the dark, her finger on the trigger of the FLUN.

"You think you've won?" The Director's voice, booming out from the darkness. "You think you've got the better of us? *You?* You *stinkin'* hepers."

I look at Sissy; she shakes her head: *Can't see him.*

"You've just delayed the inevitable. Listen: can you hear it?"

Nothing but the wind.

And then I hear it. A faint rustling, like dry autumn leaves trampled on. But mixed in, sharp, nattering sounds, metal filings rubbed in glass shards. Sissy turns in the direction of the noise, towards the distant Institute. Her face drops, aghast with horror.

A hazy wall of deeper darkness rises up like a tsunami wave crashing towards us.

"The good citizens are coming," the Director jeers. "All the guests, all the staffers, all the media. Hundreds of them. Somebody disengaged the lockdown. Once they realised that, there was no holding them back, the good citizens, no containing them. I could only hope to beat them, the hunters and I, by using the hunting accessories to get a head start. Alas . . ." His voice droops off.

More sounds from afar now, distant cries and squeals of desire.

"My goodness, can you imagine the frenzy when they realise *all* the hepers are still alive?"

I grab the reins, pound them on the horse. We lurch forward. Towards the only option left to us. The boat. If it even exists.

I'm sorry, Ashley June, I'm sorry . . .

"They're coming!" he screams, his voice trailing us as we begin to fly across the plains. "They're coming, they're coming, they're coming, they're . . ."

We skim along the harsh terrain, the horse flying faster than ever before. But where its form was once graceful, it is now jerky, desperate, panicked. As the minutes pass, the strain becomes more obvious.

The pursuing wall of dust has faded slightly. But it is the deepening darkness, and not increasing distance, that gives the illusion of disappearance. The volume of snarls and screams has only grown. Sissy sits next to me now, looking at the map. With sunlight long gone, the map is fading on the page, colours receding into the blankness of white. Her fingers trail a rough path across the map, her head swivelling around for landmarks.

"We've got to go faster!" she yells into my ear.

Blood still seeps from the cut on my hand. I do my best to stem the flow, pressing a cloth against it, a tricky manoeuvre while trying to steer a horse.

I feel fingers on my hand, prying the cloth away.

She folds it over, presses it in hard. "You've got to stop bleeding," she says.

"It's OK, it doesn't really hurt that much."

She presses in deeper. "I'm not worried about the pain. I'm worried about how your blood is giving our position away."

I reach out and pull off the cloth. "Don't worry about stanching the blood. They can see us perfectly fine in this darkness."

She looks back for a few second, and when she turns around, worry is etched on her face. I don't need to ask. The sound of the charging masses behind us grows by the minute.

"The map's gone white," she says, disheartened.

"It's OK," I say, eyes focused ahead. "We don't need it. Just need to keep going straight, and we'll hit the river. Follow the river north, and soon enough we'll come upon the boat. Simple as that."

"Simple as that," she repeats. She shakes her head. "That's what you said about your plan against the hunters. It was a catastrophe back there. I thought you said there were only going to be three of them, not five."

"All of you assured me you could handle the FLUNs. Instead you had Epap in utter panic and shooting off all his rounds in the first five seconds. And then there's Jacob, who couldn't get off even a single shot. How many more times could I have said: 'Don't forget to disengage the safety'?"

She turns her head away, biting her tongue, I realise.

After a few minutes, I say, "Thanks for not abandoning me. For staying to fight with me."

"We don't do that."

"What?"

"We don't desert our own. It's not our way."

"Epap was—"

"Empty talk. I know him well enough to know that. We don't abandon our own."

Her words sink into me deeply. It's my turn to be quiet. I'm thinking of Ashley June, alone in her cell. And then I'm hearing the Director's accusing voice: *You, running away like a squirrel and leaving her all by her lonesome.*

I flick the reins to tease out more speed. The horse pounds on, snorting, sweat glistening all over its body now.

A wail breaks clear across the sky. Too loud, too close, too fast.

And then I feel it. Drops of rain, splattering on my cheeks. I look up at the sky in horror. Dark clouds, blacker than the night sky, swollen and bulbous. The rain will soften the ground; to the horse, it will feel like glue.

Sissy feels the drops, too. She turns to me, her eyes gripping mine. They are asking: *Did you feel those drops? Did you feel those drops?* There is answer enough in my silence; she bites her lower lip.

Then she stands up, right on the bench, the horse still galloping away, the carriage jostling and rattling. Her clothes are pulled back by the wind, fluttering madly behind her. Rain starts falling down in earnest, the drops splatting on her bare arms, neck, face, and legs like miniature stars.

"There!" she shouts, and her long arm, muscled and creviced like a bronze statute, points directly in front of us. "I see it, Gene! I see it. The river! The freaking river!"

"What about the boat? Do you see the boat?"

"No," she shouts, getting back down, "but it's only a matter of time."

Behind us, the thundering of the ground grows louder, the snarls, the hisses. So much closer. I steal a quick look. Can't see anything, just darkness now. *Only a matter of time*. Sissy is right. Either way, it's only a matter of time now.

The river is a marvel. Even over the rattling of the carriage and the clamour of the chasing mob, we hear it from afar, a gentle gurgle that is deep and sonorous. When we come upon it minutes later, its size initially catches us by surprise, the banks spread far apart with a masculine broadness, at least two hundred yards across. Yet even under a sky weighed down with heavy clouds, the river seems light and feminine, filled with a sprinkling of sparkles that I at first mistake for fireflies. Its waters flow down like slowly undulating plates of smooth armour.

The horse has slowed considerably. Its breathing grows laboured even as its stride shortens. A few times, it veers dangerously close to the riverbank before correcting itself. I have pushed it too far. It slows to a trot, then to a stop. I snap the reins, but I know it's useless. The horse needs to rest.

"Why are we stopping?" Epap shouts from the carriage. When no one answers, he jumps out. "What's going on? We can't afford to stop."

"We can't afford not to," I say. "This horse is about to drop dead. Just for a minute, let it catch its breath."

"We don't have a minute. In a minute they'll be upon us!" He's pointing now into the darkness from which squeals of excitement shoot out.

I ignore him, because he's right, and jump down. The horse's leg muscles, when I place my hand on them, are convulsing. "Good horse, good horse, pushed you too hard, did I?"

Epap spins around, his arm gesturing at me in disbelief. "Would you believe this guy? Trying to be a horse whisperer at a time like this? Sissy, where are you going?"

Sissy is running for the river. She bends down at the bank, comes running back with a bowl, the water inside sloshing about. The horse dips his muzzle in, messily slurps in the water. In less than five seconds, it's done. It whinnies for more.

Sissy strokes the horse's head. "Wish I could give you more, but there's no time. You keep going, though, find us that boat, and I promise you, you'll have all the water you'd want. But find us that boat. Quickly. Quickly!" And those last words come out as a shout as she slaps the horse on its haunches. It blinks, whinnies, then bullets forward. We all leap back onto the carriage. The horse is off again.

The sounds from behind roar closer. Raindrops fall down, fat and heavy.

We plough on. First figuratively, then literally. The ground becomes sodden and soaked, soft sponges sucking in the wheels of the carriage, the hooves of the horse. Even the bracing wind works against us, fierce as a gale, pushing us back, flushing our scent backward to the enclosing horde, inciting them further. Rain cuts into our eyes.

Then the darkness, saturating the air, dissolving the horse into the night. Only the sound of its laboured breathing and the forward push of the carriage are evidence that it is even there.

Sissy has withdrawn into silence. With quick sideways glances, I catch only her lips, tightly drawn, her eyes squinting against the rain. Strands of her hair are matted down against her forehead, cutting diagonally across her face. A howl sounds across the plains, disconcertingly close. She looks at me and I nod.

She straps the FLUN around my back, grips the other FLUN in her hand tightly.

A snarl hisses, joined by a phalanx of other snarls and jaw snaps. Not behind but now *adjacent* to us.

Sissy disengages the safety switch.

Thunder rumbles, a deep reverberation in the skies. I snap my head up, suddenly hopeful.

A howl breaks out, filled with displeasure.

And then lightning strikes across the skies, a harsh, overpowering flash. The land is instantly illuminated in an embossed black and white, the eastern mountains riven with black crevices, the river reflective like melted silver. I shoot my head for a look backward, and in that millisecond before the land plunges into darkness again, I see them: an endless number streaming towards us, momentarily flattened like cards against the ground, cowering from the lightning. But so many. So close. A stone's throw away. Their eyes shining in the glare, fangs glistening.

A violent clap of thunder explodes, shaking the land. It rumbles away, and in its stead, the cries of agony and anger. They've all been blinded. By the lightning. That'll buy us maybe one more minute.

"Did you see it?" Sissy yells at me, her hand suddenly gripping my arm. "Did you see it!"

"I know, I know, but don't worry—"

"The boat!" she shrieks, and she's jumping up and down. "I saw it, I saw it, it's really there!" She spins around, yelling to the others, "I saw the boat, it's right in front—"

The carriage suddenly hits a mud patch; the wheels sink into the sludge and get caught. Sissy goes flying in the air, disappearing into the night. I'm flung off the seat as well; my feet catch the railing in front, cutting short my trajectory. I land on the horse, his back slick with sweat and rain.

The whole world is spinning as I pick myself up. Where is up, where is down, left, right, north, south, everything has become intermingled and indifferent. The sound of a young boy crying to my right: Ben. I run over to him, pick him up out of the mud. Like me, he's all covered in it.

"Ben! It's OK! Does anything hurt? Did you break anything?"

The sound of growls, the snapping of teeth, drawing close.

Ben's not saying anything, but he's looking at me and shaking his head. I pick him up. "We have to move. Sissy! Where are you?"

A short flicker of lightning, briefly illuminating the landscape. Too short to see anything but the hepers, all picking themselves up off the ground. Except Sissy, farthest away, still lying in the mud. I run to her as a peal of thunder ripples across the skies.

"You've got to get up, Sissy! We've got to move." She's groggy, but I stand her on her feet. "Sissy!" I yell, and her eyes snap to. Panic and fear clears out the cloudiness in them.

"Where is everyone? Are they OK?" she asks.

"They're fine, we've got to get going. Point us to where the boat is!"

"No! Our supplies, the FLUN, we need them!"

"There's no time, they're on us already!"

"We won't survive without—"

Peals of hyena-like laughter rip towards us, so close that I can hear the individual intonations, the salivary wetness slung between syllables.

"Sissy! Listen to me," I shout, pointing at the other hepers, "they won't listen to me. Only to you. Make them run for the boat. Make them—"

A flash of lightning lights the sky and wet land. I see it, the boat, blessedly close by, a hundred yards away. But then I see the teeming masses.

They are already upon us. Even in the short flash, I see their pale, glistening figures bounding towards us with frightening speed, like skipping stones.

In the flash of lightning, they all flatten against the land, like the quills of a porcupine in retreat, howling with anger.

"Now, Sissy!" I shout.

But she's already running, already gathering up the others, urging them on. I take after them, racing, the muddy ground squelching beneath me. The mud sucks eagerly at my shoes like kisses of death, turning my speed into slow motion.

Darkness again. Then peal after peal of thunder rumbling the sky. Slivery shouts of desire rain down on us again.

They're coming.

I hear the wet sludge of mud being stepped on behind me. Whispers, whispers, whispers, breathing at my neck.

"Dear God!" I shout. Words I have not uttered in years, words I used to say every night to my mother, her eyes soft with kindness, my clasped hands enfolded by hers. Words forgotten, embedded so deep in me, only the shovel of abject fear dislodges them. "Dear God!"

It is not a single strike of lightning that lights the sky, but a network of intersecting flashes that rips across the dome of the world. So bright that even I am blinded momentarily, the whole world bleached an impossible white. But I don't stop running, even as my eyes close. Because I can still see the boat, its negative image singed in my shut eyes, black and white.

"Don't stop, keep going!" I shout, even as the howls of anguish and pain break out all around us. When I open my eyes, I'm at the dock. "Over here!" I shout before I realise they're all ahead of me, running down the dock, their feet echoing hollowly on the wooden boards. I race down after them. They're jumping into the boat, Sissy already throwing off the anchor rope, Epap manning a long pole curiously hooked at the top, to push away from the shore.

Because I'm bringing up the rear, I'm the only one who can see what's wrong. What is so terribly wrong.

I spin around, trying to see up the dock. It's too dark.

"Get in!" Epap shouts at me. "What are you waiting for?"

I bend my knees to jump in, pause.

"Get in!"

And I'm frozen in place, unable to push off my legs. I spin around again. The dock is still empty.

The howls of anguish are building. Soon they'll be on their feet again. On us in mere seconds.

"Start without me," I shout. "Keep going, I'll catch up with you!"

"No, Gene, leave the horse, don't be stupid—"

But I'm already sprinting up the dock.

Small flashes of lightning, aftermaths of the apocalyptic one, sweep across the sky. Enough to keep them at bay for a few seconds more, to give me the light I need to see.

There. In front of the carriage. Not the horse.

But Ben.

Frantically working the reins, trying to untie it, his face covered in mud except where rain and tears have smeared it away. His mouth is open, and random odd sounds escape: "Ahh ahh no no please ugg . . ."

I grab him by the chest and heave him over my shoulders even as I spin around to race back to the dock. As I do, he undoes the last knot, and the horse breaks free. Its eyes are bulging with fear;

it's ready to bolt. An idea comes to me; I grab the reins before the horse can get away.

From around me, I hear the sloshing of mud, mewling sounds of desire.

I throw Ben atop the horse.

Piercing, ear-shattering screams fall all around me. Behind me, behind me, they're leaping for me.

I bend my leg, readying to mount the horse.

The horse shoots off into the dark, leaving me behind. I see Ben clinging around its neck for dear life, then they quickly disappear into the darkness.

I grab the FLUN strapped around my neck, disengage the safety.

Primal screams fill the air.

I start sprinting, hands at the ready on the FLUN, head turned back, on the watch. *Don't get disoriented, don't lose your bearings*. I shade closer to the riverbank on my right.

Be quick.

I steal a look backward. Dark shapes bob like floats in a pool, a wave of them flowing towards me. Another shape comes screaming at me, its stark naked body glistening like wet marble, its bared fangs almost a halo of light. I fire the FLUN. The first beam misses but the second strikes its stomach, and it doubles over in the air, landing right at my feet, its eyes clenched in pain, its scream unbearable. I feel its spindly fingers grip my ankle, its warm breath on my shin.

"Ja!" I shout as I force my legs to turn and run.

A hiss to my left. I turn—

And duck. A shape sails over me, landing on its feet. Spins. Is at me, hands on my neck, mouth open. I see the fangs, then the dark well at the back of its mouth. If I miss, my flesh, my blood, my bones, will disappear down that black well.

The beam hits right into the open mouth, right down the throat. It doesn't scream; it can't.

I fling the FLUN away, completely expended now. And I'm running again, the dock coming into sight.

A wave of them seep into view on my left. In front of me. They've cut me off. Half of them streak down the dock for the boat, the other half come after me. I'm trapped on all sides: behind, my left, in front. They're everywhere.

Except the river.

I make a harsh right, dashing for the riverbank now. The ones who were behind me, they're on my right now and closing in on me with furious intent.

I'm thirty yards away.

They pour into view from the right, like the waters of a broken dam a hundred yards away.

Twenty more yards. My knees buckle.

Then it's over. Just like that, they've cut me off. I see a string of them pour in front of me, lining the bank, crouched down, readying to pounce on me.

But I don't stop. Even as my eyes tear over, even as my legs threaten to collapse under me, even as my lungs finally burst in a spray of acid within, I don't stop. I will not die standing. I will not die kneeling. I will die fighting and running. I will meet them head-on. And a sudden surge of anger flushes into me, hotter and brighter than the lightning that streaked the night sky, a bolt of energy that charges my body.

Never forget. The voice of Ashley June so clear in my ears.

Never forget who you are. And it is the voice of my father, deep and solemn.

With a shout, I hurl myself towards them.

They charge at me.

And then I leap in the air, higher than I ever have, sailing over them, flying towards the river. The waters rush up to meet me.

"*The forbidden stroke!*" I scream.

And then I am in the river, its waters surprisingly warm. The quietness underwater is a momentary but wonderful reprieve from the howls and screams. Just the sound of bubbles and a background churning. Then the sound of splashes, one after the other. They're jumping in after me.

I extend my arm in front of me, gloriously stretched out, and stroke down. I feel the propulsion of my body, the flow of water past my head. Then I start kicking, extending my other arm and stroking down. The way I've always wanted to swim, the way it has always felt to swim. I lift my head for a moment: they're in the river now, but harmless. In here, they're the plodding dog to my swift dolphin.

The boat has pushed off the dock and is safely downstream, in the centre of the river. The dock is overflowing with people hissing and snarling with anger. I see Epap and Jacob working the poles, pushing away at good speed.

I try calling out to them, but I can't be heard above the din of rage or the pelting of rain on the river. I shout louder, but the wind now carries my voice away from the boat, from the hepers. I swim a few more strokes, but though I'm fast, the boat, catching the downstream better than me, is faster. It pulls away just as I feel a sudden drop in energy. My body feels impossibly heavy, arms and legs bloated with heavy fluid. My lungs seem unable to draw in air.

"Hey!" I shout. "Wait!"

It's my clothes, I realise. Soaked through, they've become dead weights. But I can't take them off; no way I can tread water and undress at the same time. So I slog on, concentrating on putting one arm after the other, stroking as hard as I can. But as much as I try, the boat is getting farther and farther away.

They are leaving me behind. The hepers.

I flip onto my back and float, too tired now; raindrops fall on my face. I finally understand what it is to be discarded. I've felt it all my life, but now I know it.

Ashley June once described to me how she would stand in the schoolyard and be tempted to prick her finger. To let the end come, to give in. It would be so easy now. To close my eyes, let my body drift, let them come after me. To finally succumb. With so many of them, the end would come quickly.

But to let it end now would be to discard the only person who refused to discard me. Ashley June.

I flip over, force one stroke after the next. My strokes are vapid, my arms feel like clumps of mud sloshing through water. I begin to sink.

Then I hear the sound of splashing near me.

Hands grab my back, turning me over. An arm snakes around my chest; a face rises up from underneath, presses up next to mine.

"I've got you now, just float, I've got you now."

In my fatigued state, I think it's Ashley June, her voice whispery, water spitting out onto the back of my neck and ear, the breathing husky and warm. I want to ask how she broke out of the pit, how she got here so quickly—

But then I am being hauled up like a net of fish into the boat. They pull me to the centre, faces gazing down at me with concern. It's David. Jacob. A body flops next to mine, wet and black like a seal.

Sissy.

"Turn him to his side," she says, sputtering water.

I feel the press of wood against the side of my face, weathered and smooth, the soft clap of water smacking the underside of the boat. I hoist myself into a sitting position.

The boat is little more than a glorified raft, but a wide and sturdy one at that. In the centre is the cabin, little more than a wooden dugout. At the back of the boat, Epap and Jacob are still pushing down on the poles, guiding the boat downstream, away from the bank. And there is Ben: sitting under an enclosure, hugging his knees. He looks at me; a small smile breaks out from his tear-streaked face. He thumbs to the back of the cabin, and when I hear a whinny sound from behind it, followed by the hollow clump of hooves on wood, I understand.

All night long, they follow us along the bank of the river, hundreds of them snarling with the hatred of the cheated and unjustly deprived. It is an endless night, filled with rain and darkness and the incessant sound of their primal screams. Eventually, the rain subsides and the clouds move on. The moon and stars come out, shining their sickly light on the hundreds of people crowding the bank, their eyes wide with desire even now. The moonlight infuriates them, but they stay with us yet, refusing to leave. The night sky lightens as it always does eventually, and a hint of grey intrudes on the blackness. Gradually they leave, just a few at first, then, with a collective howl that lasts over a minute, filled with the rage of unconsummated desire, they turn as one and sprint back. Back to the Institute, back to the cloistered darkness within its walls.

We decide to go on shifts throughout the day: two working the poles, one on lookout. When not on a shift, we sleep in the cabin – or are supposed to, anyway – a simple shack-like structure built of wood, opened on the front end.

They let me have the first shift off, but I'm too wired to sleep. I spend my time dousing my shirt in the river and letting the horse chomp down on the shirt for water. Like the others, I keep scanning the Vast for signs of movement, even though I know the hot and bright sun is protection enough. An hour later, my legs eventually tire and I lie down in the cabin. Sleep flitters in and out like a butterfly with a missing wing: lightly, erratically.

But when I awaken, it is late afternoon. They've let me sleep through two shifts. Next to me, Ben and Epap are snoring away, Ben murmuring incoherently. Sissy is standing at the front on watch duty, and I join her.

"They'll be back tonight," she says.

I nod. "And tomorrow night. And the night after that, maybe."

She runs her arm across her nose. "We better hope this river goes on. If it comes to an end today, tomorrow . . ."

She doesn't need to finish her sentence.

We are quiet for a while.

"Will they ever stop coming after us?"

"No." I stare out at the eastern mountains. "So long as they know we're out here, they will keep coming. They'll never stop. They'll build halfway sanctuaries to shelter in the daytime, use them like stepping-stones, gradually make their way to us."

She takes a drink from her cup. Looks out into the plains. "We can stop in the daytime," she says, "for food. If we see any game, we can hunt it down. We need food."

"We have weapons?"

"David grabbed a spear. I have my daggers. That's all we have."

"That's all we had time for," I say.

"We could have done better. *I* could have done better. I didn't grab a single thing. Even Epap grabbed the Scientist's journal. And Jacob grabbed Epap's bag. Not much in it, just some clothes and his sketchbook, but at least he grabbed *something*."

"It was pretty crazy," I say softly. "There wasn't any time at all."

The water laps against the side of the boat, a rhythmic knocking. She stares down at her hands, shuffles her feet a little. "Thank you for going back for Ben," she says, then walks to the back of the boat.

And when nightfall arrives, they come again, even more in number, ravenous and filled with a hatred I didn't know was possible. With hordes of them crowding the bank, the river is transformed into a hideous half-tunnel of torment. We are up all night, watchful and afraid. I worry about the river, that it will narrow or even end. But it never does, not this night, anyway. And when the moon dips and the skies begin to lighten, their shrieks come to an end. One by one, then in a collective cry, they turn and leave.

The sun arises, and the landscape has changed overnight. Instead of the dour brown silt of the desert, green patches of grass steal into the scenery. By noon, the landscape has evolved into a lush green pasture, daffodils and rhododendrons scattered here and there. Large trees clump together, and a prairie dog or two is sighted. We dock the boat. The horse is the most grateful for the change, bounding so fast into the green pastures that we think it's gone for good. But it's only hungry; it stays close to us the whole time, chomping away at the grass. When we leave an hour later, all of us eager to put distance between us and them, no matter how inviting the land here might be, it whinnies and trots back to the boat.

They arrive that night many hours after dusk. It is taking them that much longer to reach us now. And the group is reduced in number, only the youngest and fittest among them, no more than a few dozen. They stay for only a couple of hours before they are forced to leave in the dark, hours before dawn, the moon and stars still shining.

I'm on watch duty when the sun rises. A subdued orange, still dim enough to stare at directly, peeking just over the eastern mountains.

"Is that it?" Ben, groggy-eyed, walks up to me. "Will they come back? Have we seen the last of them?"

Yes, we've seen the last of them, I am about to tell him. But I have not forgotten, even now, that below this green earth, beyond the reach of this sun, and away from the gentle brooking of water, waits a girl in cold and darkness who once took my hand into hers.

"Have we?" he asks again.

I flick my eyes away, unable to answer.

That afternoon, we dock again. David has seen a rabbit; sure enough, within ten minutes of hunting, he spears one, a fat, grey-and-white hare. He sprints back to us, his smile wide, holding up the bunny like a trophy. Sissy glances at the sun. There's still time, she says. Let's build a fire and have a feast today. Ben jumps up and down with joy, his voice barking out across the meadows.

Everyone sets to work. Sissy and David start skinning the rabbit. Ben and Jacob set off looking for firewood, but there is little to find. Just some dead grass, a few branches. Epap is furiously rubbing two branches together, trying to get a spark. I stand about, trying to look busy. There is some talk of breaking off parts of the boat, but that is quickly shot down.

"My sketchbook," Epap suggests. "We can burn that. One page at a time."

"Are you sure?" David asks.

"It's fine," Epap answers, and gets up.

"I'll get it," I say, trying to be useful. "In your bag, right?" I run off before he can respond.

His tassel bag is in the corner of the cabin. I undo the strap and flip open the flap. The sketchbook, its leather cover pockmarked with age, is large; I have to twist it out of the bag. A gust of wind sifts through the pages of the sketchbook, opening to a page with a drawing of the Dome. I pick up the sketchbook. He's a fine artist, I'll give him that much, his lines clean and his strokes restrained but expressive. I turn the page, then a few more. Almost all are portraits of the hepers, one on each page, their names written at the top. David. Jacob. Ben. Sissy. Most of them Sissy. As she cooks, reads a book, runs with a spear, washes clothes at the pond. Asleep in bed, her eyes closed, her face soft and peaceful. I start flipping towards the front, going back in time. The hepers, in their portraits, get more youthful.

"C'mon, Gene, what's taking you so long?" Epap shouts, his voice afar.

"Be right there." I turn over the page, am about to slam the sketchbook shut, when something catches my eye.

A different name at the top of the page. This one reads: "The Scientist".

I look down at the portrait . . .

And the sketchbook falls from my hands.

It's my father.

Acknowledgements

I WOULD LIKE to offer thanks to certain individuals who have supported and encouraged me over the years:

My teachers: Mr Pope of King George V School, and Professor Dan McCall of Cornell University. Their love for stories was intoxicating and infectious.

Early supporters of my writing career: Terry Goodman, Peter Gordon, and Many Ly.

Colleagues and friends from the Nassau County District Attorney's Office, especially: Tammy Smiley, Robert Schwartz, Douglas Noll, Jason Richards, and Mehmet Gokce.

Catherine Drayton, who is amazing, and who has been everything I ever hoped for in an agent, and more; the Inkwell Management team, in particular: Lyndsey Blessing, Charlie Olsen, and Kristan Palmer.

My wonderful editor, Rose Hilliard, whose keen eye, sage advice, and warm support make me want to high-five myself every day; my publisher, Matthew Shear, for making me feel not only welcomed but special at St. Martin's Press.

My two sons, John and Chris, who broaden, deepen, and enrich my life; and, above all, Ching-Lee, to whom this book is dedicated.

The story continues in... **THE PREY**

ISBN: 978-0-85707-544-4

On the run and hunted by society, the remaining hepers must find a way to survive in the Vast – but have they just exchanged one evil world for another?